ChangelingPress.com

Stargazers
Sci-Fi Action & Intrigue Romance
Anne Kane

Stargazers
Sci-Fi Action & Intrigue Romance
Anne Kane

All rights reserved.
Copyright ©2026 Anne Kane

ISBN: 978-1-60521-961-5

Publisher:
Changeling Press LLC
315 N. Centre St.
Martinsburg, WV 25404
ChangelingPress.com

Printed in the U.S.A.

Editor: Chrissie Henderson
Cover Artist: Bryan Keller

The individual stories in this anthology have been previously released in E-Book format.

Table of Contents

Wanton 4

    Chapter One 5

    Chapter Two..16

    Chapter Three 27

    Chapter Four 37

    Chapter Five 47

Willful..60

    Chapter One 61

    Chapter Two..78

    Chapter Three 88

    Chapter Four 98

    Chapter Five 110

Wild 117

    Chapter One 118

    Chapter Two..131

    Chapter Three 146

    Chapter Four 157

    Chapter Five 167

    Chapter Six 176

Wayward 185

    Chapter One 186

    Chapter Two..199

    Chapter Three 210

    Chapter Four 222

    Chapter Five 231

    Chapter Six 242

Sinful..255

    Chapter One 256

    Chapter Two..266

    Chapter Three 276

    Chapter Four 286

    Chapter Five 295

Anne Kane 303

Changeling Press E-Books..................................304

Wanton
Sci-Fi Action & Intrigue Romance
Anne Kane

When Tarik's brother is captured by the Intergalactic Council, the handsome cyborg realizes he'll need the help of a Stargazer if a rescue mission is to succeed. Problem is, as the leader of the rebellion he can't just advertise for a Stargazer willing to flout the Intergalactic Council.

But when he kidnaps Krystal, he is completely unprepared for the irresistibly sexy young woman with a gentle soul. Now he's torn between rescuing his brother and his growing attraction to the talented witch.

Chapter One

Tarik watched the young woman pacing the cargo bay of his ship. Tall and willowy, she stalked the width of the cell with angry strides of long, slim legs. A short, fitted tunic did little to hide her shapely figure, and he felt a spark of heat ignite in his gut despite his mistrust of her kind. Wisps of wavy, chestnut hair escaped from the single braid that hung to her waist, and her green eyes sparkled with rage.

He felt the corner of his mouth tilt upward as she aimed a kick at the wall. He'd bet if he could hear what she was muttering, it wouldn't be very ladylike. Of course, she wasn't really a lady. Krystal de Mylar was a Stargazer, one of the few who hadn't yet sold her talents to the Intergalactic Council. Probably holding out for a better deal, he thought cynically.

The lack of military security surrounding her had made her an ideal target when he realized he needed to acquire one of the accursed witches in order to rescue his brother. Tarik's renegade status made it impossible to post a job proposal with the Stargazers' Guild, so he'd simply used his resources to plan and execute the perfect kidnapping. Unfortunately, none of his cybernetic enhancements would help him explain to the infuriated redhead why he'd spirited her away from her home without her consent.

The woman stopped pacing and pivoted to face the hovering droid, her eyes narrowed so that the green irises sparkled like gems. She'd obviously realized someone was monitoring her. A flicker of heat ran up his spine as she stood still, legs spread and hands on hips. Her mouth moved, and his attention dropped to her full, luscious lips as they moved slowly in exaggerated speech.

You are going to regret this.

It wasn't hard to read her lips. Or the threat in her eyes. He sure hoped she didn't know how to wrap the interplanetary energy lines around his neck.

"Not exactly what I'd expected." He turned to address his second-in-command. "I pictured someone older, and tougher."

Ryan grinned. "And a little less mouthwateringly attractive? Might have made it easier to deal with her. Do you want me to go in first and soften her up a bit? Your reputation with the ladies doesn't bode well for gaining her co-operation."

Tarik sighed. They'd managed to spirit Krystal out from under the noses of her parents and her bodyguards without a problem, but they needed her to co-operate if they hoped to accomplish their mission.

Stargazers could sense the energy lines that connected the stars and planets. They had the ability to grasp those lines and harness the energy for their own use. If she agreed to help them rescue his brother Cynn, all they'd need to do was narrow down his location and the witch could use the energy lines to get them in and out of Intergalactic space undetected by the patrolling warships. He didn't understand how the Stargazers accomplished it, but the results were irrefutable, which explained why the unscrupulous bastards running the Intergalactic Council made a point of hiring as many of the witches as possible.

Before his parents were murdered by the Council, they'd likened the Stargazers' abilities to the witches of Old Earth, who used the planet's ley lines to feed their magic. They'd been baffled though, by the Stargazers' tendency to accept employment with the restrictive Intergalactic Council. He sighed, running his fingers through his short hair. The longer he put this off, the angrier the witch would get.

"Get her into a set of restraints and bring her up to the interrogation chamber." He turned to leave, pausing when Ryan grabbed his arm. He looked pointedly at the offending hand, raising one eyebrow questioningly.

Ryan let go of his arm. "Restraints? Are you serious? She's already pissed. You need to convince her to help us, and treating her like a criminal isn't going to win you any brownie points."

That might be true, but he wanted her under control until she agreed to help. "Just the wrist restraints, then." He ignored Ryan's glare of disapproval. "If I understand the theory, she can't hook into the power of the energy lines without lifting her arms, so we should be safe enough."

Ryan's disbelieving snort told him what his second-in-command thought about that.

"Get her up there. Now." He issued the command in what he hoped was a stern tone, pivoting to stalk out of the room. The damn witch hadn't been on his ship for a full solar cycle and already she was causing trouble.

* * *

"Let me see if I have this straight." Sarcasm dripped from Krystal's voice. "You launched an unprovoked attack on my parents' estate, abducted me, left me cooling my heels in a cold cargo bay holding cell for goddess knows how long, had my hands bound behind me with a set of barbaric and extremely uncomfortable restraints, and then had me brought to what is obviously an interrogation chamber." She paused to sweep a scornful glance around the room, her gaze lingering on a padded rack with leather straps dangling from the various parts.

"And now you'd like me to do a favor for you?" She lifted her chin and fixed him with a glacial stare. "Thanks, but I don't think so. I'd like to go home now."

He had to give her credit for poise. Her haughty stance and the way she held her head high, chin tilted just so, gave the impression she was used to giving orders -- and having them obeyed.

He glanced away from her for a moment and gestured at the guards. "Please remove Ms. de Mylar's restraints and wait outside the door until I summon you." He was gratified to see a faint shadow of alarm cross her face. She knew he wouldn't give in quite this easy. He gave her a bland smile. "We need to discuss how best to accommodate her request."

The shorter of the two guards stepped forward to remove the restraints. Tarik had to think for a moment before he could place him. Brent was a new recruit, a refugee from the Intergalactic Council's recent annexation of the Utan home worlds.

Krystal stepped away from the guard and rubbed her wrists. The restraints hadn't been that tight, but they'd obviously annoyed her.

A loud click signaled the departure of the guards and Tarik leaned back, stretching his long legs out under the table. "Have a seat." He nodded toward the empty chair across from him.

"No, thank you."

He shrugged. "Suit yourself. This might take a while."

The witch raised a brow at him. "I can't imagine why."

He didn't say anything for a moment, letting his gaze wander from the sprinkling of freckles on her nose, down her lithe figure to the foot that she tapped impatiently on the floor. Luckily, the table hid his body's reaction. He didn't need her to know she could arouse him with just a glance.

"Fine!" She threw herself into the chair, crossing her arms on her chest and glaring at him. "Discuss away."

Tarik had to suppress the urge to grin. She certainly had the supercilious attitude down pat. He leaned forward, focusing on her emerald green eyes. Bad idea. A man could drown in those eyes. He shifted his attention lower, only to find himself wondering what those lips would taste like.

Okay, time to lay my cards on the table.

"I'm Tarik, the leader of the miners' rebellion. The Intergalactic Council tried to buy me off, and when I refused, they abducted my brother, Cynn. They hope to use him to force me to abandon the rebellion and give them the mining rights we inherited from our parents. I can't betray all the people who rely on us, and I can't abandon Cynn to the mercy of the Council."

He sighed and ran a hand through his hair. "We're determined to bring justice to this corner of the galaxy and stop the Intergalactic Council from terrorizing the outer planets. It's time for them to stop forcing colonists to sign over their mining rights without adequate compensation. If the colonists and miners all stand together, we can stop them from sending their thugs to murder anyone who disagrees with them."

He paused. "I've only got one option. Rescue. I need to get to Cynn before they realize I'm coming. If my intelligence is correct, you can find him, or at least locate his energy signature. We think he's being held somewhere in the Kelverian asteroid field. If you can get us in without being detected, we can snatch him and get back out before they realize what we're up to."

He met her gaze, hoping she could read the sincerity in his eyes. "I don't usually condone kidnapping people, but I couldn't very well go to the guild and say I wanted to hire a Stargazer willing to flout the Intergalactic Council."

She ignored his quasi apology, a frown marring the perfection of her brow. "What will they do if you don't agree to what they ask?"

He decided to be brutally honest with her. If she agreed to help, she deserved to know what kind of beings they were dealing with. "Most likely execute him. First, they'd torture him a bit. Make sure I know how much he's suffering. Send me vid clips of the proceedings, perhaps a few body parts in case I thought they were faking the vid."

He paused, taking a deep breath to quell the rage building inside him. "But that's not going to happen. You are going to help us." He let the steel show in his voice. No matter what he had to do, Cynn was not going to suffer the way their parents had. He wouldn't allow anything to interfere with the rescue. Not even a Stargazer with mesmerizing green eyes and the body of a sex goddess.

She leaned forward, staring intently into his eyes, and he got the feeling this wasn't the first time she'd discussed military tactics. "How good is your intelligence? Are you reasonably sure of his location?"

"Are you going to help us?" he countered, studying her face hopefully.

She smiled, a slow, bewitching movement of her lips that revealed two rows of even white teeth. "Maybe; tell me the whole story. What's so special about you?"

He let himself relax slightly. She didn't look quite as angry. He sure hoped she'd do this the easy way, because no matter how much he loved his brother, he wasn't sure he could order anyone to harm this woman, much less do it himself.

He sucked in a deep breath. "My birth family lived on the mining colony on Radian V. Two decades ago, a group of miners there discovered a deposit of a rare, radioactive mineral and claimed the rights to it as per galactic regulations." He leaned back, focusing on the wall behind her. "The Intergalactic Council offered to purchase the rights to the deposit for a fraction of their worth. The miners refused, and one by one, they and their families suffered a series of fatal accidents." He paused to let that sink in. "My brother and I are the lone survivors of that group of miners."

* * *

Krystal could see the suppressed rage emanating from the man in front of her. He'd kept his feelings and emotions hidden for so long, she wasn't sure he even realized how angry he was. She reached out with her senses and felt the cold rage, the heart-wrenching sorrow that lurked behind his expressionless face.

"There were only about a dozen of us left on-planet when they sent in a ship full of mercenaries to finish us off. They took the adults out first, murdering them in cold blood. They were dead before any of us knew what was going on. Then they started in on the kids. They thought they'd killed all of us too, but I wasn't about to lie down and die for them. I hid Cynn in one of the escape pods on the very ship that brought them to destroy us, and while they celebrated how clever they were, I set the self-destruct sequence on their ship. I squeezed into the pod with Cynn and blasted us into orbit. We'd just cleared the atmosphere when the explosion rocked through their ship."

He paused to lift an iron bar in his hands,

bending it as if it were nothing. "We were picked up by a passing colonist ship. Their med-tech had some experience with cybernetics and he fixed me up." He straightened the bar and laid it gently back on the counter. "You see, the thugs that worked for the Council enjoyed listening to me scream while they didn't quite kill me. The colonists took Cynn and I into their homes, treated us like family. They never knew where we came from and they didn't care. They were good people, and we owe our lives to them."

The bleak devastation in his eyes made her want to weep for that little boy. No one should have to live with that kind of emotional pain. Although she didn't approve of his methods, and definitely didn't like being kidnapped and transported off-planet without her consent, she conceded he did have a point.

The ruthlessness of the Intergalactic Council was legendary. They wouldn't hesitate to kill to achieve their ends. Power and money were the only things they cared about, and the value of the mining deposits would be their only consideration. He definitely needed a Stargazer if he hoped to have any chance of rescuing his brother from their clutches.

Of course, she didn't intend to give in quite yet. He needed to learn to ask nicely. Possibly even beg a bit. She repressed a smile at the thought of this wickedly handsome cyborg kneeling worshipfully at her feet. She let her gaze drift down his body as she wondered exactly how much of him was human and how much was machine.

"Do you have a plan? Other than kidnapping me?"

A wry smile curled the corner of his mouth, and she could see the cloud of anger receding slightly from his aura. "Not yet. I was hoping you could explain what you needed from me to track Cynn. You're the first Stargazer I've ever actually talked to face to face, so I'm not sure how much of what I know is myth and how much is fact."

"An apology." She watched those perfectly sculpted brows rise in disbelief, and smothered a giggle. She'd be willing to bet most people jumped to obey him.

"An apology?"

"Yes." She gave him the indulgent look she usually reserved for small children stealing fruit from the estate gardens. "If you want me to help, you need to apologize for kidnapping me and treating me like some kind of rabid animal." An interesting shade of red stained his cheeks, and she almost felt sorry for him. Almost. "And then you have to ask me nice."

"Ask you nice?" He looked confused as he echoed her words.

"Ask me nicely to help you rescue your brother." She rolled her eyes. "You can't expect to just go all alpha cyborg and have me groveling at your feet."

A ghost of a smile flickered in his eyes. "It would simplify things."

She felt herself wondering what a real smile would look like on those full, sensuous lips. His comment certainly didn't warrant a reply, so she sat, staring pointedly at him.

"I'm sorry." He leaned forward to capture her hands and she felt the full impact of those sapphire blue eyes. She could read the sincerity in them, and felt herself relenting a bit.

"I suppose that will do, although you might want to work on your delivery." She attempted to pull her hands free, but he held them in a firm grip, refusing to let her go.

"Now, what did you want from me?" She stopped tugging. If he really wanted to hold her hands, she supposed it couldn't hurt to let him.

"I need you to find my brother and take us to him." He turned one hand over and studied her palm, running his thumb over it in an unconsciously sexy rhythm. "Can you do that?"

Krystal frowned, struggling to find the words to explain her gift. "It's not that easy. I have to know someone, know their aura, their energy signature, before I can find them. Even then, I'd have to be reasonably close. Energy dissipates over time and distance." She looked up into his eyes. "If your intel is correct about which system he's in, and you can tell me something about him, I can try. Some vid footage to help me get a sense of his character would be good. I can't make any promises, but I'll try."

"What about the ship?" His thumb still caressed her hand. "Can you really use the ley lines to power her without being detected?"

Krystal smiled. That part she knew she could deliver. "Piece of cake. I've been practicing with ley lines since before I could walk. So long as you have a spot for me to work and are willing to protect me while I'm in the trance, that's the easy part." She noted the puzzled look on his face, and her heart sank. "You do know how a Stargazer works, don't you?"

The big cyborg shrugged. "Not specifically. I assume you'll need a quiet space to concentrate." He looked sheepish. "I never thought to ask for details."

She took a deep breath, hoping he didn't belong to one of the many fundamentalist religious groups that abhorred nudity. "I need to be able to feel the ley lines with my whole being. If your ship has a view screen on the bridge, that would be perfect." She looked down at the desk between them. "I will need to be naked, so I can use my body to manipulate the power lines."

Chapter Two

Tarik felt like someone had sucker punched him right in the gut. The thought of this gorgeous woman naked on the bridge of his ship sent the blood racing to his groin, and he struggled to keep his face expressionless. "Are you serious?"

She nodded, wisps of red hair bobbing around her face. "Clothing impedes the flow of energy." She raised her head to look into his eyes. "Do you have a problem with nudity?"

Hell, no. He'd be quite happy to have her nude body spread beneath him so he could explore every delectable inch of it. He wasn't so sure he'd be happy to have her parading naked in front of his entire crew. An unfamiliar twinge of possessiveness tweaked him, and he scowled. "I don't think it's a good idea for you to be prancing around nude in front of my crew."

She glared at him. "I don't plan to prance around. And I didn't see any innocent-looking crewmembers when you descended on my home to abduct me. I doubt I'd be scarring anyone's innocence." She paused, her delicate nostrils flaring as she took a deep, calming breath. "Surely you can set up a small area for me, screened off from the rest of the bridge crew." Her gaze settled on a metal rack with soft padded cuffs, designed to hold prisoners without injuring them. "Ideally, you would have a Stargazer platform for me to use. It helps if we can spread ourselves without worrying about falling while we channel the power. I could probably adapt that to work."

He almost choked at the mental image of her spread naked and restrained. Did those freckles appear on any other part of that delectable body? He gave his libido a stern order to knock it off. "Adapt? How?"

She bounced up from her chair and walked around the apparatus, eyeing it critically. She grabbed a couple of the leather straps and repositioned them higher up on the outstretched metal tubing. "Like that. My hands will be reaching up toward the ley lines so these need to be higher. A padded strap around the center, to hold me up while I'm in the trance would be good as well. And my legs need to be spread exactly one leg-length apart." She looked up from under her lashes, and his cock jerked to attention.

"I'm sure we can find something suitable." He needed to get himself under control here. "I'll have someone show you to your cabin while I look for some vid footage of Cynn for you to watch."

"That cute officer who locked me in the cargo bay?"

He brought his head up sharply. What did she mean, cute? Ryan was not cute. "On second thought, I'll have Ryan search the archives and I'll escort you myself." He activated the com-link, his voice a little sharper than necessary. "Ryan, report to the interrogation chamber. Immediately."

He looked up to find Krystal staring at him, a mischievous grin tilting the corner of her mouth. Before he had a chance to wonder if she'd deliberately manipulated him, the door opened to admit Ryan.

"Hey, boss. Need some help handling the witch?"

Tarik glanced over to see Krystal smiling at his second. She stiffened at the word "witch," sending him a quelling look. He made a mental note to chastise Ryan later. The man had the tact of a Martian sled pup.

"No." He frowned, and, as usual, Ryan ignored him completely. "Ms. de Mylar has agreed to help us rescue Cynn, and I need you to get some vid-footage of him so she can get a sense of who he is. I'm hoping she'll be able to locate him for us."

A big grin broke out on Ryan's face. "Great. I told you she looked like a reasonable gal." He turned to Krystal. "Welcome aboard. And sorry about the witch crack. Sometimes I just don't know when to shut up."

"No problem." She bestowed a dazzling smile on Ryan, and Tarik had a sudden urge to deck his old friend. She stepped toward him, and he noted the graceful sway of her hips. "You were going to show me to my cabin?" She made it sound like an invitation and his cock jerked sharply in its tight prison. A slight widening of her eyes let him know she'd done it on purpose. The little witch was flirting with him!

"Certainly." He captured her hand, enveloping it in his larger one. He looked over at Ryan. "I'll be back later to see what you've dug up. Try to make it a good mix so she can get a clear picture of him."

He led her out into the corridor, holding her closer than necessary. His cybernetic implants could sense her elevated heart rate and breathing patterns. She wanted him as much as he wanted her. The question was, would she admit it?

He decided to take the risk. If she planned to wander around his bridge buck naked, there was no way he could keep his hands off her. He stopped in front of the cabin he'd assigned to her, and waited while the door slid open.

"This is nice." She stepped through the doorway, her gorgeous green eyes sparkling with enthusiasm.

Tarik looked around the undersized space. A small counter took up all of the space between the clothes locker and the comp station. The sleeping platform filled most of the floor space, and someone had thrown a pink floral cover over the standard issue sheets. He suspected Ryan's irrepressible sense of humor, but he had no idea where his second could have found such a feminine item onboard his ship. His attention wandered to her shapely butt as she crossed the room to inspect the locker.

"I don't suppose you thought to grab some of my clothing when you..." her voice trailed off and she turned to face him, "...decided to have me join your little expedition."

"Clothing?" Tarik felt like a small boy caught in the act of peeking. "No, but I'm sure we can find something onboard that will fit you." His gaze swept her mouthwatering figure. "Although not as attractively as that."

"Well, then." Krystal's hand went to the hem of her tunic. "I'd better be careful to keep this in good shape."

She pulled the material over her head with one smooth motion, and Tarik found himself staring at one very naked, very gorgeous Stargazer. He stood rooted to the spot, her wanton display rendering him speechless.

Krystal ignored him, folding the tunic neatly before stowing it in one of the drawers under the counter. "There's one other thing I forgot to mention." She slid the drawer closed and turned to face him. "My abilities are enhanced by physical union with a male."

Tarik stared, not sure he'd heard that right. "You mean, like sex?"

A ghost of a smile crossed her face, but her expression remained serious. "Yes. The act of joining with a male generates a great deal of psychic energy, which enhances my natural abilities. It's said that the effect is even stronger if there is an emotional bond between the Stargazer and the male, but I have no experience of that personally."

She studied his face earnestly, and he got the impression there was something important here that he was missing. Something she didn't want to tell him. A sudden suspicion crossed his mind. "You said you thought my second was cute. Ryan. Were you saying you want him to bed you?"

For a moment, she stared at him in confusion. Then she broke out in a peal of laughter that sent a shiver of excitement down his spine. "Moon kits are cute too, but they don't excite me." She licked her lips, suddenly looking nervous. "I had hoped you might be unattached and available."

Tarik stood very still, using his considerable will to control the wave of lust that swept through him. He needed to be sure she meant what she said. "Are you sure you want me? I'm not going to take it easy, or follow orders, or stop when you think you've had enough. I need to be in control." Another thought occurred to him. "You mean to tell me that you fuck someone every time you use your talent?"

It came out sounding a lot more judgmental than he'd intended, but he found it hard to control the surge of jealousy at the thought of her coupling casually with someone just to enhance her powers. The angry glint in her eyes told him he'd pushed the limits of her patience.

"Why do you think I'm not employed by the Intergalactic Council?" She gave him a frosty stare. "I refuse to sleep with someone I'm not attracted to. They've given me until my twenty-fifth naming day to either change my mind, or find one of their officers to bond with. My parents don't have the political backing to defy them, so I'd resigned myself to a union with one of their less obnoxious officers. Perhaps I should thank you for kidnapping me. The grace period ends in two days, so it seems you've saved me from their clutches. At least for now."

"And you're attracted to me?" Tarik grinned wickedly, jealousy quickly giving way to a molten heat that sent blood rushing to his groin.

Krystal tossed her head, looking haughtily down her nose at him. "Mildly, but if you're not interested, I'm sure I could find someone amongst your crew that's suitable for my use. I'll need to be in top form if I'm going to outwit the Council."

Tarik crossed the space between them with an inhuman burst of speed, wrapping her firmly in his arms. "I don't think you're going to be bothering my crew, witch." He lowered his head, inhaling her intoxicating scent. "I'll be more than happy to fuck you until you're begging for mercy."

* * *

Krystal melted against Tarik's hard frame, fitting herself against his deliciously muscular body. For just a second there, she'd thought he was going to refuse her. She looked into his eyes, the blue darkening to black. A fiery ball of liquid heat slid through her as his breath fanned her cheek, his lips tracing a path from her ear to her mouth, teasing her lips open to sweep in to explore. He circled her tongue with his, swirling, tasting, enticing her to join him in an erotic game of taste and touch.

She lifted her hands to his shoulders, shaking with a fierce need she struggled to control. He reached up to loosen her hair from its braid, his fingers running through the heavy mass and spreading it over her back.

"You're so beautiful." He whispered the words against her throat as he used his teeth to nibble gently on her tender skin. "How could I not want you?" His lips moved over her, gentle despite the urgent need in his voice. Putting her aside for a minute, he shed his suit with careless haste, discarding it in a heap on the floor.

Krystal stared in awe at his heavily muscled body. Scars were scattered across most of it, giving mute testimony to the torture he'd suffered as a child. Her gaze dropped lower, to the magnificent shaft jutting proudly out from a nest of dark blond curls. The plum-shaped head strained eagerly upward, and Krystal's breath caught in her throat as she imagined it invading her tight channel.

"You're sure about this?" Tarik hesitated for a second, searching her face for confirmation before he pulled her back into his embrace, lowering his head to sear his lips across hers.

A flood of emotion filled her, his emotions, his need. She relaxed, knowing he'd gone too far to stop. The thick evidence of his arousal pressed hard against her belly. She'd never felt this incredible attraction before, this sense of desperate need. Her past experiences with sexual partners had left her wondering what all the fuss was about. Now she understood. She felt the burning need, the unquenchable desire that the other Stargazers described when they talked about their partners.

"Yes, very sure." She ran her hands across his chest, marveling at the hard play of muscle that tensed beneath her palm. This was no data-coding Council flunky. Despite his cybernetic enhancements, Tarik was all male. Anticipation ignited fingers of heat that caressed their way up her spine.

With an impatient growl, he lifted her up and laid her on the sleeping platform. Following her down, he straddled her hips with rock-hard thighs. His sapphire eyes glittered darkly, and she stared, mesmerized by the naked lust on his face

He lowered himself to lie beside her, one leg thrown across her belly to hold her in place while he laced his fingers in her hair and reclaimed her lips. Less gently now, his impatience showing in the aggressive thrusts of his tongue as he explored more fully, demanding her surrender, anchoring her in place with firm tugs on her hair. His tongue slid over hers, coaxing and claiming, blatantly seductive.

Krystal opened her mouth wider, allowing him in, wanting more, his dominant posture triggering a primal need she'd never known she had. She tilted her chin up to allow him better access, and he rewarded her with a growl as he quickly took advantage. Their tongues met, clashed, danced around each other in an erotic duel.

His lips left hers, traveling across her cheek as he licked and tasted his way down to the tender hollow of her throat. He feathered light kisses in the sensitive hollow, pausing to run his tongue across the vein pulsing erratically as liquid heat pooled low in her belly.

His hands wandered lower, exploring every inch of her and making her acutely aware of her body. He cupped the curves of her breasts, his large hands kneading the tender flesh, until she arched up into them. With a knowing chuckle, he tweaked one nipple between his thumb and forefinger.

She gasped at the incredible sensation, darts of pleasure slipping along her nerves. Before she managed to catch her breath, Tarik lowered his head and sucked the tip of one plump mound into his mouth, his teeth scoring gently across the nipple. Krystal gave up all pretence at control, whimpering in pleasure as she grasped his short hair and held him tight. He suckled greedily, using his tongue and teeth to drive her pleasure higher and higher. He smoothed his hand down across her belly, his fingers toying with the shallow dimple of her belly button.

Krystal twisted and squirmed beneath his aggressive assault. She could feel the moisture gathering in her pussy as his hand inched its way closer, stopping to explore the angle of her hips. He bit down gently on one sensitive nipple just as he cupped her sex, parting the soft folds to run his thumb across the swollen nub of her clit. He stroked the heated flesh and a shudder of pure erotic pleasure ran through her. She arched into his hand, pressing herself against his hot body with wanton abandon. She didn't care if he knew how much she wanted him, how hot he made her. Only feelings mattered; the feeling of his hands stroking her body, his mouth suckling at her breast.

He slipped a finger into her slick channel, and the breath exploded from her lungs in a strangled gasp. A slow heat flared deep within her core, spreading along every nerve as he worked his finger in and out, pausing occasionally to flick the hard nub of her clit with his thumb.

"Please." She wasn't sure how much more of this she could take. "I need you."

He raised his head, gazing into her eyes. "I know."

The simple admission sent her blood pressure soaring as he wriggled down to place his mouth over her pussy, his tongue stabbing between the slick folds of her labia to feast at the moist entrance to her sex.

Krystal arched up into his mouth, offering him everything. She writhed beneath his talented tongue, drowning in sensation until she lost herself in a fiery burst of heat that sent her hurtling over the edge on a wave of pure passion.

Tarik quickly scooted up to replace his mouth with his cock, the heavy shaft prodding impatiently at her wet entrance. Krystal opened her eyes, staring up at him in a daze as her body shuddered under the force of her orgasm. He gripped her hips tightly, holding her down while he buried himself to the balls with one swift, hard thrust of his muscular hips.

Krystal screamed at the incredible sensation, his name an endearment on her lips as she felt the molten intensity of a second orgasm racing through her, her torso bucking uncontrollably.

Tarik rode her hard, pistoning in and out of her sex with long, hot strokes of his thick shaft. She bucked and twisted beneath him, pleasure so intense it bordered on pain filling her every pore, every nerve, until she thought she'd go insane if he didn't stop. She wrapped her legs around his waist, tilting her hips to allow him maximum penetration.

He kept going, harder, faster, every stroke of his wonderful cock driving her higher and higher until she begged him for release. She couldn't think of anything else, only the taste of him, the feel of him inside her, the explosive chemistry between them.

He shifted a bit, changed the angle of his penetration, and her world shattered as she rocketed over the edge yet again, her tight channel rippling hard around his shaft as he followed her, his hot seed jetting into her. Wave after wave of sensation pulsed through her, and she clung, holding him tight as the world fell away and there was only the two of them. Together.

Clinging to each other as a million tiny aftershocks rippled through them.

Tarik collapsed, rolling onto his side without letting her go, careful not to crush her beneath his muscular body. "Damn." He lifted one hand to smooth a damp strand of hair behind her ear. "I think I could become addicted to the feel of your body under me, witch." He brushed a light kiss across her lips, his touch gentle.

Krystal smiled up at him. After an encounter as hot as that, even the word "witch" wasn't enough to upset her. Tarik's aura glowed a gentle blue, the rage dissipated for the time being. She'd hazard a guess that it had been a long time since he'd felt so at peace. A contented sigh left her lips as she felt herself drifting off into sleep.

Chapter Three

Krystal watched the two young men on the holo-screen. The clip had been taken years ago, when Tarik and his brother were in their early teens. Even at that age, Tarik had the confident air of a leader, his eyes constantly moving, looking for potential danger. Some of his movements seemed awkward, and she guessed that his cybernetic implants had taken time to adjust to the growth spurts of a human child. The scars on his body were newer and more pronounced than when he'd stripped in front of her yesterday.

She felt a rush of liquid heat in her core at the thought of their encounter the previous day. She hadn't been entirely honest with him. Sex in and of itself didn't enhance her power; it had more to do with her feelings. She'd experimented with several of the males in the palace guard, and while she'd felt a mild enjoyment at their practiced attentions, it hadn't been enough to bolster her powers. She just couldn't seem to let go and throw herself into the erotic encounters the way she'd seen some of the other Stargazers do.

One of the main reasons she'd resisted the increasingly persistent recruitment officers from the Intergalactic Council was the contract clause that required her to "exercise due attention to building her powers through the use of targeted sexual encounters." The idea of prostituting herself for power left a bad taste in her mouth.

She turned her attention to Cynn. Although physically similar to his older brother, with the same wide grin and sparkling blue eyes, his aura was brighter, with less of the angry red overtones. Tarik had mentioned that Cynn was five years younger than he was; he'd probably been too young to fully understand what had been going on during the massacre. She watched as the two brothers played an animated game of laser tag. She swore Tarik held back, letting the younger child score often enough to keep him interested in the game.

She sighed, impatient with herself. She needed to concentrate on Cynn, not moon over his sexy older brother. She studied Cynn, realizing he shared many of the traits that she found so attractive in Tarik.

"Finding what you need?"

She turned to see Tarik's second leaning against the doorway, the ever-present grin curving the corner of his mouth. "Yes, thanks. These are quite good." She tucked an annoying lock of hair behind one ear. "How well do you know Tarik's brother?"

Ryan shrugged. "Pretty well. Cynn and I have been shipmates for about six years. What do you want to know?"

"Just tell me about him. Is he a clown? Does he have a quick temper? I need to be able to identify his energy signature, and it's much harder if I've never met the person."

Ryan frowned. "He's a lot like Tarik, but without the hard edges. He's loyal to a fault, he'd do anything for a friend. And he's got the wackiest sense of humor this side of Ursa Major. He loves to play practical jokes."

Krystal watched the emotions play across Ryan's face as he described some of the stunts Cynn had pulled during their years together. Tarik's younger brother sounded like a very thoughtful, caring person with a zany streak a mile wide. She wondered what Tarik would have been like if he'd had the chance to grow up without the memory of his parents' murder to color his perceptions. She felt her heart going out to that child who'd had to set aside his grief in order to save what was left of his family.

"Do you think we'll be able to find him and get him out?"

Krystal nodded, her gaze going to the two boys on the holo-screen. "I think we stand a good chance."

"Well, that's certainly good to hear." Tarik strode into the room, and Krystal felt a delicious wave of anticipation rippling through her veins. "Ryan, don't you have to check on the deflectors before we get to the asteroid field?"

"Yes, but it'll be hours before we're anywhere near it." He turned to give Krystal a conspiratorial wink. "I thought I'd see if Krystal here could use some help figuring out what makes your brother tick."

Krystal watched in amazement as a tinge of green streaked its way through Tarik's aura. He was jealous! Not one to waste an opportunity for mischief, she grinned up at the meddling second. "Thank you. You were a big help."

"No problem." He spoiled the effect by ruffling her hair in a big-brotherly gesture. "I'd best go check out those deflectors now before our fearless leader here decides to throw me in the brig."

Krystal glanced up at the unsmiling Tarik, enjoying the feeling of camaraderie. "I don't think he'd do that."

"I might." A reluctant grin crooked the corner of his mouth as he watched their playful exchange. "He wouldn't look so cute after spending a couple of days in isolation."

"Cute?" Ryan raised his brows in exaggerated horror. "I'm not cute. I'm ruggedly handsome in a holo-vid star kind of way."

Krystal burst out laughing. "And so modest."

She noted the green receding from Tarik's aura as he realized the two of them were just kidding around. "Go check on your deflectors, and thank you for the help."

"No problem." He sauntered over to the doorway, pausing to address Tarik. "Shouldn't take more than an hour or so to run the diagnostics on the deflectors. I'll send you a status report when they're done."

Krystal turned back to the screen. "You and your brother have a lot in common."

Tarik shrugged. "I suppose we do. Does that make it easier for you?"

She looked over at him. "Yes. I should be able to detect his energy signature if we're within a reasonable distance of him."

Tarik gave her a searching look. "Are you sure? That you can identify him if we get close enough?"

She laid her hand on his arm, sensing how important her answer was. "Absolutely. Now show me the star charts. Where do we need to be?"

Tarik strode over to the console and laid his hand on the sensor pad. He closed his eyes as his internal comp connected with the ship's computer banks. Krystal watched, fascinated. She'd never been in close contact with a cyborg before. She could see the large vein in the side of his neck twitching as he communicated with the ship. The pictures of Cynn faded, replaced by a star chart. He manipulated the image, muttering under his breath when the display didn't respond quickly enough. Finally, he opened his eyes, and she stared at the chart, a feeling of dread settling in her gut.

"That's restricted Intergalactic space." She let out her breath with a low whistle. "Are you sure?"

He nodded grimly. "I have a few contacts in their organization. The Kelverian asteroid field is right here." He pointed to a small cluster of asteroids in the center of the chart. "They don't want to chance me getting Cynn back." He gave her a wry grin, but she could see the edge of desperation in his eyes. He knew how difficult this would be. No wonder he'd felt it necessary to kidnap a Stargazer. Even with her help, this would be dangerous.

She turned her attention back to the chart. "Where would they be holding him?"

Tarik indicated one of the larger planetary bodies. "The main holding center for dissidents is located here. They might be keeping him in there along with the political prisoners, but I doubt it They'd want him somewhere isolated in case I decided to mount a rescue mission." He pointed to another cluster of small asteroids located to the left of the main field. "I'm thinking they've got him in a detention center on one of these. The military uses them for holding high risk prisoners."

Krystal frowned. A military base located deep inside the restricted area would be a tough target. They'd have to weave unseen past four inhabited planets in order to get to the asteroid field. She'd need to be very sure of her control of the energy lines in that sector. Any mistake could prove fatal.

* * *

Tarik watched the witch as she studied the star chart. He hoped she'd be able to deliver what she promised. His brother's life depended on it.

Krystal looked up and he felt his heart jump at the gentle sympathy in her eyes. "I can get you there, but you're going to need a plan." She worried her bottom lip between her teeth. "Even if we take them by surprise, it's a military base. It's going to be heavily defended."

"I'm aware of that." He had a feeling she wouldn't like his plan. "You just need to get us there."

"And then what?"

"And then we rescue him." He reached out to draw her into his arms. "We disable their sensors, sneak in past the guards, locate him, and get the hell out."

She stared at him in disbelief. "That's it? That's your plan?"

He grinned. "Yeah. We like to keep them simple."

She shook her head. "There's a difference between simple and non-existent, you know."

He tilted her chin up so he could look directly into her green eyes. He could drown in their sparkling depths and die a happy man. "We've pulled off lots of clandestine missions. We know what we're doing. This time it's one of our own whose life is on the line, and we never let down one of our own."

He lowered his head to the sweet temptation of her mouth and moved his lips over hers in a gentle caress, cajoling, blatantly seductive. His tongue traced the shape of her lips, teasing them open to allow him access. His tongue touched hers, slid along the side, and engaged in an erotic dance that left them both breathless.

He nibbled his way across her cheek, pausing to whisper in her ear. "Do you still think Ryan's cute?"

She giggled, and ran a hand down his chest. "Yes, he's cute, but..." She paused, her eyes sparkling with mirth.

"But?" he prompted

"But he doesn't make me feel like ripping off my

clothes and impaling myself on his thick, hot cock."

Tarik felt the blood rush to his shaft at her blunt statement. The woman would be spending the better part of the voyage flat on her back if she didn't learn to control her tongue. He pulled her in hard against him so she could feel how much her statement affected him.

"We might want to retire to the sleeping quarters," she pointed out, shamelessly rubbing herself against the outline of his swollen cock.

With a growl of frustration, he used his comp to send a mental command to the door. It closed with a subdued *whoosh*, followed by an audible click as the lock engaged.

He let her go, backing up a step as he slowly and deliberately stripped off his clothing. Her gaze dropped to his cock, and her eyes widened, her pink tongue coming out to run across her lips in a gesture that made his shaft swell even harder.

She raised her head to stare into his eyes, and her hands went to the fastening of her bodysuit. She swayed in a gentle rhythm as she proceeded to strip off her clothing in a blatantly sexual display. When she stood completely naked before him, a slow, sexy smile spread across her face. His comp display told him her heartbeat was fast and her blood pressure elevated. She knew what she wanted and he thanked the merciful gods that she wanted him.

He took his cock in one hand, stroking slowly down the length. He pointed to a spot just in front of him. "Come here."

She did, covering the distance in a graceful glide. Her attention on his jutting shaft, she lowered herself to her knees. She reached out to touch him, her fingers teasingly exploring the length.

He drew in his breath in a ragged gasp, and darts of lust thundered through his veins. He wondered if she had any idea how much she affected him.

"Can I taste it?" She tilted her head up to look into his eyes.

He nodded, not sure if he could still talk. His cock was so engorged, it almost hurt. Krystal cupped his balls gently in one hand, the other guiding his shaft to her eager lips. She swirled her tongue around the swollen head, then licked her way down the side, pausing to explore the swollen veins that ran along the length.

Tarik closed his eyes and laced his fingers through the strands of her chestnut hair. Witch's hair. Witch's eyes. If she didn't take him in her mouth soon, the witch was going to find out just how little patience a human cyborg had when he wanted someone. And by all the gods in the skies, he wanted her. Wanted her sweet mouth around him. Wanted her soft skin against him. Wanted her clever hands sliding along his naked flesh.

She opened her lips and engulfed his shaft in the sweet, hot cavity of her mouth. He swore softly as a fever ignited in his groin, burning its way through his body. She danced her tongue along his length, teasing and tempting as she sucked on the aching shaft. He held her head steady, with fingers still entwined in her hair while he thrust shallowly with his hips, the feel of her soft mouth almost more than he could handle. If he didn't stop her soon, he'd spill his seed in her mouth, and he didn't want that. He wanted to feel her slick, hot channel tighten around him when he came.

She let out a breathy little moan, his cock still buried deep in her mouth, and it was the sexiest sound he'd ever heard. He thrust a couple more times, and then reluctantly pulled out.

"I want to feel your pussy milking my cock." He whispered the words into her ear as he reached down to plunge a finger into her sex, checking to make sure she was ready for him. She arched up eagerly into his hand, and he didn't need to scan with his neural comp to know she was more than ready.

He picked her up, bracing his legs as he slowly lowered her until his cock pressed eagerly against the wet heat of her entrance.

Krystal wrapped her legs around him, locking her heels behind his back as she wriggled wantonly in his hands. He thrust his way in through the tight folds until his balls were snugged up against her butt and she started to ride him with easy rocking thrusts of her hips. She wrapped her arms around his neck, and buried her face in the hollow of his shoulder as she met him thrust for thrust.

"Hang on, my little witch." He took over the lead, thrusting up into her deliciously tight channel. Faster. Harder. He couldn't help himself, couldn't hold back. He wanted her. Needed her.

He'd never felt this loss of control with a female before, and it shocked him. She was a witch. She could betray him. Sooner or later, they all joined the Council's ranks. She could destroy them all. And yet, he didn't want to believe it of her. She had a gentle soul and she gave herself to him with such joyous abandon.

He could sense her spiraling up out of control and he abandoned all pretence at restraint, surging into her welcoming heat harder and faster. He covered her lips with his own as she screamed out his name, her channel rippling with waves of pleasure that milked the seed from his shaft. His knees felt like rubber and he sank to the floor, taking her with him as a million tiny aftershocks ran through her body and into his.

She opened her eyes and he could see wonder shining in the enormous green depths. "That was so incredible." She said it with a trace of awe in her voice. "I can't believe I'm having wild, abandoned sex with the man who kidnapped me."

Tarik grinned and traced a finger across the dusting of freckles on her nose. "And I can't believe I've got myself buried balls deep in a witch with emerald green eyes and hair the color of a Tlanier sunset." He dropped a gentle kiss on her forehead. "We'd better get dressed and unlock the door before one of my cute crew comes to see what's going on."

"Your whole crew isn't cute." She gave him a saucy smile that made his heart do a flip-flop in his chest. "Just Ryan."

"I see I need to teach you some respect, witch." He gave her butt a playful swat before he lowered his head to sear a kiss across her lips. His crew would just have to wait.

Chapter Four

"It needs to be closer to the center of the bridge." Krystal eyed up the makeshift Stargazer platform. "I need to have as wide a visual as possible when I'm tapping into the ley lines."

The shorter of the two men looked up at her. He'd been the guard who had removed her restraints in the interrogation room. "Would there be all right?" He pointed to a spot to the left of the pilot's console.

She felt a chill go down her spine as she met his flat, black eyes. He obviously thought she was being a prima donna. She nodded. "Perfect. Thanks."

"How much longer are you going to need to set this up?" Tarik walked around the bulky apparatus.

"Not long, once we get it where the lady wants it. We just need to check a couple of connections." The two men inched the heavy platform over to its new resting spot.

Tarik had utilized the apparatus she'd first pointed out. With a few minor alterations, it made a serviceable platform to keep her upright while in a trance. She needed to have her limbs stretched out to the four corners of the universe in order to feel the energy lines and direct them to where she wanted them. She glanced over at Tarik, worrying her bottom lip with her teeth. Would he be okay with her nudity while she worked? She didn't need to be distracted by male ego.

She sighed. She'd better find out now. She had the feeling he wasn't going to like it. That flash of jealousy when he'd found her in the reviewing room with Ryan pointed to a very possessive nature. She left the two men straining to move the heavy platform, and went to stand beside him in front of the view port.

"It's beautiful, isn't it?" He looked out at the stars twinkling brightly against the velvet backdrop of the sky.

"Yes." Krystal studied the stars, seeing the faint lines of power that ran from each, joining them in a huge net of pulsing energy. "You do understand the basics of how a Stargazer works, don't you?" She found herself holding her breath, hoping he hadn't conveniently forgotten her need for nudity.

Tarik shrugged and placed his arm on her shoulder, drawing her against his warm body. "You capture the ley lines and direct them to the engines. You can also see the energy signatures surrounding people and identify them if you know them well enough." He turned to glance at the platform. "I'm not sure why you need that, but it doesn't matter. As long as we get to Cynn before the bastards hurt him, you can stand on your head and chant in ancient Gaelic."

"Nothing so dramatic. I just strip bare-assed naked and go into a trance so deep I can't trust myself to stay upright." She peeked up at him from under her lashes. His eyes narrowed and she cringed, waiting for him to speak.

"Then I guess I'll have to make sure the bridge crew knows I have first claim." He swung her around so they were standing eye to eye. "I may joke about witches, and I may have some trust issues because most of your kind side with the Intergalactic Council, but I am willing to let you do whatever it takes to find my brother." The corner of his mouth twitched with the beginning of a smile. "Perhaps the question should be: Are you sure you're going to feel safe, naked and bound with me standing in front of you?"

She relaxed. He didn't like it, but he was going along with it. "When did you want to get going?" She eyed up the platform.

Tarik looked grim. "As soon as we can. What do you need to do to prepare before we start?"

She nodded. "I like to meditate and make sure I'm properly grounded before I attempt to reach for the power lines. Channeling that kind of power isn't easy, and the backlash can be wicked if I'm not careful."

"It's not dangerous, is it?" He frowned, his eyes dark with concern. "I don't intend to exchange your life for Cynn's."

She shook her head, touched by his concern when she knew how guilty he felt about his brother's capture. "No. I'm not a novice and I'm very careful. I know my limit and make sure I don't draw any more power than I can safely handle." She reached up to caress his cheek. "I trust you to make sure I'm safe while I'm channeling."

* * *

Krystal rose gracefully to her feet, her mind at peace. She'd run through the meditation exercises her teacher had taught her, and a serene confidence flowed through her. She could do this. She was a Stargazer, a woman that fate had bestowed with a special gift.

She removed her clothing, folding it carefully and placing it beside the makeshift Stargazer platform. She placed her feet in the loops of leather, attached to the floor of the platform at exactly one leg-length apart. Pulling the straps tight around her ankles, she tested each to make sure they were secure. She reached behind her and wrapped the padded belt around her waist. If she faltered, the belt would hold her in position, keeping the flow of energy directed properly. Satisfied with the fit, she reached up and threaded her hands through the loops above her head. They too had been spaced exactly right.

She raised her head, her gaze sweeping the deck in front of her. The bridge crew were all at their stations, their backs to her. All except one. She looked into Tarik's eyes, and nodded.

The heavy curtain of her hair slid down her back as she lifted her chin, closing her eyes. She let her mind expand, seeking the bright energy of the ley lines. They shimmered into view behind her closed lids, a glittering maze of greens and blues. She felt them with her consciousness, one after the other, searching for the connection that would lead her to the Kelverian asteroid field.

There!

She couldn't have explained it, how she knew when the correct line presented itself, but there was no doubt. She concentrated, drawing the sparkling energy into her, capturing it with her outstretched arms, directing it to the engines that lay waiting. She could feel the engines take life, the power flowing into them and through them. Silently, the big ship started to move, following the path of the ley line as it flowed across the velvety stillness of space.

She reveled in the feeling of the power flowing into her, through her. That was the danger that every Stargazer faced. The temptation to draw more and more power, to fill herself with the shimmering light until it burned her out, was so hard to resist.

Without a mate to anchor her to this world, to pull her back from the edge of madness, the danger grew every time she touched the ley lines. Her teacher had warned her, time and again, urged her to choose a mate. But she'd refused. She didn't want just any mate. She wanted someone to love, someone who would cherish her, put her happiness ahead of his own. She wanted a home and children. She wanted the kind of relationship her parents had, and she refused to settle for anything less. If she couldn't have true love, then eventually she'd give in to the temptation and merge completely with the ley lines, her earthly body left behind.

She felt the ley line getting shorter, its source near. Reluctantly, she let some of the power slip from her hands, slowing the engines. She sent a tendril of power out to touch Tarik's aura, reassuring herself that he stood guard over her, waiting for her to complete her task. The touch was oddly soothing, compensating for the loss she felt at releasing even a bit of her hold on the lovely power of the line.

She recalled everything she knew about Cynn, his personality, his laughter, his energy and life force. Carefully, so as not to alert anyone nearby with telepathic abilities, she probed the planets and asteroids ahead, evaluating each energy signature, discarding them one after the other when she assured herself they weren't the one she searched for.

She had no concept of the passage of time. It could have been moments or whole solar cycles. Time had no meaning when the power flowing through her induced a trance. She discarded planet after planet, asteroid after asteroid. She turned her attention to a cluster of smaller asteroids off to the side of the main field.

And she found him. His life force felt weak, and she fed him a little of the energy that flowed through her, felt his surprise at her touch, his confusion. She tried to reassure him, but he didn't understand. She sensed others near him, and she withdrew carefully, leaving no trace of her visit.

She needed to tell Tarik, let him know that his brother was alive and that she'd located him.

Reluctantly, she released her hold on the ley line, sorrow beating at her as the power faded from her grasp. Her body sagged against the restraints, and she opened her eyes to find Tarik standing in front of her, his face a mask of concern. She opened her mouth to speak, but all she managed was a hoarse croak.

He reached for her wrists, fumbling with the straps, and she realized he intended to release her from the platform. "No!" She couldn't let him do that. He still needed her talents. "I found him, and he's alive. When your rescue team is ready, I'll get you in as close as I can." She closed her eyes and shuddered, her body suddenly cold.

"Forget it. You're worn out." She snapped her eyes open as he released her first wrist and started to work on the second. "I'll find some other way to get him out."

"No." She reached up, fumbling to reattach the straps. "I want to do this. For the first time in my life, I'm using my powers to help someone. Let me help you. Let me help your brother." She paused to suck in a deep breath, searching for the words to explain her feelings. "I've always thought of my talent as a curse, one I'd eventually be forced to use for the Intergalactic Council. I told myself that I wouldn't let it happen, but I always wondered if I'd be strong enough to refuse, to let the energy lines absorb my soul rather than serve the corruption of the Intergalactic Council." She lifted her chin to meet his gaze, willing him to understand.

* * *

Tarik paused, his hands on the padded strap at her waist. The sight of her outstretched on the platform, her skin almost translucent as the energy flowed through her in visible surges of light, had terrified him. He'd wanted to wrench her off that platform and kiss the life back into her. He'd wanted to crush her body under his and bury himself in her repeatedly until he knew she was safe. He hadn't felt so totally helpless and out of control since the day he'd found the lifeless bodies of his parents.

"You're frozen and exhausted. You brought us over ten light years from our starting point in less than a solar day." He chose to concentrate on something he could fix. He stripped off his shirt and wrapped it around her slender shoulders. "At least take a break while I brief the team, and we get ready for the assault." He tipped her chin up to place a gentle kiss on her lips. "Do it for me."

Krystal hesitated, and let her hands slide out of the restraints. She nodded and a tired smile lit her face with a gentle glow. "For you."

* * *

"We need to get in and out as quickly as possible." Tarik looked at the four men he'd picked to accompany him into the stronghold. They'd all been with him for years, and he'd be willing to trust his life to any one of them. Blade was a mutant. part human, part lizard, and he had the ability to sense the presence of warm-blooded creatures from several hundred yards away. He would be able to warn them of the enemy's position before they showed themselves.

Zack and Timmi were both enhanced humans. They'd been sold to the Galactic Council as toddlers and altered in ways they'd never fully revealed to him. They could move through any terrain without making a sound and kill a target without leaving a mark on the corpse. They'd escaped from the Council on their very first mission, seeking out Tarik's rebel band to offer their services. They delighted in letting the Council know every single time they used their enhancements to thwart the Council's plans.

He'd chosen the fourth member of the rescue squad for sheer size and brute strength. Paden weighed in at over one hundred thirty kilos of pure muscle. If they had to fight their way out, Paden would lead the way.

Tarik used his neural implants to access the ship's computer banks, and called up a dimensional image of the compound, the display hovering just above the group. "Krystal pinpointed Cynn's position as somewhere in this area." He indicated a cluster of rooms at the back of the complex. "We have to assume there's more than one guard. She detected a large mass of energy signals in that area. It may be a barracks building."

"Are you sure this isn't a trap?" Paden cocked his head in thought. "I've never worked with a Stargazer before. I thought they all belonged to the Intergalactic Council."

Tarik lowered his voice to an icy calm, holding on to his temper with difficulty. Somewhere along the line, he'd come to trust Krystal, and he expected no less from his men. She'd drained herself to get them this far without detection. "Well, Krystal doesn't belong to them. She says Cynn is here and he's heavily guarded, so we go in and get him. If you're not okay with that, speak up and I'll take you off the team."

He glared at Paden, holding the bigger man's gaze until Paden looked away. "Okay, if you trust her that's good enough for me. I'm in."

Tarik looked around the room. "Anyone else want out?"

The other three shook their heads, and Tarik took a deep calming breath. "Okay then, let's get on with it." He pointed to an area at the top of the dimensional image. "We'll be coming in from this side. There's a lot of scrub brush and small hills so we should be able to get up to the walls without being detected." He moved his hand. "There's an old underground aquifer at this point and we can use it to get inside the building."

"Won't it be guarded?" Blade leaned forward to study the image.

Tarik nodded. "Probably just one guard, according to the intel I could find. Zack goes in first and takes him out." He paused. "We can't risk the guard raising an alarm so it has to be a clean kill."

"No problem." Zack nodded thoughtfully. "Shouldn't take long. I can hide the body inside the tunnel."

Tarik traced the route of the aquifer with one finger. "We stay in the tunnel. We should be able to get most of the way to where Cynn is being held without being discovered. Once we're there, we'll have to take down whatever guards are aware of our presence and retreat the way we came. Hopefully Cynn will be able to walk. If not, Paden is going to have to carry him while the rest of us hold off any defenders that we haven't dealt with yet. Once we get back to the ship, Krystal can get us out of there." He looked around the room. "Any questions?"

Timmi looked up, a slow smile of anticipation spreading across his face. "When do we go in?"

Tarik straightened up and let the image dissolve. "We suit up as soon as possible and meet in the cargo bay. Once we're ready, Krystal will get us in place to launch the rescue." He looked around at the faces of his team. "We'll only get one chance at it, so we need to make this a clean extraction. Once the Intergalactic Council realizes we're here, they'll kill him." He consulted his interior clock. "Gather whatever you think you'll need and meet me in the cargo bay launch area in twenty minutes."

The men filed out, and Tarik headed to Krystal's cabin. He hoped she'd had enough rest to regain her strength.

Chapter Five

Krystal collapsed on the sleeping platform, groaning in frustration. It was one thing to use Tarik for a very pleasant interlude that just coincidentally boosted her control. She could accept that, even plan to do it again. Sex didn't mean anything, didn't imply need, or commitment. But to reach for his presence while in a trance, and to use that presence to brace herself against the gut-wrenching void that invariably hit her when she let go of the ley lines -- that was totally unacceptable.

She relived that moment in her mind, when she'd unconsciously reached for him. She felt again that incredible feeling of being grounded, of having someone anchoring her in the real world. Tarik. Her kidnapper. The damn cyborg who insisted on calling her a witch. She buried her head in the mound of pillows. This just couldn't be happening. It must be the stress of worrying about the Council's ultimatum.

She thumped her fist down into the soft coverings. She'd help him rescue his brother and then she'd get as far away as she could from Tarik the sexy cyborg. She wanted a gentle man for her life mate, one who would look after her and bring her presents, write her beautiful love poems and play with their offspring. Tarik wasn't anything like her dream man. He was angry and intense, and those eyes of his could see right into her soul. She closed her eyes, exhausted, and drifted off into a fitful sleep populated by pint-sized blue-eyed cyborgs who kept calling her Mommy.

* * *

Tarik looked down at the sleeping witch, and his heart did a little dance in his chest. Asleep, she looked young and so very innocent. Her chestnut hair spread out across her chest in riotous abandon, clothing her naked body with tempting streaks of red and brown.

He felt a smile curve the corner of his mouth. She really needed to learn some modesty, for his sake if not for hers. He could feel the blood rushing to his groin as his gaze followed the gentle curves of her figure and came to rest on the nest of soft curls at the apex of her thighs. He took a deep breath and struggled to control his raging lust. Once they'd rescued Cynn, he'd have time to work out the growing relationship between them. She'd somehow managed to charm her way past the ice surrounding his heart, and he didn't intend to let her go. Ever.

He leaned down and ghosted a gentle kiss across her lips. "Time to wake up, witch."

Krystal's eyes fluttered open, and in that first unguarded moment he could have sworn she looked up at him with love shining from the sparkling green depths of her eyes. Then she blinked, rubbing a hand across her face. "I had the strangest dream..." Her voice trailed off and an impish smile curved the corner of her mouth. "You must have been an adorable child."

Tarik stared at her in confusion. He'd never understand the witch. "The team's ready."

She nodded, her expression sobering. "Give me a few moments to prepare, and then I'll get up to the bridge. I'll have us under way in ten minutes."

He nodded and turned to leave. The door *whooshed* open at his approach, and he pivoted, striding back to the sleeping platform and the irresistible female perched on its edge. He cupped the back of her head in one hand, tilting it to sear a hard kiss across her lips. Their gazes met as he released her. "Be careful." He ran his hand through the silky fall of her hair. "I need to know you'll be safe."

She nodded mutely, her eyes wide in the pale oval of her face. He wished he had the words to express his feelings. She deserved a gentle man, a poet who could love her and cherish her, let her know how special she was. Instead, she had him.

* * *

The team crouched in the scrub brush surrounding the detention center. Tarik nodded to Zack, and they watched as the enhanced human seemed to flow across the terrain toward his unsuspecting target. Moments later, the guard dropped lifelessly to the ground, blood trickling from the corner of his mouth. Zack rose silently to his feet and grabbed the corpse, quickly dragging it out of sight.

"Go!" Tarik whispered the word into his com unit, rising to make the short dash across open ground to the aquifer. The other members of the team followed silently behind him, pausing just inside the tunnel to regroup. Blade and Tarik took the lead, the two mutants placing themselves next, while Paden fell into position behind them, his huge bulk moving with surprising grace as his restless gaze swept the tunnel, watching for any sign of pursuit.

The tunnel wound its way under the detention center, side tunnels branching off into darkness at odd intervals. Tarik kept a glowlight balanced above them, his internal comp controlling it so that it shed just enough light to allow them to make their way silently along the aquifer.

Tarik followed the interactive map superimposed over his optic nerve by his internal comp. It indicated the branch they needed to follow was directly ahead, and he signaled the team that they were approaching the target zone.

Moments later, Blade laid a hand on his arm, stopping him in his tracks. Tarik turned, and the mutant motioned him to get down. Someone or something lurked in the tunnel ahead.

Blade waited until his teammates settled on their haunches in the dark before he disappeared into the blackness ahead. They heard a brief scuffle, followed by a muffled thump, and the mutant rejoined them, wiping his hands carefully with a scrap of material he hadn't had a moment ago. He nodded grimly to Tarik and fell back into position.

Tarik kept the glowlight dimmed, and swung into the branch in the tunnel. "We're close. Should be an access chute ahead to the left." He spoke softly into the com unit. "Holding cells are to the left when we exit the chute." He spotted the access chute, and headed for it, using his comp's sensors to probe the dark shadows for any sign of a trap. "Blade?"

The mutant slipped into place in front of him, his head swiveling back and forth as he searched for any sign of body heat beyond the exit. "All clear."

Tarik signaled with his hand, and the team slipped into the corridor, turning left into a short hallway lined with doors. Blade indicated the one at the far end. "Life signs are in there," he whispered into his com unit.

They slid into position, two on either side of the door. Tarik waited until they were in place, weapons at the ready, before he laid his hand on the locking mechanism and used his comp to override the door lock. The panel slid into the wall, and he could see his brother tied to a chair in the center of the cell. A thick gag prevented Cynn from talking, but his eyes were wide with panic, sliding from Tarik to the corner of the room.

Tarik nodded. He crouched down, clicking the safety off his blaster before he threw himself into the room in a quick tuck and roll, coming up in front of Cynn with the weapon aimed firmly in the direction his brother had indicated.

"Tarik. It took you longer than I expected." Brent, the newest member of his crew, lounged against the wall, a crooked grin on his face. "But then, I came in the front door. So much easier that way."

Tarik stared at the man, stunned. A movement in the dark corner behind the traitor drew his attention.

Krystal! The Stargazer lay bound and gagged on the floor, her eyes dazed. One cheek was swollen, the imprint of a hand outlined in ugly red. Tarik forced himself to control the deep rage he felt. He met Brent's cold stare. "What's going on here?" He moved toward Krystal, unable to resist the need to comfort her.

Brent's eyes narrowed. "Back off. And get the rest of them in here." He pointed a lethal-looking blaster at Krystal's head, but his eyes never left Tarik. "Do as I say or the witch gets really hurt."

Tarik stopped and stared at the man who'd claimed to hate the Council more than anyone else in this sector of the galaxy. "Zack and Timmi, come in here real slow. Brent knows you're out there." He addressed the traitor. "Why?"

"Money. And power." Brent laughed, the sound harsh and humorless in the small room. "Do you have any idea how much the Council is willing to pay for both you and a Stargazer? All I had to do was deliver Cynn to them, and tell you that you needed a Stargazer to get him back. I never thought you'd fall for the damn witch, but that turned out to be a plus. You were so busy lusting after her you didn't realize I was setting you up."

He prodded Krystal carelessly with his foot, and Tarik felt a tight ball of anger coiling in his gut. The man had just sealed his own death warrant.

"The Council rep says she's the strongest witch they've come across in a long time. They knew she'd rather burn herself up in the power lines than submit to the Council, so they wanted her here, away from the arbitrators, while they convinced her to join." A nasty smile crossed Brent's face. "Maybe if you're good, they'll let you stick around to keep her ramped up to speed. The witches thrive on getting fucked."

Tarik gauged the distance, blocking the sound of the traitor's voice as he waited for him to make a mistake, to let his arm relax just enough. The man was a fool. He must have known Tarik would come armed to the teeth, and bring the best fighters from his group with him. Why hadn't he brought his own backup, or arranged for the Council to intercept them before they reached their target? Brent had to be insane to think he could take down the leader of the rebellion with just a blaster, no matter how lethal it looked.

He'd turned Cynn over to be tortured, and abused Krystal. An entire troop of Intergalactic soldiers wouldn't be enough to save him from Tarik's wrath. And yet, he stood there all alone, bragging about his treachery.

"We're waiting for a signal." Paden's voice was barely audible over the com unit, and Tarik didn't make a movement that might alert the traitor. Brent should have realized there were more men out there.

"They're going to give me my own ship, and a full troop under my control." Brent's gun hand moved, a fraction of an inch, and Tarik held his breath. *Just a little more…*

Cynn groaned, and Brent turned sharply toward

the sound. Tarik seized the opportunity, launching himself directly at the traitor, twisting left to let his cybernetic arm take the blast as Brent pulled the trigger. The sickening smell of burnt synth-flesh filled the air, and Krystal whimpered.

Tarik raised his good arm and punched Brent square in the face, crushing his nose and driving the splinters up into his brain cavity. Brent fell to the ground, his agonized scream cut short when Tarik raised his foot to stomp on the other man's chest with every bit of his weight and cybernetic strength, crushing his rib cage and ensuring he wouldn't ever betray a friend or lay an abusive hand on a female again.

He looked up to find the rest of the assault team crowded into the small cell, Timmi using a laser blade to cut the restraints from Cynn. Tarik pulled off his shirt and wrapped it around his charred arm. The damage looked worse than it actually was. The blaster beam fire had been too brief to damage the titanium framework and intel-chips that formed the core of the arm.

He crouched down, gently pulling the gag out of Krystal's mouth before he made short work of the restraints. She threw herself at him, running her hands over his body again and again, as though to convince herself he was really there.

He hugged her close, smoothing his hands through the tangled mess of her hair. "It's okay, my little witch. He's gone. He's not going to hurt you or anyone else ever again."

"But you could have been killed!" She glared at the bloody corpse on the floor. "He said if I didn't do exactly as he said, he'd kill you."

Tarik grinned. "I'm not so easy to kill. Now calm

down, we still have to get out of here." He glanced over at the other men. "Any idea what we're up against on the way out?"

Cynn grinned, taking a blaster from Blade and checking the charge. "Not a clue. I've been a little tied up since I got here, but I'm looking forward to repaying some of the hospitality I've been shown. Nice to see you, bro." His gaze shifted to Krystal. "I take it you're the Stargazer everyone's been buzzing about. They're not going to be happy to see you plastered to my older brother."

Krystal gave him a shy smile, and Tarik felt his heart swell with pride at her courage. He'd ripped her from her safe home and put her smack dab in the middle of the rebellion, and she worried about him being hurt. He gave her a quick, hard kiss before he stood and checked his own weapons. He pried the blaster out of Brent's hand and handed it to Krystal. "If you have to use it, aim for the chest. It's the biggest target, and if you miss, there's a good chance you'll at least slow the attacker down."

He looked around at the team. They were all standing at the ready, waiting for orders. "We're going out the same way we came in, but there's bound to be some resistance." He looked at Paden. "You and Blade lead the way. Timmi, you and Zack follow, with Cynn in front of you. Krystal and I will bring up the rear." He looked around. "Everyone ready?"

The men nodded, faces grim as they got into position.

"Go!" Tarik shouted the command, and the group surged out the doorway.

* * *

Krystal kept her head down as much as possible, making sure her weapon pointed away from the men in front of her. She followed Timmi out into the corridor and around to the access chute, the comforting bulk of Tarik following behind her.

She'd been horrified when Brent yanked her off the Stargazer platform, taking advantage of her weakness immediately after they'd landed to slap the restraints on her and carry her off-ship. In a post-trance daze, she hadn't been able to focus enough to fight back. She didn't know what he'd done to the rest of the crew, whether he'd hurt them or if he'd fabricated some story to explain his bizarre behavior.

She shuddered, remembering the insane gleam in his eyes as he bragged about how much he'd sold them out for.

She paused, shrinking back against Tarik when Paden and Blade opened fire on a small group of snipers in one of the branch tunnels before signaling the all clear. The team hustled along the deserted aquifer, methodically working their way back to the ship.

At last, they reached the exit, and Paden held up his hand, halting the group. He sent out a signal on the com link, and moments later Krystal watched as the ship hovered into view, landing gently in the clear area in front of the scrub brush. The noise of the engines was deafening, but surprise was no longer an issue.

The team regrouped, putting Krystal in the middle of them as they moved toward the ship in a tight group. The crew on the ship laid down a thick blanket of covering fire that kept the enemy troops from taking advantage of their run across the open ground.

Moments later, the seven made it to the ship, and Krystal sagged in relief as the airlock slid closed behind them. She turned to Tarik and threw herself into his waiting arms, ignoring the teasing hoots and whistles from the rest of the men.

* * *

Three long solar days later, they were finally clear of the pursuing Council ships and could afford to relax. Krystal sunk into the warm water, letting the aromatic bubbles rise until only her head was above water. "Mmmmm. This feels so good. I can't believe you own an authentic jetted bath tub."

Tarik grinned wickedly. "I didn't until you expressed a desire for a bubble bath. I had the engineering unit fabricate it while we played hide and seek in that damn asteroid field." He lifted his arms and pulled the snug body shirt over his head.

She tilted her head and stared at him in amazement. "You had an antique bath tub replicated just for me?"

"No." He hooked his thumbs in the waistband of his leggings and skimmed them down his lean thighs. "I did it for me." He tossed the clothing carelessly aside. "I figured if I had one of these in my quarters, I could keep you naked and available all the time." He stood and stalked slowly across the room toward her, his cock bobbing eagerly as it curved upward from his groin.

Krystal waited until he got close enough, and splashed the soapy water at him. He raised his eyebrows at her as the bubbly drops slid down his chest, and she giggled. She'd never imagined all those years ago, when she'd realized she was different, that life could ever be this carefree and happy again.

Tarik growled in mock severity and climbed into the tub, straddling her body with his long legs. "You need to learn a little respect, witch."

"Really? And who's going to teach me?" She

stuck out her tongue impudently.

"I guess it'll have to be me." Tarik wrapped one hand around his shaft, stroking slowly along the thick length.

Her eyes followed the movement and she gulped as she watched the thick cock swell even larger. "Are you planning on using that on me?"

"I think in you would be more effective."

"I'll squirm and wiggle."

"Can't be helped."

"I might even scream a bit."

"I certainly hope so." He knelt down and pulled her legs apart, positioning the swollen head of his cock at her hot, wet entrance. "You might want to start squirming now."

Krystal obliged, moaning as he slid himself deep inside her slick pussy with one powerful thrust of his hips.

"Ready to acknowledge me as your master and become a permanent member of my crew?" Tarik slid his cock in and out of her tight channel with measured thrusts of his hips, running his hands down the sensitive flesh of her inner thighs.

"Master is such a strong word." Krystal gasped as he lowered his mouth to nip the sensitive skin in the hollow of her throat.

"True, but then I'm a very strong cyborg," he pointed out, as she wrapped her legs around his waist. He gripped her hips and raised her up, hesitating for a brief moment before lowering her back down over his delicious shaft.

"Yes." She whimpered as he held her in place with one hand and reached down to score his thumbnail across her swollen clit.

"Yes, you acknowledge me as master, or yes, you

want to join my crew?"

Krystal moaned in frustration. Why did she have to be stuck with the only male in the galaxy who wanted to carry on a conversation while he fucked her? "The crew thing!"

Tarik ground his pelvis into hers, his cock stretching her, filling her impossibly full, and she felt a hundred tiny flames dance down her spine on their way to her core.

"Call me Master." He pulled her in toward him to nibble a line of fiery kisses across her breast.

"No." Her breath came in short pants. She could feel her body spiraling higher and higher, molten heat flowing along her every nerve as Tarik pumped his enormous cock in and out of her slick channel. The water splashed and bubbled around them, the warm wetness adding to the erotic sensations that flowed through her.

"Oh, come on. I'll be a good master." He lifted up, tilting her so that his cock rubbed across her clit with every thrust, sending flashes of heat racing through her. She squirmed helplessly on his shaft, closing her eyes as sensations rocketed into her, one after the other, so fast she no longer knew where she ended and he began. The orgasm burst over her with lightning speed, hurtling her into a chasm of pure feeling.

She clutched at Tarik, screaming his name as her channel gripped him, and he came with her, his cock emptying its thick load deep inside her. Wave after wave of sensation rocketed through her until at last she floated back to earth on a cloud of sheer bliss, tiny aftershocks still rippling through her core.

She opened her eyes to find him watching her with his sparkling blue eyes, his cock still buried deep inside her.

"You really are a witch." He trailed a gentle finger across her cheek. "You've stolen my heart, and I didn't even know I had one. You're really going to stay with me and join the crew?"

Krystal grinned happily at him. "Yes, Master!"

Willful
Sci-Fi Action & Intrigue Romance
Anne Kane

Born both a Stargazer and Daughter-Heir to the throne of New Zanadles, Jazlyn is used to a life of pampered luxury. But when the planet runs into financial trouble, her father agrees to bind her to a five-year term of service aboard a vessel with two very virile interplanetary merchants.

Her leisurely life is replaced by a whirlwind of Intergalactic Council intrigues and the lusty attentions of her new employers, but when space pirates attack, a routine delivery turns into a deadly struggle for control of the ship.

Chapter One

"You did *what*?" Jazlyn stared at her father.

He had the grace to look slightly sheepish. "The Finance Minister said it was the only way to keep the Intergalactic Council from foreclosing and taking over New Zanadles." His gaze silently implored her to understand. "It's only a five solar year contract, and you'll get to travel. You've always wanted to travel."

Jazlyn snorted. "As one of the nobility, not the main power source. Do you have any idea how humiliating this will be? I'll be taking orders from peasants!"

Her father's mouth thinned into a harsh line that always preceded one of his moral tirades. "They are not peasants! I had the palace guard investigate them thoroughly before I even considered the proposal. Mr. Rance and Mr. Nuevo are both law-abiding citizens, well respected in the merchants' guild. They've promised to treat you fairly, and the amount they've agreed upon for your services will be enough to pay off New Zanadles' loan to the Council." He reached out to place a hand on her shoulder. "Being one of the nobility comes with responsibilities. You should be proud that you're able to save our planet from being subjugated by the Intergalactic Council."

"I know. We really do need the money." She sighed and ran her fingers through her long sandy hair. "I just never pictured myself as a working girl." She lifted her chin. "So how long do I have to prepare for this great adventure?"

Her father dropped his gaze to study the intricate pattern of the tiles on the floor, refusing to look at her. "They're waiting in the green room. I thought it best if you met them just before you board their vessel. Their launch window is at the start of the next solar period and they have a shipment of perishables that needs to be delivered to the Globar system as soon as possible."

"Now?" She stared at him in dismay. "I can't possibly pack and say my goodbyes in less than a full moon cycle."

Her father looked up, and she could see the steely determination in his eyes. She knew that look. He'd given his word and nothing she could say or do would change it.

"Fine! I'll go supervise the packing." She flounced toward the doorway, only to stop when he called after her.

"That won't be necessary. I've instructed Mika to have your clothing and personal items delivered to the space station."

Jazlyn pivoted to face him, hands on her hips. "What about Mika? I do get to take my personal maid with me, don't I?" Mika, a distant cousin, had grown up with her and was more of a confidante than a servant. Leaving her home world would be hard enough without losing Mika's support.

He nodded. "It took a bit of negotiating, but they've agreed to let Mika accompany you, provided she doesn't interfere with the ship's routine."

"So I guess I should go and greet my new..." Jazlyn's voice trailed off. She had no idea what to call them. Employers?

Her father gave her an exasperated look. "They are people, Jazlyn. They need your help to deliver their goods, and we need their help to avoid financial ruin." He reached out to pull her into his embrace. "I know you'll make the people of New Zanadles proud that you are the Daughter-Heir."

* * *

Bryce paced impatiently across the lush carpet. The waiting grated on his nerves. They'd paid for the services of a Stargazer, and he was eager to get on with their voyage. Drought had swept through the Globar system this past season, and the settlers were desperate for the foodstuffs packed in the hold of his spaceship. The Intergalactic Council would be quite happy to let the settlers starve unless they agreed to be ruled by the Council. He wasn't about to let that happen.

He'd tried to hire a guild-sanctioned Stargazer, but none of the available witches were willing to take the contract. Approaching New Zanadles and offering to take an untried Stargazer had been a last resort. He hoped her father's confidence in the witch's abilities proved warranted. He'd paid a good sum for her services, and with the cargo bay full, they couldn't afford any lost time.

He pivoted as a quiet swishing signaled the door opening. A young woman swept into the room, her chin held high. Neon blue streaks shone brightly in the sandy brown hair that fell in a silken curtain to her waist. A tight bodysuit showed off her figure in a mouthwatering display of lush curves. Dozens of gaily-colored bangles decorated her arms and ankles, jingling cheerfully with every stride of those long, shapely legs. Her green eyes glowed with a haughty temper. She ran her gaze over him dismissively before she turned her attention to his partner, Tyler.

"On behalf of my family and my subjects, I welcome you to New Zanadles." She bowed formally. "I'm Jazlyn, Daughter-Heir to the throne. My father informs me that he has contracted me to serve on your vessel and I understand you are in a hurry to proceed."

Tyler came to his feet in a smooth move and took the proffered hand, bowing low. Bryce found himself annoyed at his partner's lithe grace. "Yes, we have a deadline to meet and we've wasted much precious time looking for a Stargazer willing to accompany us." Tyler's gaze flickered to Bryce, a wry smile curving his mouth. "Allow me to make introductions. My name is Tyler Rance, and this is my partner and best friend, Bryce Nuevo."

The corner of the witch's mouth curved upward gently. "I see." She looked from one to the other. "You look well with each other. Have you been together long?"

Bryce blinked, not sure what she meant until Tyler guffawed loudly, a wide grin on his face. "We're not a couple."

Jazlyn gasped, lifting a hand to cover her mouth. "Oh, I'm sorry. When you said partner, I assumed..." Her voice trailed off, heat staining her cheeks bright red. "I didn't mean to insult you."

Bryce grinned at her sympathetically. "Not to worry. If I were inclined that way, Tyler would be my first choice." He stepped forward to offer his own hand, bowing low when she accepted and placed her soft fingers within his hand. "We're honored you've agreed to serve aboard our ship." The feel of her smooth skin, warm and silky in his grasp, left him wondering what the rest of her would feel like. He gave his head a mental shake. She'd agreed to serve as a valued member of the crew, not a body slave. He obviously needed to take a quick side trip to one of the local pleasure houses before they shipped out. He hadn't been this affected by a woman since his initiation on Qualar.

"How much time do I have before we depart?" Her voice had a musical lilt to it that reminded him of the birds singing in the palace gardens.

He lifted his head, and found himself staring into the depths of those witch-green eyes. "The next clear launch window is just before the second moon rises. We'd like to utilize that. Your father indicated you'd be able to accommodate." He glanced over at Tyler. "Have her personal effects been delivered to the shuttle?"

Tyler tapped a finger against his earlobe, activating the implanted com unit. "Just getting there now." He frowned. "Were we expecting a passenger? There's a female demanding boarding privileges, and she's giving old Harold a hard time."

"Mika!" Jazlyn swiveled to look at Tyler. "Father said you'd agreed to let my companion accompany me."

Tyler nodded slightly. He pointed at the table and a holo-image shimmered into view. He lifted his eyebrows in disbelief. "Is that your companion?"

Bryce looked at the tiny image of a female, her outlandish outfit showing off more of her than it hid as she stomped her foot and gestured rudely at their supplies clerk.

"Yes." A grin curved the corner of Jazlyn's mouth, and Bryce stared, fascinated by her plump pink lips. "You might want to do your man a favor, and tell him to let her in. She doesn't know the meaning of the word 'no'."

"Not a problem." Tyler watched the tiny figure for a few seconds before he glanced over to Jazlyn. "You said her name was Mika?"

Jazlyn nodded. "She's a distant cousin and my dearest friend. Please treat her with respect."

"I'll go down and personally welcome her onboard." Tyler grinned, and Bryce could see the interest in his old friend's gaze as he practically drooled over the display. He had no doubt Tyler would be very welcoming. They hadn't had time to visit their usual haunts and blow off a little steam when they'd gotten into port. The settlers' position was too precarious for them to waste precious time at the pleasure houses.

"Get the companion and the clothes stowed away. I'll answer any questions Jazlyn has and be along as soon as I can. Oh, and tell the crew to prep for launch."

Tyler snapped to attention and gave him a mock salute. "Yes, sir!" He headed to the exit with long strides of his lanky legs, and then paused. "Oh, and nice to have you aboard, Jazlyn. I can see this is going to be a very interesting voyage."

"Thank you." Jazlyn turned to Bryce. "Perhaps you can fill me in on where we're heading." She led him to the seating area under the great tapestry. She sank into the cushions of the overstuffed sofa, leaving him to choose from several large chairs. "My father didn't tell me why you contracted me instead of one of the Council Stargazers. I've never performed on any vessel but my father's."

She stared at him with those gorgeous green eyes, and he felt the blood pool low in his groin. This would definitely be an interesting voyage.

"We have a shipment of flash-dried subsistence packs for the Globar system. They're in the midst of the worst drought in recorded history and they're getting desperate." He hesitated to mention the Intergalactic Council's interest in the system, unsure of her political leanings. "We need a Stargazer's talent to cut travel times and get the shipment to them before anyone starves. Your father was the only one who expressed an interest in the contract."

Jazlyn raised a hand to sweep the hair back from her face, and the bangles on her arm jingled melodically. A frown marred the perfect line of her brow. "I had no idea the situation was so serious. You might want to reconsider taking on an untried Stargazer."

"None of the others were willing to take the contract." He held up a hand. "I'm sure you'll do fine. Your father seems to have a great deal of confidence in your abilities, as does the Commander of the Imperial Fleet." And he did not intend to trade this gorgeous morsel for one of the hard-eyed Council witches. "We've had a Stargazer platform installed, and I've arranged a meditation chamber just off the bridge for your use. We've never utilized the services of a Stargazer before, so if there's anything else you need, just ask."

"You've never used a Stargazer before?"

"No, usually we're fine with standard means of transportation." He grinned at her. "And we'd never make any money if we had to pay your father's rates on a regular basis."

She cocked her head and his eyes followed the shimmering blue streaks as the silky mass flowed down her back. Were they a sign of her talent or just nano-enhanced strands? He'd never paid much attention to the Stargazers he'd encountered before, but then none of them had caused his cock to harden so that it chafed behind the cloth of his snug leggings.

"Do you know how we work?"

The look of dread on her face caused him to smile gently. "I know enough. You can see the energy lines that join the stars and planets and can tap into them." He paused. "And I know you have to be naked in order to manipulate the energy, although I don't understand why."

Jazlyn visibly relaxed. "Clothing impedes the flow of energy. I use my body to channel the flow, so I don't want anything blocking that energy flow. Part of the reason for the specialized platform is to shield me from the crew." She wrinkled her nose in an endearing expression that made him want to drag her into his arms and kiss her until she couldn't breathe. "Some people have a real problem with nudity."

Bryce nodded in what he hoped was a comforting gesture, and shifted in his seat to ease the pressure of his clothing on his rock-hard shaft. He didn't have a problem with nudity. Right now, he'd be happy to have both of them naked, preferably somewhere other than in her father's palace. He didn't think the king would be overly impressed with what he had in mind for the Daughter-Heir.

"And then there's sex." Her gaze swept over his body in a frankly assessing manner. "We use sex to bolster our power. The chemicals released in the body during copulation heighten our talents and enable us to absorb more of the power of the ley lines without burning out. I'll need someone to partner with me several times during every voyage." She paused, and he watched, fascinated, as she wet her lips with her tongue. "You and your partner would be acceptable, but if you'd rather not participate, perhaps you could suggest a member of your crew. I'd need to approve your choice, of course."

Bryce stared, shock radiating through him. Had she just suggested a threesome with him and Tyler? The thought had electric charges of heat racing through his veins. He leaned toward the little witch. "You want Tyler and me to fuck you? At the same time?"

A ghost of a smile hovered on those delicious

lips. "To be honest, I'd prefer to phrase it a little less bluntly, but yes. That's the general idea. I've never had multiple partners before, and the idea is intriguing."

"Well." Bryce felt like a newbie at the flight academy, propositioning his first female. "I'm sure we'll both do our best to help you achieve your goal."

She smiled wickedly. "Perhaps you'd care to demonstrate?"

* * *

He blinked. Had the little minx just propositioned him? "Now? In your father's palace?"

She rose gracefully and glided over to key something into the locking device. The door slid shut with an audible click. "There. Now we won't be interrupted."

Bryce crossed the distance between them. He'd been playing the gentleman until now, but he wasn't about to ignore such a blatant invitation. Sliding one arm around her waist, he tilted her head back, teasing her lips open with little nibbles. She tasted of jasmine and honey, things he'd almost forgotten during his long years in space.

She opened to him and he slid his tongue in deep to explore, his other hand sliding down to grasp her buttocks and draw her up against his aching shaft. She arched into him and he could feel the heat of her sex through the thin material of their clothing.

"Damn, you're gorgeous." He trailed a row of kisses across her cheek before stopping to nibble on the soft lobe of her ear.

"You're not so hard on the eyes, either. I was wondering how to get you away from your partner, but he conveniently decided to leave." Her warm breath caressed his neck.

"I think the sight of your companion motivated

him. We haven't had time to visit the pleasure houses since we docked." He nipped the delicate skin of her neck. "I thought you wanted both of us."

Jazlyn ran her hands down his chest. "Later. Right now, I want you. Let's hope Mika leaves your friend enough energy to perform his duties. My cousin is quite a handful."

Bryce slid the fastener of her suit down, letting her breasts spill into his hands. "You're quite a handful yourself." He cupped the heavy mounds and Jazlyn moaned softly. He leaned forward to suck one dark nipple into his mouth, swirling his tongue around the turgid peak. He licked and sucked, first one and then the other, pausing briefly to skim the tight suit down over her hips and legs.

"That's not fair." Jazlyn grinned wickedly. "I want you naked too."

"As you wish, Daughter-Heir." He bowed mockingly, and quickly proceeded to strip off his clothing, discarding it in an untidy heap on the floor. He watched her eyes widen as his cock sprang free, curving upward.

"Oh, my." She eyed up his shaft. "I think I'm going to enjoy this voyage." She closed the distance between them in three graceful steps, dropping to her knees in front of him.

When she reached up and gently cupped his sac he thought he was going to come right then and there. Heat coursed through him, electrifying every nerve in his body. It took all his self-control not to drape her over that sofa and bury himself deep in her hot sex.

Mischief danced in those witch-green eyes, telling him she knew exactly what she did to his control. He took a deep breath and watched as she licked her lips, her tongue slowly wetting them so that they glistened red. Then she leaned forward and engulfed the head of his cock, swirling her tongue around it in long, smooth strokes.

By all the gods, that felt incredible. He braced his legs and cupped the back of her head, urging her to take him deeper. She obliged, tilting her head to let his shaft slide in farther, her tongue busily lapping along the sides while she gently squeezed his sac.

He closed his eyes and allowed himself to enjoy her amazing mouth as her tongue explored the length of his cock. Her cheeks hollowed as she worked her way down his shaft, the sensations sending heat coiling in the depths of his belly. The little sucking noises she made were incredibly erotic. He gave himself up to the blissful joy of her attention for a few more minutes, and then gently pulled her back.

"I want to feel your tight pussy around me when I come." He pulled her to her feet and led her over to the seating area. She followed his lead silently, her eyes dark with lust. He urged her up onto one of the plush seats, draping her hips across the high back, her buttocks up in the air. Bending over her, he urged her legs farther apart, allowing him easy access to her hot pussy.

"Damn, you have no idea how gorgeous you look from here." He met her gaze as she turned her head to look over her shoulder. "I could look at you all night." He reached down and ran his hands across the silky smooth skin of her ass, down the deep cleft, stopping briefly to finger the tight rosebud of her anus before he parted the damp lips of her pussy and inserted a finger. Heat and wetness greeted his questing finger, her inner muscles clamping greedily around him. He brushed his thumb across the hard nub of her clit, enjoying her whimpering cry as she pushed back against his hand. He teased her for a few moments, pumping two fingers in and out of her slick channel while she squirmed against his palm.

He withdrew his fingers and took his cock in hand, pressing it against her eager sex. Gripping her hips tightly, he slid himself into her tight pussy. Slowly. One teasing inch at a time. She tried to push backward, force him deeper, but his fingers dug into the flesh of her hips, holding her steady, making her wait. She'd made the first move, and the second, but now it was his turn, and he wanted her to acknowledge his lead.

He inhaled deeply, taking her scent into his lungs. Sunshine. She smelled like sunshine, and flowers, and all those things he missed during long voyages. He pulled his shaft out, then rammed it back into her and reveled in the feel of her sex as it clamped tightly around him. Bending over, he brushed his lips across her neck. He bit down on the tender skin, and then soothed the pain away with a flurry of tiny kisses.

She whimpered loudly, writhing beneath him. "Please. Fuck me harder."

"Yes!" He wrapped his arms around her to cup her breasts while he picked up the pace, ramming himself into her repeatedly. She met him thrust for thrust, crying out as they both thrashed, winding higher and higher until, with one last hard thrust, he spilled them over the edge, his hot seed spurting deep within her.

They collapsed across the seat, spent, the only sound in the room their ragged breathing as they struggled to drag oxygen into their starving lungs.

Jazlyn looked up, her eyes dazed. "That was amazing. I've never been fucked like that before."

Bryce smoothed a lock of blue-brown hair off her

face and brushed a gentle kiss across her lips. "Thank you. You're quite the amazing partner yourself." They lay quietly together for a few minutes, still wrapped in each other's arms, until Jazlyn sighed and slipped out of his embrace. Retrieving her bodysuit, she shrugged back into it. "I'd better go make sure Mika didn't miss anything in the packing. I'll see you aboard your vessel."

Bryce, scrambling awkwardly to his feet as she turned to leave, watched the gentle sway of her hips as she strode toward the doorway. The bodysuit left little to the imagination, and his was working overtime. He could still imagine the feel of that nicely rounded butt snugged up against his groin as he buried his shaft in her. This promised to be the most bizarre mission since he and Tyler had teamed up to purchase the ship.

* * *

Mika shook out a pair of green silk pantaloons, folding them carefully before she stowed them in the garment locker. The departure had been so hurried she hadn't had time to unpack before they left the docking station. They'd used conventional propulsion to depart the planet. The partners said they didn't want to advertise the fact that they had a Stargazer onboard. "They're quite the pair, aren't they?" She slanted a mischievous look at her cousin. "You shouldn't have any trouble getting your talent tuned up with that twosome."

Jazlyn stroked the brush through her thick hair. "They are quite yummy, aren't they?" She grinned. "I wonder if Daddy dearest actually met them before he decided to sign the contract. He looked more than a little uncomfortable when he delivered me to the docks."

"Well, it's too late for him to change his mind

and marry you off to one of those buffoons who show up at court to beg for your hand. We left the docking ring two cycles ago, and we'll be clear of the civilian shipping lanes soon." Mika transferred clothing from the transport pods to the lockers with a quiet efficiency. "You'd never be happy with one of them. Remember the ambassador from Roheda?"

Jazlyn rolled her eyes. He must have been the fattest male she'd ever seen. With his reptilian features and the sickly green tint to his skin, she wasn't sure she could have stomached eating in the same room as him, let alone having him touch her. Luckily, he'd found out about the state of New Zanadles' finances and had disappeared with a very undiplomatic haste. "A real winner that one." She put the brush down and studied her features on the plasma display. "So what do you think of Bryce?"

Mika wrinkled her nose. "He's okay. He seemed kind of serious and bossy, though. I think I prefer the other one. Tyler, was it?"

Jazlyn laughed and threw a wadded-up shirt at her cousin. "It was, and you know it. Do you really prefer Tyler? Bryce has those dreamy blue eyes and all that long, dark hair."

"It doesn't really matter." Mika tossed the shirt back to her. "You'll get both of them anyway. Now, I've been scouting out the crew, and there's lots of potential there. Did you know they have a mixed crew? I even saw an Asylian, and you know their reputation for stamina." She laughed. "I think I'm going to enjoy this little adventure."

"You always do." Jazlyn regarded her cousin with affection. Despite being orphaned at birth, Mika had a sunny personality and never failed to see the best in every situation. Throughout their childhood, she'd always found a way to turn every situation to her advantage. Jazlyn almost pitied the crew. They had no idea what they were in for.

"Can you pull up the star charts? I'd like to see where we're heading." Jazlyn shoved the last of her clothing into the built-in clothes chest and flopped down on her belly on the bed closest to her.

Mika sat beside her, and held out her hand to point her finger straight in front of them. Using the microchip embedded under the nail on her left index finger to access the public areas of the ship's computer system, she called up the star charts for the Globar system. With the casual proficiency of long practice, she projected a holo-display into the air in front of them.

"Can you get a fix on where we are now?"

"No problem."

Jazlyn studied the display as it shifted, more planets popping into view as it reconfigured itself to show their ship's current position. She noted the green line that signified the outer limits of the Intergalactic Council's territory. She'd never been outside that line before, and the Globar system was at least six parsecs beyond it. An icy finger of fear slithered down her spine.

"That's a long way from here." She mentally calculated the nexus points and likely energy lines. "It'll take us several solar cycles, with separate jumps from system to system. I'll have to talk to Bryce and Tyler, although, if they've agreed to make a delivery, I assume they know how much distance is involved." She frowned. "They must know I can't make that in one non-stop trip."

"Oh, I'm sure they're aware of that." Mika tilted the holo-vid and absently set the little planets to twirling around their suns. "You should probably go talk to them now that we've settled in." She looked up at Jazlyn and her eyes sparkled with mischief. "How about we do a walk through the ship first? I want to see what my options are, since you get those two to play with." She lowered her hand and the holo-display winked out of existence.

Jazlyn grinned. It had been a while since the two of them had run amok in the civilian quarter, and she'd missed the happy-go-lucky days of their schooling. Maturity was highly overrated. "Sure. Let's go see what kind of trouble we can get into." She stood and linked her arm through Mika's. "How about we try the food dispensing area first? No point in going hungry while we hunt down a male or two for your pleasure."

Mika skipped happily at her side, palming the door controls to lock as they exited their cabin. "Sounds like a good plan to me. Any idea where that might be?"

Jazlyn shrugged and started out down the corridor. "No, but that will give us something to ask when we run into a likely target. You can ask him where the food dispensing area is."

Mika rolled her eyes and giggled. "You noble types are so devious! Why not just ask him if he's interested in some mind-blowing sex?"

Jazlyn tilted her head and imitated Mika's high-pitched giggle. "You working types are so direct! Why not make him work for it?"

"Like you're going to make Bryce and Tyler work for it?"

"That's different."

"Really? How?"

"I need sex with them to build my strength, and they know it."

"You don't need both of them."

"No." Jazlyn grinned at her cousin. "But I'm greedy."

Mika laughed, and eyed up two brawny cadets striding toward them. "Must be a family trait. I'm feeling a little greedy myself at the moment."

Chapter Two

Jazlyn looked down the long corridor and wondered how she'd managed to get lost in the close confines of a starship. Maybe she should have taken a right at the bottom of the drop tube instead of a left? She sighed. Or maybe she should have paid more attention when Mika gave her directions.

She was already overdue for the preliminary meeting with Bryce and Tyler. This was not a good way to start their professional relationship.

She closed her eyes and centered herself. Maybe she could locate one of them if she concentrated. She called up a mental image of Bryce, with his sexy blue eyes and dark hair. She recalled the sense of mastery, the air of authority that tinted his aura. Immediately, a strong sense of his presence filled her. He was in front of her, and high above. A wry grin curved her lips. She wasn't even on the right deck.

She let the image go and headed back to the drop tube. It surprised her that she'd been able to sense his presence so strongly. Sensing people's whereabouts was one of her lesser talents. Generally, she could only locate people if she knew them well. Strangers or people she'd only met casually took a lot more effort. Bryce must have made a bigger impression on her than she realized.

On a whim, she called up an image of Tyler, and tried to locate him. The figure remained stubbornly lifeless, and after a few minutes, she gave up. Apparently, he hadn't made as much of an impression on her as his attractive partner.

* * *

As soon as she landed on the upper deck, she spotted the strategy room. She paused to calm her suddenly racing pulse before she entered. She didn't need to let Bryce know how excited she was at the thought of seeing him again in all his naked glory. Or Tyler either, she added belatedly.

But first, they needed to get the formalities out of the way.

"Ah, there you are." Bryce stood as she entered the room. With his hair tamed back by a leather band around his temples, he reminded her of a picture of an ancient warrior.

She favored him with a smile. "Sorry to be late. I took a wrong turn, but I'm here now." She looked around the sparsely furnished room. An oval table of smoothly polished stone dominated the small space, with seats placed around it in a haphazard fashion. Slowly shifting star charts covered the walls, and she guessed they were generated from within the walls themselves.

Bryce gestured her to one of the seats. "Shall we get started?"

She nodded, glancing over at Tyler. He seemed to be lost in thought, nodding absently at her from the far side of the room. He placed a cube in the center of the table and sat back down as a star chart projected up from the crystal cube. Stars and planets shimmered into view. She recognized her home and some of the closer systems. She took her seat and waited patiently for them to explain what they expected of her.

"Here's our destination." Tyler pointed to a cluster of five planets circling a small sun. "As you know, the settlers are rapidly running out of food, and..." He shot a glance at his partner, who nodded slightly. "We know the Intergalactic Council has been discouraging merchants from making deliveries in the region. They want to annex the inhabited planets, and the settlers have been less than welcoming. We're not sure if the Council is aware of your presence onboard, but we have to assume their intelligence officers have alerted them. We can't take the chance on them pulling some sort of diplomatic crap and delaying us, so we're going to take an indirect route."

He traced a zigzagging path through the myriad of stars that twinkled above the table. "We plan to utilize hyperspace jumps combined with your talent to avoid leaving a path that points directly to our destination. We hope to sneak in and deliver the subsistence packs before the Intergalactic Council realizes we've ignored their 'suggestion'."

Jazlyn studied the projection. She would have chosen a more direct route, but she had to concede that they weren't likely to see anybody or anything along the deserted route he'd proposed. "Do you really think the Council cares that much about a backwater planet in the outer fringes?"

"Oh, yeah." Bryce nodded. "That backwater planet has enough raw minerals on it to keep the Council supplied for the foreseeable future. And they can't touch it unless the settlers either grant them open access, or agree to join the Council and be ruled by them." He gave her a lopsided grin that made her heart do a little flip in her chest. "What do you think the chances are of settlers turning their hard won homes over without a fight?"

She shrugged. "Probably not great." She found it amusing that the money from this contract would help buy her own home planet's way out of the Council's clutches as well. A win-win situation all round. She watched the smooth play of muscles in Bryce's biceps as he leaned casually against the stone table. Definitely a win-win.

She cleared her throat, suddenly nervous. Bryce looked up and caught her glance, holding her in place with a look while he slowly circled the table and took her hand in his. He drew her hard up against him and she could feel the barely restrained power in his grip. He framed her face with his hands, tilting her head back. His eyes were liquid pools of lust, mesmerizing her. A rush of heat raced through her, pooling in her belly, and she swallowed, hard. For the first time in her life, she felt herself losing control. She'd felt lust before, used it to boost her abilities, but never this raw urgency, this craving that had every nerve in her body on edge.

He was so big, so hard, so... male.

And she wanted him with every fiber of her being.

* * *

Bryce lowered his head and his lips brushed across hers in a featherlight caress that sent erotic flames licking across the surface of her skin. His tongue came out to tease, tasting and tempting until she opened her mouth with a small sigh, surrendering to the inevitable.

He engulfed her lips, and his hands brushed the material of her top off her shoulders, baring her chest to his warm, questing hands while his tongue invaded her mouth. He cupped her breasts in hands that seemed to know exactly what she wanted, what she needed. She moaned and leaned into his hard body as he tweaked one tender nipple between thumb and forefinger, causing a liquid heat to dampen her pussy.

His lips left her mouth, and he nibbled his way down her cheek to her throat, burying his face in the tender hollow while he grazed his teeth across her rapidly beating pulse.

She gasped as a second set of hands circled her from behind. *Tyler!* She'd been so intent on Bryce that she'd totally forgotten they weren't alone in the room. Trapped between the two hard male bodies, she felt small and very feminine. She arched her back, rubbing her bare breasts against Bryce while Tyler fumbled with the fastenings on her leggings, his breath hot on the back of her neck.

"Looks like we've got ourselves a Stargazer sandwich," he drawled as he managed to undo the last of the laces holding the leggings up.

"Mmmmm. And it's quite tasty." Bryce nipped playfully at her breast. "Pity we don't have any sauce to spice it up."

"Oh, I'm thinking it's going to be spicy enough with a little help from us." Tyler hooked his thumbs in the waist of the leggings and skimmed them down over her hips. "I'm betting she tastes as good as she smells."

Bryce swirled his tongue around one taut nipple, and Jazlyn sucked in a deep breath as scalding tongues of lust ran down her spine. He sucked the tender tip into his mouth and feasted on it, now suckling, now scoring the tender bud with his teeth. He looked up at her, his eyes shining darkly. God, she could drown in those gorgeous eyes. She brought her hands up between them, palms flat on his rock-hard chest.

And all the while Tyler's hands roamed across her body. Caressing. Stroking. Exploring. She shouldn't be enjoying it this much; the feel of four hands caressing her, two mouths licking, sucking, nibbling on her heated flesh.

"Don't look so serious." Bryce raised his head to recapture her mouth, his lips harder now, more demanding. She opened and his tongue swept in to duel with hers, aggressive in its demand for her surrender.

Honeyed heat coiled in the pit of her stomach, and radiated outward to her breasts, her thighs, her pussy. She moaned softly, and Tyler chuckled behind her. His warm presence disappeared for a moment and she heard the soft rustle of clothing hitting the deck. Then he was back, and she could feel the thick length of his cock press up against her ass.

"Now that's hardly fair." Bryce cupped her breasts, tweaking the nipples sharply between thumb and forefinger. "I'm the only one still clothed." He stepped back and quickly stripped off his clothing. Striding over to the door, he engaged the privacy locks. "That's better. Now, where were we?"

Jazlyn licked her lips as she watched his enormous shaft bob gently with each stride. Damn, she remembered how good that felt buried deep inside her. A single drop of pre-cum glistened enticingly on the plum-shaped head, and she wanted to reach out and taste it. But Tyler still held her from behind, his large hands slowly working their way toward her eager pussy.

Bryce reached them and grasped her hips, pulling her to him so that his cock pushed hard against her belly. Tilting her chin up, he kissed her hard. His tongue dueled with hers and he bit down sharply on her lower lip before kissing the hurt away. "Time to get you up on the table."

"Definitely a good idea." Tyler loosened his grip and Bryce scooped her up, depositing her on the hard stone table.

The partners quickly joined her, one on either side. They propped themselves up on one elbow and continued to caress her naked body while the vid image of the star chart danced in the air above their heads. She closed her eyes and concentrated on feeling. She could no longer distinguish between the partners as they used all of their experience to turn her body into a mindless mass of writhing pleasure.

Bryce took the lead. He flicked the ball of his thumb over the tight bud of her clit, and she went wild with lust, turning toward him. Tyler captured her arms from behind, and wrapped his legs around hers, rolling so that she was spread out on top of him, legs splayed wide. His hard cock pressed into the cleft of her butt, hard and thick, and a shudder of delicious fear ran down her spine at the thought of that huge shaft invading her virgin anus. What would it feel like? Would it hurt?

As if he had the ability to read her thoughts, Tyler whispered in her ear, "Don't worry, little witch. I'm not going to hurt you. I think my partner would toss anyone who harmed a hair on that pretty little head of yours out the nearest airlock." He nipped her earlobe. "You've got him spellbound."

"I've got him what?" Her question turned to a gasp as Bryce slid one large finger into her slick channel, stroking inside with teasing little caresses while his thumb brushed over her clit.

She bucked forward, trying to force him in deeper, but Tyler held her back, spreading her thighs a little wider. "You just be good and wait until he's ready."

"He's right." Bryce scooted down and positioned himself between her splayed legs. "You've got me bewitched with those gorgeous green eyes. You're irresistible." He raised his head and caught her gaze, holding it firmly as a slow, sensuous smile spread across his face. "I'm not even sure I want to break free." He lowered his head and swiped his tongue across her entrance in a long, slow lick that had her screaming for more.

"Easy, darling." Mischief sparkled in his eyes. "I'm just getting started."

He proceeded to lick and suck, feasting on her sex like a man who'd been starving for days. Tyler held her still, licking and nibbling on her neck, her shoulder, wherever he could reach. Trapped between the two of them, she writhed and whimpered, careening out of control. She didn't think she'd be able to take much more of it, and then Bryce stopped. He reared up on his knees so that he towered over the pair of them, a monstrous hard-on jutting aggressively out from his groin. He slipped his hand over the shaft, slowly stroking the long length. Jazlyn watched, mesmerized as his hand moved back and forth from the huge, plum-shaped head back down to the heavy sac nestled in the dark curls.

"Do you want it?" His eyes shone, lust darkening the blue to almost black. She licked her lips and nodded. His hand stroked once more, and he grinned darkly. "I want to hear you beg."

She started to say she didn't beg. She was a Stargazer, one of the elite. But then a single drop of pre-cum slipped out of the slit, a glistening drop. She swallowed hard. "Please."

The word hung in the air between them for a second, and then he dropped to all fours, bracing himself above her on gloriously muscular forearms. The head of his cock pushed against the soft folds of her sex, and she arched up to try to impale herself on it, but was stopped by Tyler who wouldn't relinquish her arms or legs.

"It's okay, sweet." Bryce drew back and then

thrust into her, burying himself to the hilt in one smooth strike. "I know what you need."

"I need you." The minute the words left her mouth, she knew they were true. There was something about Bryce that made her crave his touch, his presence.

He started to fuck her with long, slow strokes of that amazing cock and she stopped thinking. His gaze held her pinned in place as his cock slid in and out. Streaks of liquid heat slid along every nerve. She could barely breathe, and her lack of control shocked her. Her whole life was about control, and he'd shattered it with that first deep thrust of his shaft.

Tyler moved beneath her, rubbing his cock back and forth in the cleft of her buttocks, but she barely felt it. Her world narrowed to Bryce.

Only Bryce. His hands. His eyes. His cock.

She could feel herself spiraling upward, higher and higher. Molten darts of pleasure caressed her spine as Tyler loosened his grip on her arms and reached around to fondle her breasts, large hands cupping them as his fingers tweaked the taut nipples, adding to the sensations rocketing through her body. She let out a low keening sound, unable to form a coherent sentence as erotic feelings looped from her breasts, to her belly, to her sex and back.

Bryce shifted his position, just a bit, and applied more pressure to her sensitive nub. She cried out his name as wave after wave of erotic heat swept her up and over the edge. The inner muscles of her channel spasmed, gripped hard around his invading shaft, pulsing until his cock jerked and she could feel the hot seed jetting deep inside her.

She wrapped her arms around his neck as he collapsed on top of her, shifting sideways so she wouldn't be pinned beneath his bulk. She buried her head in the warm hollow of his shoulder as a hundred tiny aftershocks rippled through her and she fought to drag oxygen into her starving lungs.

"Well, I'm glad the two of you enjoyed yourselves."

Jazlyn peeked out from her warm haven to see the wry grin on Tyler's face as he slid off the table. His cock looked painfully engorged and she realized she'd been so engrossed in Bryce that she'd totally ignored his partner's needs.

"I'm sure you'll manage to find a female willing to take care of that." Bryce didn't sound the least bit repentant. Jazlyn raised her head to see his blue eyes dancing with mirth as he looked as Tyler.

Tyler dragged his pants up over his hips. A barely suppressed smile teased the edge of his mouth. "I saw Jazlyn's companion heading toward the crew lounge just before we started. She mentioned she'd be available later if I fancied a rendezvous."

Jazlyn smiled, rolling her eyes. Mika always managed to make her wants very clear, and it appeared this voyage would be no exception. She ran her hand over Bryce's heavily muscled chest, enjoying the feel of hard flesh as Tyler grabbed his shirt and strode out of the room whistling cheerfully, his well-muscled torso still naked.

"That's enough of ogling Tyler." Bryce rolled onto his back, wrapping his arms around her so that she landed on top of him. He met her gaze, his eyes already deepening with lust.

Chapter Three

Jazlyn snuggled deeper into the pile of covers, luxuriating in the feel of Bryce's warm body spooned tightly against her. She felt deliciously sated. It had been a long time after Tyler had left before they'd stumbled back to his cabin and fallen asleep in the spacious bunk.

Warm breath wafted across her ear. "Good rising, little one." He draped an arm across her rib cage in a casually possessive gesture.

"Good rising, yourself." Jazlyn rolled over, covering her mouth as she yawned. "I guess it's about time I started to earn my keep."

Bryce turned to capture her lips, his hand cupping the back of her head while he kissed her thoroughly.

A wry smile curved the corner of his lips as he let her go. "As much as I'd like to spend the next few solar cycles here naked with you, we do have a hold full of food to deliver." He propped himself up on one elbow and laid his warm hand on her belly. "Of course, your contract is for five solar years, so I'm sure I'll have plenty of time to explore your delightful company."

Jazlyn wrinkled her nose, unwilling to admit how very much she'd enjoy spending time in his company. "I'm sorry I ignored Tyler last night. I'm not usually that selfish."

Bryce laughed. "Tyler's no youngling. I'm sure he managed to find a willing female, possibly even your friend. I notice neither of them has come looking for us yet this rising."

"Still." Jazlyn felt sheepish. "My behavior was unacceptable. I'll apologize to him the next time I see him."

Bryce caught her chin in his hand and seared a kiss across her lips. "I'm not sure I want you alone with him. Tyler's quite the ladies' man, and I find I'm not willing to share you."

She raised her eyebrows, staring at him in shock. That was so far out of line, she didn't know what to say. A casual coupling, no matter how wonderful, didn't give him the right to dictate whom she could or couldn't see. "I think it's up to me whether or not I wish to share my body." She glared at him. "The contract you arranged with my father does not give you any rights over my body or my behavior."

Bryce ignored her outburst. "I may not control you, but the rest of the crew knows better than to cross me." He scored a thumb across one nipple, giving her a smug smile when it hardened to a taut peak. "Tyler and I never compete over females."

"Females?" Jazlyn attempted to sit up, shrugging off his arm. "I'm a Stargazer, not some body slave you picked up at a spaceport auction."

"I know that." He let her go. "But I want you."

"Do you always get what you want?" She stood and pulled on her leggings, re-doing the laces Tyler had fumbled with the previous evening.

"Always." Bryce wrapped his warm arms around her and drew her back against his hard body. She could feel his cock stirring to life as it pressed into her buttocks.

"Well then, it's about time you learned some restraint." She grabbed her shirt.

"We could certainly try restraints next time, if you desire to."

He'd deliberately misunderstood her. Jazlyn tried to hide the grin that threatened to spread across her face. The man was incorrigible. She reached behind her and encircled his shaft with her fingers, stroking it gently as it hardened. She'd always wondered how it would feel to wake up in the arms of a lover.

* * *

"We had the bridge totally redesigned when we decided to hire a Stargazer." Bryce held her close as they stepped into the transport tube. She took a deep breath and concentrated on the shift of muscles underneath his tight shirt. No matter how many times she used them, drop tubes unnerved her. Mika thought it was the lack of control, but knowing that didn't help her with the sudden sick feeling in the pit of her stomach. They reached the bridge and Bryce stepped out of the tube, taking her with him.

She looked around the oval room approvingly. The observation screen covered an entire third of the wall, giving a comprehensive view of the space surrounding the vessel. The Stargazer platform was in the center of the room, with high sides designed to give her comfort and privacy as she worked. Workstations for the rest of the bridge crew were located at random intervals around the outer walls, with the captain and first officer stations in front of the platform. Someone had put a lot of thought into the layout.

Bryce let go of her hand and strode to the empty captain's chair. "We're still on auto-pilot. Tyler will take over once you get us connected to the energy lines. We'll take turns captaining the ship, and one of us will be monitoring you at all times." He gave her that lopsided grin that made her heart beat faster. "You're too valuable to take chances with."

Jazlyn lifted her hand to sweep her hair back from her face. The nano-bots she used to create the blue streaks were reacting favorably to the richer atmosphere of the ship. Their color had deepened several shades since she'd boarded. She paced around the deck, familiarizing herself with the layout. The platform was one of the newer models, she noted thankfully. The older models didn't adjust to accommodate the Stargazer's size. She fingered the straps, noting with approval the soft leather and ample padding. She'd be able to work long hours without discomfort.

"Will it be adequate for your needs?" Bryce wrapped his arms around her from behind, nuzzling her neck with his warm lips.

She nodded. "Yes. I'm amazed, everything is exactly the way I like it."

Bryce rested his chin on her shoulder. "I consulted with the captain of your father's flagship. He gave me the specs and a few tips."

He let her go and she turned to frown at him, suspicion bubbling in her mind. "Exactly how long ago did my father agree to this?"

He shrugged. "Two moons, maybe three. Enough time for us to refit the bridge to accommodate you."

"And yet the day I boarded was the first I heard of it." She felt a flash of anger for her absent parent. "He could have warned me!"

"But he didn't. I'm sure he had his reasons."

"So am I." He didn't want to give her time to think of an alternative, or just flatly refuse to cooperate. She knew her father cared about her, but he always put the welfare of the people of New Zanadles first, and he knew she'd balk at being sent off-planet for an extended period. He could be incredibly stubborn when he thought he was right.

She felt a wry smile curve the corner of her

mouth. They were very much alike. "We should be far enough out from the system core to avoid detection. When did you want me to start?" They'd probably been far enough out last night, but then she'd been busy. She studied her toes so he wouldn't see the color she could feel rising to her cheeks.

"As soon as you're ready." She could hear the restrained mirth in his voice. He'd been every bit as preoccupied as she had. She glanced around and realized that Tyler and Mika still hadn't surfaced.

"There's a meditation chamber over here." Bryce led her to an alcove to the left, with a small doorway in it that led to a small, white room. A single padded bench stood in the middle and there were shelves on one wall, presumably to hold her clothing while she worked. She nodded in approval.

She looked at Bryce, admiring the way his shoulders filled out the tight suit. "Since the delivery is urgent, I should get started. I'll need some time alone to center myself."

He stepped forward to frame her face with his hands, tilting it up to place a kiss on her lips. "I'll be on the bridge if you need anything." He nodded to a series of touch pads on the wall. "They give you access to all of the star charts for this sector, if you need to check on anything." He kissed her again, and strode out the door, thumbing the control to close it behind him.

* * *

Jazlyn removed her clothing, one item at a time. Folding each carefully, she placed them on the shelves. Her tunic. Her leggings. Her footwear. Her undergarments. Completely naked, she closed her eyes, stretching her arms above her head. *Breathe in. Breathe out.*

She leaned to the left side, feeling the gentle stretch of her muscles. *Breathe in. Breathe out.*

She returned to her upright position and repeated the movement, stretching to the right. *Breathe in. Breathe out.*

She padded over to the bench, lowering herself to sit cross-legged on it. Taking a deep breath, she emptied her mind, reaching for the calm deep inside herself. She ran through each of the meditation exercises that her mentor had taught her, taking the time to do them correctly. Channeling the power of the ley lines required her complete concentration; a single moment of inattention could trigger a dangerous backlash.

A quiet confidence filled her as she finished the last of the mental exercises. She was gifted, a Stargazer. She could handle the power lines and their shining energy.

She crossed to the doorway and entered the main area of the bridge. Bryce turned to watch her as she climbed onto the platform and settled into the frame. She met his concerned gaze with a serene smile. She slipped her feet into the soft leather anklets, set at precisely one leg-length apart, and pulled the straps tight around her ankles.

Next, she grasped the ends of the thick leather belt and wrapped it snugly around her waist. If she faltered while in the trance, the belt would hold her upright and make sure that the energy flow to the engines remained constant. She reached above her head and threaded her hands through the loops. They, too, hung a precise distance apart. Satisfied with her preparations, she lifted her chin and caught Bryce's gaze. Worry clouded his face, and she gave him a reassuring smile before she nodded firmly. Time to start.

Closing her eyes, she tilted her head back. She let her consciousness expand out into the cold void of space, seeking the brilliant energy that signified the ley lines. Behind her closed eyelids, the lines shimmered into view, their seductive energy calling to her. The blues and greens were darker in this quadrant, clearer in the absence of man-made clutter, but they still formed that glittering maze that tempted her to immerse herself in its power. She ignored the temptation, searching amongst the strands for the one she needed to follow to reach their destination. She examined each strand, discarding one after the other. Instinct would tell her when she'd found what she needed. Greens. Golds. Blues. The lines were seductive, tempting her to lose herself in their beauty. Still, she searched.

And then she found it. The line that would lead her to the Globar system. She narrowed her focus, concentrating on that one line, drawing the twinkling energy into herself, and using her hands to direct it to the massive engines of the ship. Dimly, she felt the vibrations as the ship began to move through space, picking up speed as she strengthened the flow of power, acting as a human conductor.

She reveled in the feel of the energy coursing through her body, captured by her, controlled by her. The temptation was there, always at the back of her mind, to draw more and more power until there was no going back. She'd merge completely with the brilliant energy of the lines, become one with that incredible maze. It became harder and harder to resist. Every time she channeled the power, she hesitated just a fraction of a second longer before letting it go. She'd always used her father to anchor her to this life -- to reach out to if the temptation were too great.

But he wasn't here.

Time had no meaning in her trance. The power flowed through her to the engines in a steady stream, and she remained passive, letting it use her. Dimly, she was aware of planets, stars and the other heavenly bodies as they came within range, only to disappear as the ship hurtled toward its destination.

It could have been nanosecs or whole solar days before she sensed her destination approaching. Reluctantly, she let some of the power slip away, loosening her hold on the line. She could feel the engine slow as she came out of the trance. Her body sagged against the harness as fatigue overtook her. When the auxiliary power kicked in, she emerged completely, and exhaustion slammed into her. She opened her eyes to find Bryce striding toward her, concern plowing deep furrows into his handsome brow.

"How long..." Her voice cracked and she couldn't finish. She must have held the power longer than she'd intended. She felt spent, every last ounce of her reserves drained.

"Too long. Why the hell didn't you let go before this?" Bryce's hands were gentle as he unbuckled the restraints. When she would have fallen, he lifted her in his arms and dragged a blanket over her naked body. "You scared the hell out of me. Don't you ever do that again."

Jazlyn smiled weakly at the rough affection in his voice. Typical male, he seemed to think he had the right to give her orders. "I'm a Stargazer. I don't take orders from merchant captains."

"So this is what you do when I'm not around." Jazlyn started as Tyler's deep voice boomed out cheerfully from the far side of the bridge. She peeked over Bryce's shoulder. Tyler had one arm draped possessively around her cousin.

Mika smiled up at him with adoring eyes, before she turned a concerned look in Jazlyn's direction. "Did you overdo it? You know your tutor warned you. Those lines can devour you whole if you're not careful."

"I'm fine." She felt silly, held in Bryce's arms like a small child while her cousin lectured her. "Just a little tired."

"You can rest for a cycle before the next jump." Tyler looked at the dark red planet visible on the observation screen. "That's Makus 1 off to our left. We stocked up on supplies before we left New Zanadles, so we don't need to dock." He glanced at his partner. "No need to alert any Council spies that we have a Stargazer onboard."

Bryce nodded. "I agree. I'll take Jazlyn down to her cabin so she can get some rest. You secure the bridge and make sure we're ready in case we have to power up in a hurry."

"You two are so paranoid." Mika ducked out from under Tyler's arm. "I'll come and take care of Jazlyn."

"Not necessary." Bryce met Jazlyn's gaze, and she felt her cheeks go red. "I can take care of her."

"She needs rest, my friend." Tyler grinned. "Not your amorous attention."

"And she'll get it." Bryce strode toward the doorway. "If you want to take care of someone, Mika, Tyler's in need of some supervision."

Mika laughed, the sound cheerful in the confines of the bridge. "Let him go, Tyler. I told you he's smitten. My darling cousin has him wrapped around her little finger."

Bryce threw the pair a quelling look, and strode out the doorway with Jazlyn held firmly against his heart.

Chapter Four

"Is there anything I can get for you?" Bryce lowered Jazlyn onto his bunk. He'd been terrified when she'd continued to hold her trance even after her body sagged against the restraints. He wasn't sure he could take watching her push her limits repeatedly.

"I'm fine. For now, I just need to sleep." She gave him a smile that lit up her eyes. "When I wake I'll be starving, so if you could get a food platter ready that would be great. And water. Lots of water."

"One food platter coming up just as soon as I get you tucked in." Bryce sat on the bed beside her, arranging the blanket over her. He brushed the hair back from her face, and placed a tender kiss on her forehead. Good thing Tyler seemed to prefer her cousin, because he wouldn't be able to stand by while another man enjoyed her charms, not even his partner.

He watched a ghost of a smile cross her lips as her eyes drifted closed, long dark lashes fanning out on her cheeks. She looked so small and vulnerable. He found it amazing that she had the stamina and power to control the vast energies of the lines. He brushed a finger across her cheek, marveling at the softness of her skin.

Satisfied that she wouldn't wake any time soon, he strode over to the food dispenser and chose a mixed protein and fruit platter from the display panel. The unit hummed briefly before a tray of brightly colored foodstuffs appeared. Balancing the tray on one arm, he grabbed a carafe of fresh New Zanadles water that they'd stocked up on before they left the planet. One of the most common causes of space sickness was the body's reaction to the minerals and foreign organic compounds contained in strange liquids.

He crossed to the bunk and placed the food and drink on a side table where she'd see it immediately upon waking. While he'd love to slide into the bunk beside her, he needed to deal with the logistics of checking the ship over before the next leg of their voyage.

Bending over the bunk, he ran his fingers through the silken strands of Jazlyn's hair. The blue streaks seemed to shimmer with a life of their own, and he suspected she used nano-bots to achieve the effect. Brushing his lips tenderly across hers, he let his tongue linger as he tasted the sweet honeyed flavor that was uniquely her.

He straightened up and turned toward the door, pausing to cast a last lingering look at the witch sleeping in his bed. If he had any say in it, she'd be spending a lot of time there.

* * *

"Warning! Warning! Unauthorized access on lower decks. Warning! All hands to battle stations!"

The shrill blaring of the ship's automated defense system dragged Jazlyn out of her sleep. Still bleary-eyed from her exhausting stint on the platform, it took her a moment to comprehend. *We're under attack?*

The cabin door slid open and Bryce strode in, his handsome face grim. "Damn space pirates were hiding in the debris field orbiting Makus 1. They came up on our blind side and breached the lower decks before we realized we were under attack." He shook his head. "I have no idea how they managed to force the airlock open, but at least they're confined to the cargo decks where they can't do a lot of damage. Tyler is working on sealing off the access tubes to keep them trapped down there. I need you to lie low while we deal with them. If we don't contain them and they realize we have a Stargazer onboard, they won't stop until they find you."

Jazlyn sat up and grabbed a handful of berries from the platter he'd left beside the bunk earlier. The post-trance hunger pangs had her stomach growling at a very unladylike volume. "Pirates? What do they want from us? You have a cargo hold full of flash-dried foodstuffs, hardly a rich haul."

Bryce shrugged, busily keying extra security into the door system. "I want you to lock yourself in the cabin until the fighting's over." He turned, and his expression softened. "I don't want anything to happen to you, and this just doesn't make sense. I'm thinking the Council has a hand in it. Like you said, we're just not a likely target for space pirates."

Her head jerked up as a thought occurred to her. "Where's Mika?"

"She's fine. She was with Tyler when the pirates attacked, so he stashed her in his cabin. She'll be safe there until this is over." Crossing to the bunk, he sat beside her and lifted her chin to sear a possessive kiss across her lips.

Satisfied that her cousin was safe, Jazlyn opened her mouth and returned the kiss, enjoying the warmth of his body next to hers. After a few moments, Bryce lifted his head, a rueful smile on his face. "I'd love to finish that, but we need to deal with the invaders first. The ship's comp system will respond only to Tyler or me. They shouldn't be able to hack it." He straightened up, keeping one arm around her. "Computer, on."

For a brief moment, nothing happened, and her heart sank. She knew that if the pirates controlled the computers, they had little hope of repelling the attack.

Computer ready.

Relief showed on Bryce's face. "Show lower

decks."

A visual appeared in the air in front of them, and Jazlyn gasped in alarm. The bodies of crewmembers littered the floor, their limbs jerking awkwardly, eyes dazed.

Bryce let out a frustrated growl. "The bastards are using neuro weapons. They were outlawed back in the twenty-third century, and for good reason. The effects on the brain cells are unpredictable. Computer, locate Tyler."

The image blurred, then solidified to reveal Tyler standing back to back with a burly crewmate in the center of the bridge, blasters held at the ready. As they watched, one of the pirates appeared in the doorway to Tyler's left. He turned slightly to make the shot, and another pirate appeared behind him. The crewmember managed to drop that one, but it soon became apparent that the pirates had the advantage of numbers. As soon as one went down, another replaced him.

"Damn." Bryce watched as two more pirates rushed his partner. "We hoped to get to the bridge and seal off the lower decks. The pirates must have managed to override the protocols on the access tubes."

Jazlyn sat with her eyes glued to the image of Tyler as he fended off attack after attack. A fine sheen of sweat covered his face, and a worried frown creased his forehead. She could see why her cousin was attracted to the virile merchant.

Then, just when Jazlyn thought the defenders had a chance, another pirate strutted onto the bridge, pushing a terrified female in front of him. The pale blue of her skin, along with the short dark hair, marked her as one of the engineers from the Orion system. The pirate shot Tyler an evil grin as he twisted the girl's arm, causing her to cry out in pain. "So, Captain, you want to negotiate, or should I see how much I can make this little tramp squeal before I kill her?" He twisted her arm again, laughing at the girl's helpless screams.

Bryce turned to Jazlyn, his expression grim. "And that's why I don't want you out there. These guys are ruthless." His gaze switched back to the holo-vid image.

Tyler froze, his eyes narrowing as he regarded the pirate. "What do you want?"

"Your ship. What else?" The pirate shrugged eloquently. "You surrender your weapons, and tell your crew to stand down, and we'll put you and your crew off at the unmanned way-station anchored outside the system. You'll have food and shelter while you wait for rescue. Nobody gets hurt." He stumbled slightly as the ship lurched sideways, and smirked down at a body slumped unconscious at his feet. "No one else, at least."

"They're not pirates," Bryce said in a disbelieving voice. "Watch how they lose their balance when the ship moves."

Jazlyn studied the invaders. The crew hadn't been able to engage the autopilot, and with no one at the helm, the gravitational fields they passed through were pulling the ship off course.

"There!" Bryce pointed at the pirate behind Tyler. He stumbled and grabbed the nav-station for support at a slight shift in the ship's progress. "What the hell is going on? Space pirates should be able to take a mild shift like that in their stride."

"Were they sent by the Intergalactic Council?" Jazlyn could hardly believe the Council would go this far. "You said they didn't want us to make it to the

Globar system with food. Would they be willing to fake a pirate attack to stop us?"

Bryce studied the invaders. "I think you may have nailed it. Those have got to be either mercenaries or Council troops. They're just not behaving like pirates. If they manage to take the ship and strand us on a way-station, the settlers will be out of options." He glared at the holo-vid.

The ship lurched sideways again, and she watched with satisfaction as all of the pirates scrambled to keep their footing. The crew, having weathered many a deep space storm, didn't even sway. "I've got an idea." She turned to Bryce. "They don't know about you, they think Tyler's the captain. If we can convince them that we're on their side, maybe they'll let me power the ship." She grinned. "If I get it up to full speed, and then drop the power lines, anyone who's not tied down is going to be thrown into the nearest bulkhead."

She looked at the holo-vid again. Tyler had dropped his weapons. She knew he didn't have a choice. He couldn't stand by and see the Orion engineer punished for his defiance. The pirates were shepherding the crewmembers toward the meditation room, which suited her plan. "We let our crew loose and they take back control before the pirates, or whatever they are, manage to recover."

Bryce looked doubtful. "I guess it could work. I count fourteen pirates, at most. Should be able to round them up without too much trouble, but how do you plan to keep the crew from getting thrown around along with the pirates?"

Jazlyn gestured at the meditation room. "Easy. We'll get you thrown in there with your crew and you can let them know what's going on."

Bryce nodded thoughtfully and slanted her a quizzical look. "How do you plan to convince them you're on their side?"

Jazlyn snorted in a very unladylike fashion. "I was born into palace life, and I've been playing at political intrigue for years. These peasants don't stand a chance." She tossed her head and bounced to her feet. "Let's go play nice."

* * *

Jazlyn looked up into the eyes of the lead pirate and gave him her best innocent smile. "My father sold me to the captain. I wanted to try out for the Intergalactic Council, but he said they weren't offering enough money." She sighed dramatically. "I'd be ever so grateful if you could get us to one of their stations." She studiously avoided looking toward the meditation chamber. If they could hear her, she sure hoped Tyler would realize they had a plan.

The pirate looked suspicious. His beady eyes narrowed as his gaze went from her to Bryce and back. Jazlyn's heart started to sink. He wasn't buying it.

"You want me to believe you and your male-friend are thrilled to see us and want nothing more than to be dropped off at the nearest port under the control of the Intergalactic Council?"

Jazlyn nodded and kept her gaze lowered. These overbearing types always bought the submissive act. Too arrogant to think a female might not be thrilled with their virile presence. She suppressed a sudden urge to giggle. "If I harness the power of the lines, I can get you wherever you want to go much faster than if you have to use the ship's turbines."

He paced over to the viewing screen. "Suppose I let you practice your witch magic, how can I be sure you won't do something to help the crew escape?"

Yes! He was buying her story. She could hear it in his voice. "You have my lover as hostage." She gestured at Bryce. "I'm not going to do anything to get him hurt." It amazed her to hear the depth of feeling in her voice.

The pirate nodded slowly and Jazlyn could see him weighing his options. His expression hardened. "Okay then. Do your little rain dance or whatever it is you do to psyche yourself up. One wrong move and I'll have lover-boy executed." He motioned to one of the other pirates who stepped up and grasped Bryce by the arm. "There's a deserted way-station close by. We'll drop this bunch off there, and then head back to Rieger Station as quickly as possible. You do know where Rieger Station is, don't you?"

Jazlyn nodded, trying not to look too eager. Bryce played along, letting himself be led away without protest. "I've never been there, but I know its position."

"Good." He turned his head to give Jazlyn the full benefit of his evil grin. "Just remember we have your lover handy in case you try to pull any funny stuff."

The pirate led Bryce to the meditation room and unlocked the door. She caught a brief glimpse of Tyler and the rest of the crew before the pirate shoved Bryce through the entrance. Bryce turned and met her gaze as the metal panel slid closed and the locking mechanism engaged with a metallic click. His confident expression bolstered her determination to defeat the pirates. She'd dropped the lines once, when she was in training, and the results had been devastating. Hopefully, she could repeat the effect.

Rieger Station had been built to house the Intergalactic Council's training barracks. Bryce was right. The Council had orchestrated the attack. She felt a surge of pride that her father had managed to avoid turning New Zanadles over to them, even if he had sacrificed her freedom in the process. A good ruler always put his people first.

"Ready?"

She raised her arms and ran her hands through her hair, remembering how it had felt when Bryce had done just that. Damn, she hoped the crew could manage to brace themselves. "I just need to meditate first." She gave him what she hoped was a disarming smile. "It helps me control the trance."

"Whatever. Just make it quick." He turned back to study the control panel in front of him.

Jazlyn sat on the deck in front of the Stargazer platform. She'd never had to work under less than ideal conditions. Taking a deep breath, she closed her eyes and reached for that small part of herself that radiated calm. Her breathing slowed and she ran through the exercises quickly. This would be harder than any other time she'd worked with the lines, since she couldn't sink into a full trance or she wouldn't be able to find the perfect moment to drop the lines.

She narrowed her focus, letting the fear of failure, the self-doubt, slip away. She couldn't let worry about anyone else's safety interfere with her control. Not Mika. Not Bryce. Unintentionally, she reached for the reassurance of his mind. He was there, and she felt a surge of peace.

She opened her eyes and stood, keeping her focus on what was to come. She removed her clothing and placed it neatly on the floor beside her. Mounting the platform, she slipped her feet into the anklets and tightened the straps. The belt at her waist was next, and she made sure it was secure enough to hold her when she dropped the lines. Ignoring the stares of the pirate crew, she reached up and threaded her hands through the wrist straps. She threw her head back and let her consciousness expand. At once, the beauty of the lines filled her senses, but she ignored their seductive pull. She had a job to do, and people's lives were dependent on her.

Bryce's life.

She found the line leading to the way station and gathered the energy to herself, reveling in the warm strength that washed through her as she directed it to the engines. Since she hadn't truly entered into a trance, it took her a lot longer to stabilize her link to the ley line. When she'd established a strong flow channeling through her to power the ship, she risked opening her eyes enough to check on the pirates.

The leader paced back and forth in front of the view screen, alternating his attention between the stars that were visible as the ship hurtled toward its destination, and her. She watched as he stalked the same path over and over. She needed to time the disruption to throw him into the solid bulk of the ship's wall, not the soft fabric that coated the center of the viewing port.

With most of her energy focused on controlling the lines, she estimated how long he took to complete his path. She needed to drop the lines just as he passed the center point of the bridge. Time slowed to a crawl as she watched and calculated.

Now!

Without hesitation, she snapped her eyes open and broke her connection to the ley lines. The groan of the engines was audible throughout the ship as the massive turbines ground to a halt. The bulk of the ship shuddered for a split second, and she held her breath.

She couldn't afford to fail.

The ship jerked, as if it had run into an invisible wall.

The inertial force threw Jazlyn's body hard against the restraints, as the artificial gravity field failed to compensate quickly enough.

The pirates fared much worse. None of them had been strapped in, and the sudden deceleration had them flying across the bridge to smack into solid bulkheads. The leader landed hard against the ship's forward control panel, his head making a sickly thunk as it connected with the solid metal. His eyes glazed with incomprehension before he slid unconscious to the floor.

Jazlyn fumbled her way out of the restraints. Not bothering to stop for her clothing, she sprinted to the meditation chamber, quickly placing her palm on the scanner to deactivate the lock. The panel slid back with agonizing slowness, and then she saw Bryce in the opening, hands up in a defensive position. She spared a quick glance at the rest of the crew. No one looked injured, although old Harold favored his left leg as he hobbled forward.

Tyler stepped up beside Bryce. His jaw dropped as he took in her naked body and the pirates lying unconscious all over the bridge. He relaxed and stared at his partner, a grin slowly spreading across his face. "That's one hell of a woman you've got yourself."

"I know, and I fully intend to keep her." Bryce gathered her into his arms and kissed her hard, ignoring the whistles and catcalls from the rest of the crew. He shrugged out of his shirt and wrapped it around her shivering body. The backlash of power had left her fingers too numb to connect the fasteners, and she could feel her strength ebbing quickly away.

"Are you okay?" He anxiously searched her face.

"I'm fine, just a little tired." Considering the stunt she'd just pulled off, she was doing great.

Bryce looked past her to the pirates lying in crumpled heaps on the bridge and addressed Tyler. "Don't just stand there ogling my girl. Go secure the ship before these cretins regain consciousness."

Jazlyn grinned. His girl. It had a nice ring to it.

Chapter Five

Bryce wrapped his shirt more securely around Jazlyn's naked body before he picked her up, cradling her against his chest. He'd let Tyler direct the mop up of the pirates, most of whom weren't even conscious yet. He felt a surge of pride when he thought of Jazlyn single-handedly outwitting the Council's group of brutes.

"I'm so cold." She buried her face in the hollow of his shoulder. "Did we get them all?"

"Ssshhh." He nuzzled his face into the silky cloud of her hair. "You need to rest. Even Tyler can take care of a bunch of unconscious Council thugs." He glanced through the doorway and chuckled softly. "That is, if he manages to let go of your cousin long enough. I guess she got tired of hiding safely in his cabin."

"He's holding Mika?"

"I'm not sure holding is the right word." He watched as Tyler scooped Mika up in his arms and engulfed her mouth with his own. "It looks more like he's devouring her."

"Devouring?" She raised her head to peek over his shoulder, and gasped. "Wow, he really is devouring her."

Bryce loved the way her eyes sparkled with delight. "Jealous?"

She turned her attention to him, and his heart melted. "No, because I'm sure that as soon as things are under control, you're going to take me down to your cabin and show me just how proud you are of me." She smiled smugly. "You find me irresistible, if I recall."

He laughed again. He didn't think he'd felt this

happy since… well… maybe he'd never felt this happy before. "That I do. Are you sure you're feeling up to another round of my attention?"

"I am a little tired," she conceded. "So I guess I'll just have to lie still and let you have your wicked way with me."

"Hmmm." He twisted his neck to nip at her perfectly shaped ear. "That sounds promising."

She arched her brows at him and her mouth curved upward in an amused grin. "Then why are we still on the bridge?"

"Because he needs to help me figure out what we're going to do with these… pirates." Tyler let go of Mika and produced a handful of plasti-cuffs from the synthesizer. "We can't just carry them around with us, and if we let them off at any of the bases, the Intergalactic Council will know they failed and send another pack of vultures to finish the job."

"We don't have enough security facilities to keep them onboard. The brig is rated for three bodies, max." Bryce prodded one of the unconscious bodies with the tip of his boot.

"We could leave them on the way-station, and disable the com-sender." Mika glared at the unconscious leader. "They won't die, but by the time anyone finds them, we'll have made our delivery to the Globar system and be long gone."

"Great idea!" Bryce headed toward the doorway, Jazlyn still held securely against his chest. "Tyler, get security to round them up and confine them to cargo bay two until we get to the way-station."

"And where are you heading off to in such a hurry?" Tyler's grin said he knew exactly where his partner was going.

"To reward our resident Stargazer for outwitting

the pirates." Bryce palmed the door locks as Tyler hooted with laughter.

* * *

"Resident Stargazer. I like the sound of that." Jazlyn nuzzled his shoulder as he strode toward the drop tube. "I've always been referred to as the offspring of the Regent, or the Daughter-Heir. No one has ever seen me as a person with my own abilities and talents." She peeked up at him from under her lashes, and he felt his cock harden at the smoldering look in her witch-green eyes.

"I think your father may have to find himself another heir." Bryce held her tight as he stepped into the access tube. Exiting on the crew deck, he carried her into his cabin and tossed her onto the bunk. Stepping back to admire her creamy limbs splayed across the dark brown covers, he started to shuck his clothing off. "I have other plans for you."

"Oh, really?" Jazlyn propped herself up on one elbow, her eyes glowing as she watched him. "Are you going to share those plans with me?"

"If you ask nice." He paused, his hands on the waistband of his leggings. "You're quite the willful little witch. Part of my plan involves teaching you to ask nicely."

Jazlyn's brows rose. "Really? And how do you propose to do that?"

"Well." He stripped off his leggings and strolled over to sit on the edge of the bed. "Perhaps ask nicely is a little misleading. What I had in mind involves begging."

"Begging?"

"Definitely."

"Me?"

He nodded and traced a finger across the mound

of one breast.

"I don't beg."

He dipped his head to score his teeth across a dusky nipple. "We'll see about that."

Jazlyn gasped and arched her back, offering herself up to him. He grinned. By the end of this cycle, she'd definitely be begging. He sucked the nipple into his mouth, swirling his tongue around it. He ran his hand down her belly, marveling at the silky softness of her skin. Shifting himself lower, he used his lips to trace a path from her breasts to her hips, stopping to delve into the sexy dimple of her belly button before he continued on down toward her mound. Positioning himself between her thighs, he raised his head and looked into her eyes. "Ready to beg?"

She snorted. "Never."

He sighed theatrically, rolling his eyes. "Don't say I didn't give you a chance."

Resolutely ignoring his painfully swollen shaft, he grasped her legs and spread them apart, his nostrils flaring as he inhaled the sweet smell of her sex. Resting her thighs on his shoulders, he lifted her tight buttocks and angled her pussy toward his mouth. The first swipe of his tongue had Jazlyn gasping and bucking her hips, and he smiled to himself. He loved how sensitive and responsive she was. Not giving her a chance to recover, he settled in to feast on her sweet juices, licking and sucking, stabbing his tongue deep into her tight pussy.

Jazlyn moaned softly, writhing as he held her to him. She tangled her fingers in his hair, holding him in place. A low keening sound escaped her lips, and he could sense her edging higher, spiraling toward her climax.

With one last deep thrust of his tongue, he lifted

his head and watched her as she whimpered. "Don't stop, please." Her voice, low and sexy, sent shivers of heat racing to his groin.

He let her legs go and rose to his knees, leaning forward until his cock pushed against the damp folds of her sex. "Ready?"

"Oh, gods, yes!" Her gorgeous eyes glowed with a desperate need that had his cock swelling even harder. She wanted him. This gorgeous, talented Stargazer wanted him.

He braced himself above her on his forearms and entered her with one hard thrust, seating himself to the balls in her tight channel. Her inner muscles clamped down hard on him, and he started to move, shafting her with long, even strokes.

"Bryce." She gasped his name out as she wrapped her arms around his neck, urging him to go faster. Her hips arched up as she met him thrust for thrust, her nails digging into the muscles of his shoulders. "It's too much. I don't think I can take this."

"Yes, you can." He nipped the delicate lobe of her ear. "This is me telling you I love you. You can take that."

The stunned look on her face told him she'd never expected him to use the L word. He grinned wickedly at her astonished expression and picked up the pace, burying himself repeatedly in the silken heat of her slick channel. He felt himself rocketing toward orgasm, and he lowered his head to take her lips in a searing kiss as the world exploded around them.

Her muscles clamped down hard on his shaft, milking the seed from him as wave after wave of climax washed over them. Her soft cry mirrored his hoarse one as the pleasure started somewhere deep in his belly and rolled through his entire body. He collapsed beside her on the bunk, wrapping his big arms around her.

"Damn." She stared at him with a dazed expression. "That was one hell of a ride." She paused, and he could see uncertainty creeping into her expression. "Did you really mean it?"

"Hell yes." He pulled her close and brought his lips down on hers, kissing away all the doubt. "I've never said that to any female before. I love you. I love your witchy green eyes, and your kissable lips and your soft sexy body. I love the way you laugh, and the way you go all serious when you're working. I love you awake, and I love to watch you sleeping in my bunk." He dropped a kiss on the tip of her nose. "So you can leave your cousin to deal with Tyler. You're mine, and no one else is ever going to make love to your sexy little body again."

The corner of her mouth twitched, and he watched as she tried unsuccessfully to stop a smile from bubbling up on her face. "My little sister Belinda is going to be one happy Daughter-Heir when she gets the news. She'll make a much better regent than I would anyway." She wrinkled her nose in disgust. "She actually enjoys formal high court functions." Her expression turned serious. "Do you think the Intergalactic Council will give us any more trouble?"

He shook his head. "We'll strand this bunch on the way-station so they won't be able to make contact until they manage to flag down a passing starship. By the time the Council realizes we foiled their plot, the supplies will be in the hands of the colonists, and we'll be long gone." He traced his finger down one of the shiny blue streaks in her hair. "We'll fly under the radar for a while until they give up looking for us. We have falsified papers for the ship and most of the crew." He laughed at the surprised expression on her face.

"I can see I have a lot of explaining to do." He nibbled a row of kisses across her throat. "Have you heard about the rebellion?"

She looked at him, an uncertain frown creasing her forehead. "Of course I have. You mean to tell me you're part of the rebel forces?"

He nodded, kissing the hollow at the base of her neck. "Yes, ma'am. And so are you. As interplanetary merchants, we get to travel all over the known worlds without arousing suspicion."

Jazlyn wound her arms around his neck, her eyes sparkling with mischief. "Well, I always wanted to travel, but I never pictured myself as the resident Stargazer on a merchant spy vessel. I'll have some interesting stories to tell my grandchildren."

Bryce ran his hand across her smooth belly. "First, we need to get to work on children. Grandchildren come later."

He claimed her lips in a kiss that promised a lifetime of love and laughter.

Wild
Sci-Fi Action & Intrigue Romance
Anne Kane

Unfairly indentured, Stargazer Anaya plans her escape carefully, stowing away on a ship belonging to the cynical bounty hunter Ryland. She just needs to avoid detection until the ship docks at the next port of call.

When Ryland discovers the beauty, he assumes she's a runaway sex slave and offers her a choice: be returned to her master or stay and serve his every desire.

Chapter One

"And what do we have here?" Ryland reached out and snagged the woman's arm as she tried to slip past him. "Did you really think you could scurry around the bowels of my ship without me noticing?" With a quick twist of his wrist, he snapped a set of immobilizer cuffs over her hands and smiled grimly when numbness slowly stilled her flailing limbs.

She let loose with a string of inventive curses, some of which he'd be willing to bet were anatomically impossible. What did she expect? Stowing away on a bounty hunter's ship had to be one of the stupidest things a sentient being could do.

Despite his anger at the inconvenience her presence on his ship would cost him, he let out an appreciative whistle while his gaze swept over her lithe body. She looked even more delectable in person than she had on the vid scans. He'd been too preoccupied with the new intel he'd gathered on his current target to detect her presence until the ship was well away from the docking ring.

Last sleep cycle, she'd grown careless and triggered an intruder alert on the lower decks. He'd searched for signs of a pirate attack before he'd realized the intruder was a lone female, scavenging food from one of the dispensers. She must have stowed away during his last docking. A runaway slave, most likely. There were quite a few slave farms in this sector where the slaves, both male and female, were bred for looks and a high sex drive.

Angry red chafe marks at her wrists and ankles suggested a less than caring owner, which would explain her willingness to risk the harsh penalties for running. He didn't approve of beings who mishandled their slaves, so he felt no compulsion to return her to whomever she'd fled from. Grunner, the serial killer he was tracking, already had a good head start. Returning the woman to her owner would set him back at least two solar cycles, and possibly give the killer enough time to find another victim.

She'd chosen his ship; she could take the consequences.

He held her at arm's length while she continued to curse. Ample curves softened the lean lines of her slender body and a mane of dark, shaggy hair framed her round face before tumbling down her back in an untamed mass. Her green eyes slanted upward, giving her a slightly exotic look. Right now, those eyes glared up at him and she twisted helplessly in his grasp. For a slave, she had quite a temper.

Which might explain the marks on her wrists and ankles.

He really didn't have time to deal with an abused female right now. On the other hand, he couldn't very well throw her in the brig and forget about her. He jerked her forward with a little more force than necessary. "What's your name?"

"Anaya. Who the hell are you?" She snarled another oath when he refused to loosen his grip on her arm.

"I'm Ryland, the owner of this shuttle, so you can shut up, Anaya, and pay attention."

The woman fell silent and stared up at him with a stunned expression on her lovely face. If he didn't know better, he'd swear no one had ever told her to be quiet before.

He lifted her hands and stared pointedly at the angry red welts on her wrists. "I don't approve of abusing one's property. There are a number of ways to administer discipline without leaving marks on the flesh. I don't have time to play nursemaid, so if you don't want me to return you to your master, you'd better come to an arrangement with me."

She looked confused. Just what he needed, a slow-witted female to deal with. He took an exasperated breath and tried to think of a way to explain the situation in simple terms.

He grasped her shoulders and glared into her amazingly bright green eyes. "I don't want to waste the time necessary to turn around and take you back." He stroked his finger down the front of her tight suit, noting the way her nipples hardened under the light touch. He smiled darkly. "You can be my pet body slave and stay on board, or I can call your master and arrange to have you returned to him -- or her -- at the next port." He traced the delicate structure of her cheekbones. "Your choice."

The woman's jaw dropped open and she stuttered, "Y-you want me to be your b-body slave? Like a sex slave?"

He nodded. "I'm not a gentle man, but I won't intentionally hurt you. Having my own body slave on board might prove to be interesting." He raised a brow quizzically, a thought suddenly occurring. "You're not running from a bond-mate, are you?" That would bring up a whole other set of problems he didn't even want to consider.

"No!" Those gorgeous green eyes widened in alarm. "I'm not mated."

He relaxed a bit, surprised at the relief he felt at her answer. "Well? Do we have a deal?"

"Ummm. Sure." She looked down, shuffling her feet on the deck. "Deal. Just don't send me back."

The submissive stance was so obviously against

her nature, Ryland grinned. The little minx thought she could fool him with a bit of third-rate acting. "Good. While I'd love to sample your talents right now, I have some work to do." He swept her up in his arms, tossing her over his shoulder before striding out the door.

Heading down the corridor, he ran an assessing hand over the smooth curves of her butt. She dangled helplessly, her head bouncing awkwardly against his back. He'd always been partial to a firm ass. The woman squirmed uncomfortably, her hands still restrained behind her. "Easy now. Don't want any more marks on that luscious body of yours." He brought his hand down smartly and laughed at her strangled gasp. "This voyage is looking up."

He used his neural implants to open the door to the holding cell, ignoring her stream of colorful insults, and tossed her into the anti-grav stasis field. He'd have to teach her to hold her tongue. For a body slave, she had a shocking lack of control.

He could tell by her stunned expression the exact second she felt the effects of the stasis field. It held her suspended within its parameters, unable to move her limbs. He reached in and straightened her so that she stood upright and wouldn't suffer any ill effects. His military-grade neural net automatically negated the field's attempt to control him. "I can't have you running loose on the ship just yet. You'll be safe here until I have time to deal with you."

He grinned at the shocked look on her face as he backed out of the cell. Turning, he sauntered down the corridor in the direction of the bridge, cheerfully whistling his favorite tune off key.

* * *

Damn!

She'd been so sure he hadn't detected her presence on board his ship. She'd just about jumped out of her skin when he'd appeared and wrapped his arms around her, dragging her up against his muscular body.

A very nice body.

She'd been watching it and hiding from it since she'd bribed the dockworker to slip her on board with the supplies. She'd planned her escape from the Colony Five government facility very carefully, researching the deep space vessels that came into the port. She'd settled on this ship because the bounty hunter always traveled alone, and she reasoned that avoiding detection would be simple with only two of them aboard his spacious ship. Apparently, she'd been wrong.

At least she still had one thing in her favor -- the man had no idea she was a Stargazer. He'd seen the marks on her wrists and ankles and assumed she was some sort of pleasure slave, running from a harsh master. If she could manage to play along until the next port, she'd be able to escape and finally taste freedom. She smiled grimly, imagining the fleet commander's frustration when he realized she'd managed to elude his evil clutches. She'd never again feel the sting of the electro lash for refusing to use her talents in ways she found repulsive, using her talent to outpace legitimate settlers to their assigned planets and cheat them out of their homes.

She sucked in a startled breath as she heard the sound of her captor's footsteps ringing out on the metal decking. It hadn't taken him long to finish his business. She schooled her features into what she hoped resembled a slave happy to yield to her master.

Submitting to his sexual appetites wouldn't be

too difficult. She was a Stargazer; she often used sex to bolster her talent, and the big bounty hunter was just the type of male she found attractive. Every part of his mouthwatering body was super-sized, including the thick bulge in those tight spacer pants. She felt her pussy cream in anticipation when he stalked through the doorway, a darkly sinful grin on his rugged face.

"Miss me?" He shrugged his shirt off his shoulders, baring a muscular chest. "I've turned navigation over to the ship's comp until we reach the next system, so we have time to get acquainted."

Anaya gulped, her attention on his big hands. He hooked his thumbs in the waistband of his pants and slid them down over his hips, allowing his massive shaft to spring free. He dropped the pants to the floor and kicked them off.

She felt a sudden twinge of misgiving. She'd always been in charge during her sexual exploits, her chosen partners willing to follow her lead and pleasure her in any way she demanded. The bounty hunter might not be quite so easy to control.

He gripped his cock in his fist, casually running it down the thick length. She watched, unable to tear her gaze away from the single drop glistening on the plum-shaped tip.

Ryland sauntered over to where she hung in midair, trapped by the field. How the hell did he manage to move through it so effortlessly? She narrowed her eyes speculatively. Only a military-grade nano system would allow him that kind of control over an anti-grav stasis field -- which would also explain how he'd managed to detect her presence.

She felt incredibly vulnerable, unable to move while he stood by her side, sweeping the heavy mass of her hair back from her forehead. She barely managed to whimper softly when he carefully eased the silky material of her suit back to expose her breasts. She'd always been proud of her breasts, pert little mounds, nicely rounded with dusky pink nipples.

He rolled one between his thumb and forefinger, nodding in approval as it came to attention. "There's something satisfying about a female that's bred to fuck. Cuts through all that annoying chatter some women require before getting down to business."

Anaya had to concede he had a point. Legally registered sex slaves commanded a premium price at flesh markets around the galaxy. They were bred for looks and a high sex drive, and were perfectly happy with their lot in life. They were well treated and often lived better than the citizens.

Ryland walked behind her. Anaya felt him grasp her hands and gently push the cuffs up higher on her arms to expose the welts circling the slender limbs. She felt the soothing caress of his thumb gliding gently over the tender flesh before he let go of her arms and came back around to face her.

"Your master deserves to be thrashed. This is totally unacceptable." He looked into her eyes, and she thought she detected a twinge of guilt at her fear. "Don't worry. I won't hurt you. Much. I've never taken a female by force and I don't intend to start now."

Anaya watched his lips descend, mesmerized. She closed her eyes, her lips parting under the gentle pressure teasing them with skillful nibbles. She could feel the restrained power of his hands exploring her body, gliding over the hollow of her shoulder, shaping the mounds of her breasts. He swept his tongue into her mouth, demanding her submission while his hands continued to stroke the sensitive flesh of her breasts.

He smiled at her, his sexy blue eyes glittering

when he trailed a path of kisses from her mouth down to the hollow of her throat. He paused there, taking his time exploring the tender skin before continuing down to nuzzle one nipple, scoring his teeth across the pebbled peak while she gasped, unable to move. Ryland sucked the tip into his mouth, and liquid heat shot through her.

"Please." She hated the pleading tone of her voice, but she couldn't stop herself. "I need to be able to move."

"You need to do what I tell you." Ryland tilted his head. "I'm beginning to see why your master punished you so harshly. You need a firm hand." He turned his attention back to her breasts, licking and sucking as she whimpered helplessly beneath his attention. Just when she thought she couldn't handle any more, he stopped and backed away from her. A wicked grin curved his sexy mouth when he deliberately slid his big fist down the length of his cock.

Anaya watched the huge shaft swell even larger, the plum-shaped tip jerking eagerly. She slipped her tongue out and licked her lips, unable to tear her gaze away.

"Want a taste?"

Anaya tried to nod, but the stasis field stopped her. "Yeah." He arched his brow at her, and she flushed. She just wasn't good at this submissive stuff. "Yes, master. Please."

"That's better." He stepped forward, catching her when the field suddenly let go. If she'd been unsure before, that confirmed it. He had a military-grade neural net and he could control the ship with a thought. He removed the cuffs from her wrists. "On your knees." He stroked the hair back from her face, and she dropped to her knees on the hard decking, wincing at the impact.

She reached out to take the enormous shaft, barely managing to wrap her palm around the thick length. Ryland cupped the back of her head with one hand while she flicked her tongue across the swollen head, tasting the salty drop clinging to the tip. His cock jerked under her questing tongue, and she smiled to herself. Being the master didn't guarantee him all the power.

Closing her eyes, she sucked the sensitive head into her mouth, swirling her tongue around the fluted edges. She scored her teeth across the slit and Ryland groaned, lacing his fingers into her long hair to hold her to him.

She leaned forward, running her tongue down the long shaft, exploring the veins that circled it. She nibbled her way to the base and sucked one of the furry balls into her mouth, earning herself a strangled growl from the bounty hunter.

She felt a surge of elation when she realized nothing had changed. She was still in control of the man who would soon be giving her pleasure. He just didn't realize it yet.

She sucked on first one ball and then the other before returning to nibble and lick at his enormous shaft. Tilting her head, she sucked the tip into her mouth and slowly worked more and more of the thick cock in. She'd never managed to deep-throat any of her lovers, but then again, she'd never tried. Usually she explained what she wanted, and if the male was lucky, she'd want to feel a cock inside her. Sometimes she just wanted to be pleasured and her partner's satisfaction didn't matter.

"Oh, yeah. Work that sweet little mouth of

yours." Ryland thrust his hips back and forth, pumping himself in and out of her mouth. She angled her head into a better position, enjoying the smooth slide of him against her lips, her teeth gently raking him with every thrust. She could feel herself going damp and slick at the thought of his huge cock invading her sex.

The power she'd harness from their joining would be incredible.

"Enough." Ryland's voice thickened with lust. He pulled his cock out and urged her to her feet. "I want to feel that little pussy of yours tighten itself around me when I come." He swept her up in his arms and strode out the doorway. "And I want to feel you squirming under me."

Anaya buried her face against his hard chest, inhaling his musky male scent. The powerful rippling of his biceps sent a quiver of anticipation through her. She was in complete agreement. She wanted him buried hard and deep inside her.

She gasped, her eyes snapping open, when he tossed her onto a hard sleeping platform. He followed her down, straddling her body as he sat back on his heels. Grasping her arms, he pulled them up over her head, one hand spanning both her wrists.

He slid his hand over her belly, pausing to trace the outline of the dragon tattooed in the hollow of her hip. He raised his head, and she could see the question in his eyes. She didn't want to tell him. She didn't want to think about that day, in her sixteenth year, when her handler decided to have his house symbol tattooed on her. The day she realized her freedom no longer existed. "It's a dragon."

He nodded, and she could have sworn she saw a glimmer of sympathy in his eyes before he moved his hand lower -- and she forgot all about slaves and masters and dragon tattoos that screamed she was just a piece of property.

He slipped off her, still holding her hands in one of his while he moved the other down, cupping her mound in his large palm before he slipped one finger into her damp heat.

Anaya cried out, bucking her hips up off the hard mattress. Fingers of erotic flame licked their way down her spine when he pushed that finger deeper, stroking the tender flesh inside her.

"Damn, you're wet." He raked his thumb across the hot nub of her clit, a wicked grin on his face. The man knew exactly how to make her beg.

And beg she did. "Please. I need to feel you inside me." She gasped when he slipped a second finger in beside the first, scissoring them in a maddening rhythm that sent her soaring out of control. She no longer had the ability to think. Rational thought fled, replaced by feeling.

She whimpered, twisting beneath him in a mindless haze of lust and need. A hot tide of pleasure surged through her with every stroke of his fingers, every teasing stroke of his thumb across her clit. Her inner muscles tightened around him, trying to drag those fingers deeper, hold them inside. She made a desperate sound, deep in her throat, and suddenly the fingers were gone, leaving a terrible yearning hunger behind.

"Noooooo." She opened her eyes, dazed with lust. Ryland grinned, freeing her hands so he could grasp her hips, lifting them high and tilting her until his cock brushed eagerly at the throbbing entrance to her pussy.

Anaya moaned, arching her back to try and force

his gorgeous cock inside her. His grin widened and he held her still for one long second. Then he thrust hard, burying himself so deep she could feel the soft fur of his taut balls slapping against her ass. He waited until she looked up at him and then slowly rolled his hips, grinding himself against her pussy.

Anaya sucked in a deep breath, flickers of heat racing through every nerve ending. Her hips moved automatically, matching his when he settled into a steady rhythm, pumping his hard shaft in and out of her slick core. She watched his eyes, the lust flaring hungrily in the molten blue, sending shivers of excitement racing through her.

He was all male, sinewy muscles and hard angles, ruthlessly plunging into her tight channel. And he wanted her. Anaya. Not the power of the Stargazer. Not the prestige that came from being chosen by a witch. He didn't know. He just wanted to fuck her. And that was the sexiest thing she'd ever encountered. She wrapped her legs around him, locking her ankles behind his back to give herself more leverage.

"You are one hot little bitch." He bared his teeth in a predatory smile. "And you love riding my cock, don't you."

It wasn't a question and Anaya didn't bother trying to answer. She closed her eyes, feeling the tiny ripples of pleasure start to roll through her, driving her higher and higher. Lust. Hunger. Need. They swirled together, overwhelming her with a searing delight that took her up to the heights and spilled her over the edge.

"Rylaaaaaaannnnd!" She screamed his name, her nails digging into his back as a blinding explosion of intense pleasure shattered her world into a million tiny points of light. He held her tight, his cock jerking deep inside her. Her inner muscles gripped him firmly as his hot seed jetted into her. He collapsed on top of her, his breath coming in long, hard gulps. They lay there for several long minutes, still joined, and Anaya felt an odd sensation.

Contentment. If she could just lie here forever, just a woman in the arms of her lover, she could be happy.

Ryland shifted his bulk and collapsed on the mattress beside her, his breath slowly returning to normal. He pulled her into the shelter of his body and fitted her against him with her head resting on his shoulder. She felt his lips brush a soft kiss across the top of her head, and she sighed happily, a lazy smile curving the corner of her mouth. The life of a pleasure slave wouldn't be so bad with Ryland as her master.

Chapter Two

Ryland stared at the vid screen, the list of open bounties scrolling across it in an endless loop. Murderers. Con artists. Escaped thugs. Space pirates.

And an indentured Stargazer whose masters were desperate to recover their property. The picture was old, the details murky. Anaya must have been barely past her coming-of-age when it was taken. The hair was shorter, cut in a jagged fashion that made her terrified green eyes look too large for the thin face, but he had no doubt the girl on the screen was the same one he'd left sleeping in his quarters.

Son of a hell-spawned asteroid field! She owed him an explanation, and it had better be good. He paused the display and used his neural connections to download the bounty information.

According to the document, Anaya had been indentured to the military junta that ruled Colony Five for an unheard of twenty-year period. The documents were signed by a man named Staavil, her court-appointed guardian. She'd vanished several solar cycles ago, and the bounty papers suggested someone had kidnapped her, since she had no way to get off-planet unnoticed. Her masters were adamant that she had no travel documents. The bounty offer contained the usual warnings about the dangers of engaging professional kidnappers. They were offering five thousand credits for her return in good working condition, plus a bonus for information on how she'd gotten off-planet in the first place.

Ryland snarled softly. The wounds on her wrists and ankles told him why she'd left, but five thousand credits was a goodly sum. More than the amount offered for his current target, the serial killer. He'd be a fool not to return the witch and collect.

And yet, he had a feeling this was one bounty he'd pass on.

He slammed his fist down on the marble surface in front of him, remembering the way her hot channel had milked his shaft while she whimpered and bucked eagerly beneath him. Stargazer or not, the little witch was the best damn fuck he'd had in a long time.

* * *

A stinging slap on her bare ass woke Anaya from a contented sleep. Ryland had proved to be an amazing lover. She glared up at him, rubbing her hand across her offended butt. "What was that for?" She studied his grim face warily, suddenly feeling vulnerable.

"For deceiving your master." Ryland paused, his eyes ice cold. "Stargazer Anaya Pretch."

Anaya cursed softly, a sinking feeling in the pit of her stomach. How the hell had he managed to discover her heritage? She eyed him cautiously, not sure what to say.

"Well?" He knelt on the bed, towering over her. "Care to explain why you let me think you were a bred sex slave?"

Anaya turned her head, refusing to look him in the eye. She had no idea how much he knew and she didn't intend to supply him with any information.

"Who put those marks on your wrists?"

She looked up at the unexpected change of topic. His tone was mild, but she could see the temper flashing in his eyes. She gulped, her hands covering the angry red welts. "My handler. I wouldn't do what he commanded, so he punished me. He wanted me to use my talent to help him cheat legitimate settlers out of their homes." She shrugged. "He couldn't afford to really injure me and he knew how much it would hurt every time I worked on the platform."

Ryland snarled, forcibly prying her fingers off her arm. "Son of a bitch needs to learn respect." He ran his fingers gently over the welts. "Your handler. Explain that to me. I thought Stargazers were in charge of their own destiny. Free to be contracted to whoever offered them the best deal."

Anaya felt her hard-won control slipping. "Unless their guardian decides to sell them." She tilted her chin up, knowing her defiant glare wouldn't win her any points with the bounty hunter. "I was fourteen when my parents failed to return from an exploratory mission to the Orion singularity, and I freaked out. I wanted to go look for them but the station medic sedated me so I wouldn't do anything rash. When it became apparent that my parents weren't returning, the courts stepped in. They didn't realize I had talent and they appointed a distant relative, Staavil, to be my guardian, with no limitations on his authority."

She paused, remembering Staavil's glee when he discovered her secret. He'd locked her in a tiny cabin on his shuttle, not bothering to tell her what he planned. She'd existed on dried spacer foods and recycled water for what seemed like ages, until he'd come to drag her, bound, to a meeting with the Colony Five government officials. She'd cursed him when he handed her over to Jorge, the soulless cyborg who'd been appointed her handler.

"You're not taking me back." She would fight this time. She was older now, able to stick up for herself. "I'll fight you with every last breath in my body."

Ryland raised his brows, laughter replacing the anger in his eyes. "Really?" He lifted her chin with his finger. "That could be interesting. I always enjoy a good fight." He dipped his head to place a hard kiss on her lips. "But you promised to be my personal slave." He ran his tongue across her lips, the soft pressure achingly tender. "And I promised I wouldn't hurt you. I always keep my promises."

He grasped her arm and raised her injured wrists to his lips. He traced the angry welts with his tongue. "What was his name?"

"His name?" Anaya frowned, confused. "Whose name?"

"Your handler. The man who hurt you." Ryland's soft tone, with its hint of restrained fury, sent a shiver down her spine.

"Jorge. He's not actually a man, he's a cyborg."

"No," Ryland corrected her. "If he gets anywhere near you ever again, he's dead."

Anaya held her breath. "You won't send me back?"

He reached up to tuck a stray lock of hair behind her ear. "They're offering five thousand credits for your return." His gaze wandered down her naked body. "That's a lot of money." He paused and a darkly wicked smile curved the corner of his mouth. "You think you can make that up to me?"

Anaya looked at the mischief dancing in those ice-blue eyes and dared to hope. "I'll certainly try." She smiled faintly. "And if I'm not submissive enough for a sex slave, you could always let me help power the ship."

"A good master can train his slaves into submission." Ryland grinned wryly. "I must be crazy. Everyone knows witches are trouble." He straightened up and grabbed one of his shirts from the bin beside the sleeping platform. "Get some clothes on and meet me in the crew lounge. We need to get some meat on those bones of yours if you're going to make a decent slave."

Anaya ducked and snatched the clothing before it sailed over her head. "Where is the lounge?"

Ryland grinned at her while he strode to the doorway. "You're a witch. You should be able to find it without any help from me." He ducked when she threw the shirt back at him. His laughter echoed mockingly as he disappeared down the corridor.

* * *

Ryland stared at the holo screen. Gone. The serial killer had managed to elude him yet again. They'd followed the trail of spent ion particles from his shuttle all the way to where the mutilated remains of his last victim had been found, and it ended abruptly in a deserted part of the galaxy with no shuttle in sight.

Ryland tapped into the computer records with his neural net and retraced the asshole's route, looking for any sign of deviation. A shuttle couldn't just disappear. There had to be a logical explanation.

"Problem?"

He turned at the sound of Anaya's voice. She stood in the doorway, one of his old shirts covering her delectable body. With her hair tousled and her eyes still hazy from sleep, she looked young. Much too young for a cynical bounty hunter like him. If he had any decency, he'd turn her loose at the next port.

He felt a grim smile tug the corners of his mouth. Lucky for his libido, he'd lost any decency he'd ever felt the night his wife and unborn child had been slaughtered by an escaped convict from New Mars. Before that night, he'd been an astronomer, quietly studying the stars and other celestial bodies. He'd spent twenty-two hours absorbed in the shower of meteorites in the Geses system on that fateful night.

His wife had stayed in their home, pleading exhaustion in her third trimester. The convict had slipped in through the window Ryland had left open to capture the evening breeze.

Ryland returned to find the room awash in blood. So much blood. He'd cried for the last time that night, holding the mutilated remains of his family. He'd laid her and their unborn son to rest in a sunny meadow before he'd hunted the convict down and administered his own brand of justice.

There were no appeals, no technicalities, and no mercy for the animal who had destroyed his family. After he'd disposed of the body, there was no going back to his peaceful life. He'd taken on one contract, bringing in a hit man. Then another, capturing the leader of a ring of child slavers. Then another murderer. He found he had a knack for tracking down criminals.

He shrugged. "Not a problem, more of a puzzle." His gaze dropped to her long legs as she crossed the room to stand beside him. "This is the third time I've been hot on the trail of this piece of spacer dung, only to have the damn trail disappear right in the middle of nowhere." He pulled up the star charts from the beginning of the voyage and showed her the trail of ion debris he'd been following. "And then it just stops in the middle of nowhere." He looked at her hopefully. "I don't suppose you can see ion trails the same way you see energy lines?"

Anaya frowned, a cute furrow creasing her brow. "The energy lines are alive, full of light. Ion trails have no life in them; they are the dust and debris left behind." She studied the charts. "He must be disguising the trail somehow, or maybe capturing the spent particles so you can't follow him."

Ryland had considered that possibility earlier, but he couldn't see how it could be done. Still, there had to be something, some fact, some kernel of knowledge, he'd overlooked.

"Maybe it's the singularity." Anaya pointed to the dense spot of blackness at the far side of the star chart. "That's a naked singularity. Since it didn't form a black hole, there is no event horizon, and the energy backwash radiating from it could be dissipating the ion trail, dragging it into the dense center."

Ryland stared at the chart. Of course! It was so simple and yet brilliant. He called up the records from his previous unsuccessful chase, studying the outlying areas. Another singularity appeared in the top corner. He looked up admiringly. "I've been studying this thing since early rising. How the hell did you figure it out so quickly?"

Anaya's eyes sparkled. "Stargazers work with energy lines, and we're very aware of anything that can disrupt them."

Moving her hands gracefully, she gestured at the screen. Ryland loved the way she used her whole body when she talked, her arms and hands in constant movement and her slim body swaying. He could feel the familiar tightening in his groin and his cock started to harden. She might not have been bred for sex, as he'd originally assumed, but she certainly had the capacity to keep him in a constant state of arousal. He dragged his attention back to the star charts. "So how do we find out where he went? Or has he managed to outsmart us?"

Anaya moved forward, and his gaze dropped to the cheeks of her firm ass peeking out from beneath the hem of the shirt. "Think of it as a big circle of darkness. Your quarry enters the circle and the trail disappears.

At some point, assuming he didn't commit suicide by letting the singularity swallow him up, he has to emerge. We need to find the spot where that happens."

Ryland reached out to circle her wrist, careful not to touch the welts that were slowly beginning to fade. He watched her eyes widen when he drew her down into his lap and fastened his mouth on hers, capturing her lips with a hungry intensity. She hesitated for an agonizingly long second, her lips soft and unresponsive, and then she kissed him back. He slipped his tongue in to tease hers, exploring the sweet taste of her. He used one hand to tilt her head back, angling her mouth to the perfect position.

He'd never felt such hunger, such need for a female. Even with his wife, there hadn't been such an intense aching lust. That had been love, young love, sweet and trusting and pure. This was something else. He didn't understand it and he didn't care. He let himself savor her honey sweetness for a few moments longer before he reluctantly let her go. Anaya quickly took two steps to the left and collapsed into the co-pilot's station.

He took a deep breath and willed his body to cooperate. He'd just finished making thorough love to her less than two hours ago. He should be able to keep his lust in check for a while longer.

"So how do we reacquire his trail?" He felt a small surge of satisfaction at the confused look in her eyes. All that lust hadn't been one-sided. She'd felt it too.

"We circle the singularity. At a safe distance of course." A visible shudder passed through her body. "We don't want to get drawn into the center."

Ryland nodded. They wouldn't stand a chance of surviving in the dense core of the singularity. He danced his fingers across the console in front of him, programming a circular sweep pattern into the computer. The ship's artificial intelligence system would do a thorough search of the path in front of them twenty times per second, looking for the fugitive's ion trail. Satisfied that it was set to notify him when it found the trail, he disengaged his neural net from the comp system and stood.

Anaya watched him warily from her seat, and he felt a familiar grin curve the corners of his mouth. It was becoming a habit with her around, this grinning. Amazing what a round of fantastic sex could do for one's outlook.

He turned, enjoying the way her gaze slid down his body, pausing to take in the noticeable bulge in the front of his spacer suit. He stalked across the space between them. No point in having a gorgeous sex slave aboard ship if you didn't plan to make use of her. She might be a Stargazer, but that didn't change their original agreement.

* * *

"Get that shirt off and get down on all fours."

The look he gave her didn't inspire confidence, but Anaya felt her treacherous pussy dampen. "I thought the fact that I'm a Stargazer changed our arrangement." She chanced a look up into his eyes while she shrugged out of the shirt and reluctantly got down on her hands and knees on the cold decking. "You know I wasn't bred for sex."

"That's debatable; you fuck like you were born for it." He looked over her naked body, causing her pussy to cream in anticipation. "I said your talents might prove to be useful. I didn't say I no longer required your..." he paused and gave her a wicked smile, "...other talents. Spread your legs a bit more and keep your eyes front. Your training is woefully inadequate."

"I wasn't trained to be a sex slave," she muttered, spreading her legs a bit wider.

"That's quite obvious." He brought his hand down on her ass in a sharp slap.

"Ouch!" Anaya twisted her head to glare up at him.

"Quiet." Ryland ran his hand down the cheek of her ass. "Your focus should be your master's pleasure, not any incidental pain you might feel."

Anaya bit back her angry reply. She hated to admit it, but being on display, naked and helpless, had a certain appeal. She spread her legs a bit more, enjoying the feel of the ship's cool air on her aroused clit.

"That's more like it." Ryland's voice had thickened. He stepped around in front of her and started to strip off his clothing with quick, efficient movements.

Anaya licked her lips, watching him drop the top of his spacer suit to the floor to reveal his muscular chest and a hard, flat stomach with a V of dark hair that disappeared into the waistband of his pants. He held her gaze, a roguish grin on his face. He hooked his thumbs and stripped the pants down over his hips, discarding them. His cock sprang free, the hard shaft curving upward from a nest of dark curls. Anaya sucked in a lungful of air, anticipation sending darts of lust dancing down her spine.

"Stay there." Ryland walked around behind her, and she twisted her neck to try to follow his movements. He reached down and swatted her on the backside. "I said stay still. I want to examine my property."

Anaya almost laughed. He might like to think he was the big bad bounty hunter, but she suspected he wasn't nearly as tough as he made out. She'd stowed away aboard his ship, misled him about her motives, and neglected to tell him that an entire planetary government would be willing to do anything to get her back. And yet he hadn't done more than throw her in a stasis field for a few hours and then proposition her because he thought she was a bred sex slave. That hardly qualified him to be a hard-assed bad guy. She ought to know. Her handler back on Colony Five had a sadistic streak a galaxy wide and enjoyed watching her suffer. He'd made an art out of inflicting the most pain without doing any lasting damage to her body.

She closed her eyes. She didn't need to use her talent to locate Ryland, bent over her from behind. His hands wandered with proprietary familiarity over her back, sliding around to cup her breasts, squeezing and massaging. She could feel his enormous erection pressing eagerly against her butt and she wiggled invitingly.

Ryland retaliated with another slap, more of a tap really, but Anaya let out a sharp yelp and he immediately rubbed the offended area.

"You need to learn who's master." He rested one hand on her back while he slid the other down the crack between her cheeks, and Anaya felt hot flames of want racing through her body. He paused his explorations at her anus, his finger resting lightly over the tight bud. "Have you ever been taken here?"

Anaya gasped at the thought. "No. I usually tell my lovers what to do. I've certainly never ordered one to hurt me." She whimpered, arching back into him. He slid his hand lower and slipped one finger into her aching pussy, probing deeply.

"Well, I'm not one of your wimpy lovers to be ordered around." He pulled his finger out and then slid it back in. He slid a second one in beside the first and started to pump them in and out, his thumb running across her clit with every stroke.

Anaya lost all logical thought, her entire consciousness focused on feeling. The cold steel of the deck. The darts of heat sliding along every nerve. Need pooled in her belly. She bucked her hips backward, wanting his enormous cock buried deep inside her. A low moan escaped her lips when he scored his thumbnail across the tender flesh of her labia.

"Fuck me, damn it! Fuck me now!" She screamed the order through clenched teeth, only to hear his amused chuckle from behind her.

"I don't take orders, darling. I'm the master." He withdrew his fingers. "You might want to remember that."

"I'm sorry." Anaya shifted restlessly beneath him and tried to sound submissive. Those fingers had felt so damned good. "But what are you waiting for?"

"I'm waiting for you to ask nice." She could hear a hint of laughter in his voice. "Or maybe just to scream and beg. Your choice."

Damn! She wanted to tell him to go to hell, tell him she was a Stargazer, she didn't beg. But she had a feeling he could make her. Make her beg and scream. And make her like it.

He reached forward, his shaft rock-hard against her ass when he bent over to nibble on the lobe of her ear, his breath warm on her neck. "Ready to beg?"

"Stargazers don't beg." She wished her voice sounded a little less breathless.

He stroked his fingers against the sensitive walls inside her channel again. "Do they scream?" He nipped the lobe of her ear.

Anaya sucked in a breath, not bothering to answer him. She shocked herself with a sudden desire to give in, to beg him to enter her, to fuck her hard.

Ryland chuckled, the sound low and knowing. He slid his fingers out of her pussy.

A groan escaped her clenched teeth and she whimpered with lust. She could feel that big shaft pressing hard against her ass, and despite her fear of the pain, the thought of his thick cock invading her body in that way caused shivers of excitement to shimmer through her.

He lowered his head to nibble a hot trail of kisses from the bottom of her neck down her spine. Licking. Kissing. Nibbling. Anaya couldn't hold back. She'd always been the one in control, the one who did the demanding.

But she'd never felt this amazing combination of want and need. Lust and desire. Her voice was low, almost a whisper. "I need you. Inside of me. Please."

"Now that's what I wanted to hear." Ryland moved up over her, his cock pushing impatiently at the slick entrance to her pussy. He used his knee to spread her legs wider, opening her for his pleasure. The thick head of his cock slipped inside her and she arched her back, bracing herself, hot juice dripping from her eager sex.

He entered her with agonizing slowness, one thick inch at a time until she felt his balls snuggled up against her. Anaya lost all attempts at control long before that point, whimpering and bucking beneath him, begging him to move harder, faster. She couldn't wait; she wanted all of him, now, deep inside her. Every deliberate move he made drove her higher, closer to losing all control.

"Not so fast. I want to try out that tight little ass of yours." He stopped, pulling his cream-slicked cock out of her channel.

Anaya hesitated. She'd never done anything like this before, but her curiosity and lust overrode her fear of pain. Reaching back, she spread her cheeks wide.

She turned her head and watched him as he squeezed some lubricant onto his hand and smoothed it onto his rock-hard shaft. Grinning at her submissive stance, he took his cock in his hand and aimed it at her ass. He looked so very male, dark and sure of himself. She could feel his shaft, slick with her own juices as well as the lubricant, pushing against the tight bud of her anus, slowly stretching the delicate tissues while Ryland forced himself inside. He took his time, letting her get used to the size and feel of his invading shaft. It burned. Pain mixed with pleasure. Pleasure sharpened by pain. He reached down and slipped two fingers into her slick channel, pumping them in and out so that she had a hard time distinguishing the pain from the fiery burst of pleasure racing through her. She pushed back, taking more of him. Something wild rose up in her, making her sizzle and burn with a savage need.

She heard Ryland growl out an oath behind her as he settled in to shaft her with a steady rhythm, holding her still with one arm, while he continued to tease and stroke her pussy, her clit, her wildly creaming channel with his other hand.

She lost all sense of herself, swept up in a spiraling wave of heat that rose ever higher. The pain was in sharp contrast to the pleasure radiating through every cell in her body. She bucked, whimpering and moaning. She felt her orgasm starting to gather, rolling through her, carrying her upward in an ever-intensifying storm of feelings. Then he slammed his cock into her a final time, and a tidal wave of indescribable feeling washed over her. She screamed his name, wave after wave of orgasm ripping through her, leaving her spent and gasping for air.

Ryland growled and she could feel his cock jerk as he came, spilling his seed into her. They collapsed in a tangled heap on the steel decking, his cock still buried deep inside her and his arms holding her close.

A jarring noise had them both twisting to look at the flashing display on the vid-screen. A mechanical voice announced, "Suspect ion trail detected at ten degrees starboard. Repeat. Suspect ion trail detected at ten degrees starboard."

Chapter Three

Ryland studied the trail they were following. It had been four risings since they'd managed to pick up the killer's trail again and they weren't getting any closer to catching him. They couldn't use Anaya's Stargazer abilities because she needed to know the destination in order to manipulate the energy lines. All they had was this trail of used ion particles, which she couldn't see any better than he could. He slammed his fist down on the console in frustration. If he really was in this for the money, he'd be far better off to sell Anaya back to the Colony Five government.

He shrugged at his own folly. He'd taken the contract because the killer targeted women. Women like his late wife. It had nothing to do with the bounty offered and everything to do with his own personal vendetta.

He'd never send Anaya back to that sadistic handler. Hell, the little minx had gotten under his skin, something no one had done since his wife. He'd never let her go. Period. He did not intend to admit it to her, but just her presence here on the ship made him feel more alive than he had since his wife's murder. It was about time he started to live again. If his wife knew how long he'd mourned her and their lost son, she'd kick his butt for wasting time worrying about something he couldn't change.

Ryland called up a chart of the galaxy they were in and studied the planets in the direct path of the ion trail. The killer could be headed for the spaceport waystation or for any one of a dozen smaller planets on either side of it. Damn, he really didn't want to wait for another murder to pick up the trail again. He needed to find this asshole now and put an end to the senseless slaughter.

"Midday meal is ready." Anaya's voice tinkled with amusement when she hailed him over the ship's com system. "It might even be edible this time."

Despite himself, Ryland felt a grin tugging at the corner of his mouth. When he'd decreed that the ship's mess was a female's domain, Anaya had warned him that her culinary skills were less than stellar. He'd thought she just objected to the menial work. After all, how hard could it be to program a couple of replicators?

He'd been surprised at how truly inept she proved to be at all domestic pursuits. The first few meals she'd managed to coax out of the replicators had looked bad and tasted worse. She'd just shrugged and resolutely chewed the unappetizing blobs, leaving him to either follow suit or admit he'd been wrong in assuming all females could cook.

"Be right there." He stood and stretched, working out the kinks in his long body before heading down to the mess.

* * *

Anaya hummed the overture to her favorite aria as she pulled the meal containers out of the replicators and sat them on the table. This cooking thing wasn't so hard once you got the hang of it.

An appreciative whistle alerted her to Ryland's presence. She turned to see him lounging against the doorway, looking rather tasty himself. His dark eyes sparkled with something she couldn't quite identify. He hadn't bothered to put a shirt on, and the thick muscles roped across his arms and chest made her mouth water for something other than the midday meal. Her gaze slid lower, over his flat stomach to his impressive shaft, outlined by the tight leggings. She felt color stain her cheeks and she jerked her attention back up to see the laughter in his eyes.

"Don't worry, witch." He straightened up and sauntered over to the table. "Right now I'm hungry for something other than your delectable little ass." He leaned and inhaled. "If you weren't so tasty yourself, I might promote you to ship's cook. This smells great." He draped himself over the seat and forked a generous portion into his mouth.

Anaya took the chair across the table and started to eat her own meal. She felt comfortable, sharing the ship and learning to do things that most free women took for granted. She'd never expected to find herself in a position where domestic chores were part of her everyday routine. She peeked at Ryland from beneath her lashes. The man was a walking menace.

"I've been trying to figure out where Grunner is heading." Ryland paused, his eyes narrowing thoughtfully. "The spaceport lies directly in his flight path, but the security is so tight he'd have to be stupid or suicidal to pull another murder there. Of course, he could be running low on supplies."

"Do you know what this Grunner looks like?"

"I've got a composite sketch from the port authorities where he committed his last kill. It's not great, but better than nothing." He accessed the ship's files and pulled up the image, flashing it onto the mess wall via the data chips imbedded in his temples. "His right arm is completely covered in an intricate tattoo of Martian origin, so he should be easy to identify."

Anaya shuddered. Even in a sketch, the man looked cold. His eyes were flat, devoid of any feeling. "I hope I never meet him. Just a sketch sends shivers up my spine."

Ryland stood and reached across the table, tilting

her chin up with his hand. She parted her lips, her pulse increasing at his touch.

"You won't be anywhere near this son of a bitch." He feathered a gentle kiss across her lips. "He's dangerous, and I intend to bring him back in cryostasis."

* * *

Anaya ran the brush absentmindedly through her hair. They were at the spaceport and Ryland wanted her to accompany him while he checked it out. Grunner's trail had led straight here, but there were so many ships coming and going from the giant complex, Ryland couldn't tell if the killer had actually docked, or if he'd just circled the huge port and taken off on another tangent.

He'd sent her to the cabin to "make herself presentable" while he cleared the formalities with the port authorities.

"We're cleared. Meet me at the airlock." Ryland's voice sounded flat, the com-unit echoing through the layers of metal between them. She put the brush down and smoothed the front of her snug bodysuit. Made of a single piece of form-fitting material, the soft green fabric hugged her body like a second skin and complemented her eyes. Covering her from her neck to the tops of her knee-length boots, it was both comfortable and practical. More importantly, it was the only outfit, besides the one she'd been wearing, that she'd brought with her when she stowed away. Since she hadn't anticipated her capture, two sets of clothing had seemed ample.

"Roger that." She grabbed her ear bud and clipped it firmly in place. She didn't want to lose contact with Ryland on a spaceport that catered to miners on leave. Playing slave to one oversexed male was more than enough.

"I said presentable, not edible." Ryland's gaze swept over her, his eyes darkening at her outfit. "I'm going to have to keep you on a short leash or you'll have every fool miner on the port drooling over you."

Anaya smiled at the compliment. "It's my only other outfit." She could feel her cheeks heating up. "And it covers me from head to toe." She tapped the deck with the tip of her boot for emphasis.

Ryland snorted. "Everything covered, but nothing hidden. Turn around."

"Excuse me?"

He sighed theatrically. "Turn around. It's a simple command. Face away from me."

She arched her brows. "Why?"

"Because I told you to."

She snorted. "And?"

He smiled. "I have a present for you, and I won't give it to you unless you do."

She rolled her eyes. "You just want to ogle my ass again."

He laughed. "That too. Turn around." Anaya twirled gracefully around, stopping when she faced precisely in the opposite direction. "Now close your eyes."

She giggled. "You're just full of orders today." But she closed her eyes. Excitement had her fighting not to fidget like a youngling at a star exhibit.

She felt something heavy resting in the hollow of her throat, and a delicate chain encircled her neck. Ryland brushed her hair aside and fumbled with something at the nape of her neck. "Can I open my eyes now?"

"Not quite yet." Amusement softened his deep voice. He put his hands on her shoulders and turned her around until she faced him. "Okay, now you can look."

Anaya opened her eyes, her hands going to the object around her neck. Ryland held up a reflective sphere, and she could see a beautiful star sapphire, cut in a multifaceted pattern, nestled against her throat. A chain of delicately woven white gold suspended the jewel around her neck.

"It's beautiful!" She blinked back the tears that threatened to spill from her eyes. "Where? Why? When?" She didn't know what to say. She'd never expected something so personal, so thoughtful. She threw her arms around Ryland's neck, knocking the sphere out of his hands as she placed a happy kiss on his mouth. "I love it!"

"Don't you be getting any ideas." He pulled her in close and kissed her. "It has a nano-sender unit embedded in it. If we get separated, I can use my neural net to locate you through the star." He nuzzled her hair, nipping gently at her earlobe. "It looks natural on you. A beautiful star for a beautiful Stargazer."

Anaya buried her head in the hollow of his shoulder, afraid to let him see the stark emotion in her eyes. He was only being practical; he didn't want to lose his new slave. "Thank you."

"You're welcome." His voice sounded gruffer than usual. "And when we're on the spaceport, I don't want people knowing what our connection is. You're just a friend who's traveling with me. Okay?"

Anaya nodded, confused. He didn't want people to know she was his sex slave?

"Good." He placed his hand on the ID pad beside the air lock and it cycled open to reveal a corridor packed with beings from all over the galaxy. "Now let's go see if we can find us a killer."

She stared in amazement at the variety of sentient beings bustling on their way to or from the ships in the docking ring. It hadn't occurred to her that a spaceport this far out in the galaxy would be this busy. She shrank back against Ryland when a two-headed reptile with beady eyes turned to stare at her.

Ryland planted his arm firmly around her waist and drew her in close to his side. "Relax. I have no intention of losing my favorite toy to a passing lizard."

His comment served to make her relax, although she still glanced around nervously while they strolled down the corridor. "What if someone recognizes me? You said there was a contract out for my return."

"No one's going to be stupid enough to try and take you away from me." He tightened the arm around her waist. "Not if they're smart."

Anaya relaxed a bit. He had a point. Even amongst the hustle and bustle of a busy port, Ryland had an air of authority that beings automatically deferred to. The crowds parted around them, giving Ryland, with his warrior's build, a wide berth.

"We'll go check out the local watering hole. If Grunner landed here, chances are he passed through the port's bar, at least briefly. The bartender is an old friend of mine."

She nodded, feeling out of her depth. She didn't want to admit she'd never been to a bar. She'd been kept on board ship during the times they were docked anywhere other than the home Colony. You don't take your slaves out for drinks at the local club.

* * *

"I've never known Ryland to travel with a female." The bulky bartender, whom Ryland had introduced as Joe, looked curiously at Anaya. She fidgeted uncomfortably on her barstool, wishing she'd stayed aboard the shuttle. Who knew showing up with Ryland would cause so many questions? "You must be one special lady."

"We're just friends." She glanced at Ryland who was nursing dark ale while his restless gaze swept the room. He wasn't paying any attention to her and appeared happy to let her answer his friend's questions. "I needed a lift and he offered to let me tag along."

"Really?" The bartender raised his brows in disbelief and a mischievous look crossed his face. "Then he won't mind if I introduce you to some of the local boys." He raised his hand and started to wave at a group of miners.

"I don't think you want to do that." Ryland grabbed Joe's wrist and forced his hand back down to the bar.

"I thought so!" Joe smirked at the bounty hunter. "Just friends, my ass. Tell it to someone wet behind the ears."

Ryland turned his attention to the bartender, and a shiver ran down Anaya's spine at the cold, flat expression in his eyes. "She's with me, although she deserves better. Our relationship is nobody's business but our own." He paused, his eyes narrowing. "And just in case that's not clear, Anaya is far too good for the likes of the scum that calls this place home."

Joe threw his hands up in a conciliatory gesture. "Hey, sorry. I was just fooling around." He laughed, the sound strained. "We've been friends a long time and you've never brought a lady with you before."

Anaya bit her lip to keep from laughing. She'd gone from being "some female" to a "lady" in less time than it took to down her drink. And Ryland had just publicly placed her under his protection. Not exactly a declaration of undying devotion, but still nice.

"So what are you doing way out in my sector of space anyways?" Joe had obviously decided that a change of subject was in order.

"Looking for a serial killer." Ryland fished a vid-recorder out of his pocket and handed it to the bartender. "Name's Grunner, although he might use an alias. He likes to kill women and slice them up into little pieces. So far the body count is at twelve and I don't want it to go any higher."

Joe's jovial expression sobered. He took the recorder and studied the image, his eyes narrowing. "He came through here about two solar cycles ago. Surly fellow. Stocked up on supplies and took off real quick." He nodded toward a slender male nursing his drink at a table in the far corner. "Blake over there would have filed his flight plan, if you're interested in where he was headed."

"Thanks." Ryland slid off his stool and crossed the room.

Anaya sipped on her drink, a surprisingly tasty fruit punch, while she waited for him to come back. Joe made small talk, telling her amusing little stories about life on the spaceport. She laughed dutifully in the right places, but her attention kept straying to Ryland.

He straightened up and turned to stride back to her side. "We need to get moving. Grunner was here all right, and his registered flight plan has him heading to New Eden."

"New Eden?" Anaya licked a stray drop off her glass. "I've never heard of it."

Joe looked glum. "You don't want to, sugar. A bunch of religious zealots founded the colony there years ago and they're trying to recreate the biblical Garden of Eden with one nasty twist. The founders blamed Eve for all of mankind's troubles, so they created a male-dominated society; the women have no rights. Mostly they wait on the men hand and foot, apologize for existing, and pop out babies."

Anaya stared at Ryland in dismay. "That's awful. Can they do that?"

He shrugged. "The colonies make their own rules, and so long as they aren't harming any of the other settled worlds, no one is going to interfere. The odd woman manages to escape off-planet, but mostly they just accept it. They were born there and don't know any other kind of life. Problem is, if Grunner gets there, he's going to have a field day. The elders aren't going to care if a few women they consider worthless turn up dead."

"You're not taking your lady friend there, are you?" Joe threw Ryland an incredulous look.

Ryland snorted. "Not likely. She can stay on the ship while I go hunting. I won't take her planet-side."

"Why?" Anaya looked from one to the other.

"Laws of New Eden apply to all women on the surface, be they native or visitors. If you broke one of their insane laws, they have the right to punish you. Just walking down the street, you'd probably break a few." He gave her a wry smile. "And they are overly fond of corporal punishment."

She wrinkled her brow. "Meaning?"

"They could whip you."

She gasped. "You can't be serious. That's barbaric."

Joe nodded. "I agree. But then religions have a barbaric history. And he's right. They are the most whip-happy bunch in the galaxy. You listen to Ryland and stay off that planet."

She looked from one to the other, not sure if they

were teasing. Surely in this day and age people didn't go about whipping each other.

"He's telling the truth," Ryland retorted impatiently. "And the asshole already has a head start on us. Finish your drink and let's get moving."

Anaya opened her mouth to point out she could get them there in short order, and then snapped it shut. She didn't want anyone else knowing she was a Stargazer. Plenty of time to discuss her abilities when they were safely back aboard the shuttle.

Chapter Four

Ryland eyed her thoughtfully. "Can you do that? I thought you needed some kind of special platform to work on."

"No." Anaya looked around the bridge. "It makes it easier, and I wouldn't want to work without one indefinitely, but it is possible. I just need something to secure myself to so I don't fall over."

"Fall over?"

"If I stay in the trance too long, I can get weak without realizing it. I need something that will hold me upright if that happens." She looked around the bridge. "Any ideas? I need to be standing with my arms above my head."

A wicked grin lifted the corners of his mouth. "Lots, but I don't think they're going to help us. This is starting to sound like a bondage scene from a second-rate vid-show."

Anaya wrinkled her nose and tried not to burst out laughing. "Especially when you consider I have to be naked to work with the energy lines."

Ryland stared at her with a bemused expression on his face. "You're kidding, right?"

She grinned. "Nope. Buck naked. And tied to an upright post."

He laughed. "Good thing I don't work with a crew. The sight of you naked would have their concentration shot all to hell." He grinned. "Luckily I'm made of sterner stuff."

"You think so, huh?" Anaya ran her hands down her body, gazing pointedly at the growing bulge in the front of his leggings.

Ryland grinned, unrepentant. "I didn't say I wouldn't react, just that I could still work with my cock as stiff as a Martian icicle."

The man was hopeless. Time to get the conversation back on track. "So, what about finding something for me to work with?"

"I think I've got a solution." He turned to the doorway. "Wait here. I'll be back in a sec."

Anaya watched his sexy butt disappear down the hallway. She worried her bottom lip between her teeth. There was something about Ryland that made it hard to keep her mind on the task at hand. Unless, of course, the task was bolstering her power with some steamy sex. She could feel her cheeks warm at the thought of his impressive cock and what it could do to her.

The jarring sound of something scraping its way down the hall snapped her out of her reverie. What was making all that racket?

She stuck her head out of the doorway and started to laugh. Ryland grunted loudly, dragging a large wooden statue representing one of the mythical gods from ancient Earth's lore. Recently, a band of wandering minstrels had revived the galaxy's interest in Thor with their operatic rendition of his life's story. Why Ryland had a life-sized statue of the god aboard his ship, she couldn't imagine. She backed away to allow him to maneuver Thor through the doorway.

He tilted the statue upright beside the captain's chair and gave her a sheepish grin. "Some of my friends have a warped sense of humor." He patted the statue. "Thor is reputed to have carried a magical hammer that smote the bad guys and then returned to its owner." He struck a pose beside the blond giant. "I don't have the hammer, but I chase down the bad guys and bring them back to face justice."

Anaya grinned. "I can see the resemblance. And you look scary enough without the hammer." She walked over and stared up at the statue in awe. "He's magnificent." She turned and stood in front of Thor, lifting her arms. "This might actually work. Do you have a belt, or a long strip of that stuff you used to bind my hands when you found me on the ship? You need to tie me to it so I don't fall or let my arms move."

Ryland nodded. "I'll go get some. I think you should get a good sleep and make a fresh start at next rising. It'll give me some time to set this up."

"Good idea." She ran her hand down the smooth length of Thor's chest, before slanting a mischievous look up at Ryland. "Care to come and tuck me in?"

* * *

"Do Stargazers really gain power from sex?" Ryland nibbled a line of kisses across her jaw. The thought of her casually coupling with random partners left a bad taste in his mouth.

Anaya stiffened under him, refusing to look him in the eye. "Yes. I never really thought about it, it was just something that needed to be done. Get plenty of rest, eat a well-balanced diet, and let whomever my handler sent fuck me."

"You didn't get to choose your own partners?" He'd always thought the Stargazers were the ones in control.

"From where? It's not like I could go check out the males at the local watering hole. They owned me." She looked at him, and he glimpsed a lifetime of misery in those eyes. She shrugged. "It wasn't all that bad. They were very skilled and the handler made sure I rarely got the same partner more than once. He didn't want me getting attached to anyone."

Ryland felt a sick feeling deep in his gut. They'd treated her like an animal. A very valuable animal, but an animal nevertheless. He had a sudden murderous urge to go find her handler.

Anaya shifted restlessly against him and he realized he'd tightened his grip. He kissed the spot where his fingers had squeezed her soft flesh. She needed to know how amazingly special she was -- even if he did plan to keep her for his personal slave forever.

He trailed a line of soft kisses down her body. Taking his time. Making sure she enjoyed every touch of his lips. Every lick of his tongue. Every nibble of his teeth.

She squirmed, whimpering and moaning. When she arched her back, rubbing her wet mound against his aching shaft, he shifted his weight, rolling her under him. Slowly, tenderly, he entered her. One deliberate inch at a time -- fighting the urge to ram his swollen shaft deep into her slick channel. She deserved to feel loved. If he were a different person, if that part of him hadn't died with his wife and child, he could love her. If she were free, she'd make someone a wonderful mate, but that was never going to happen. He did not intend to ever let her go.

Anaya's nails dug into his back and she jerked her hips under him. "Faster, damn it. Bury that big cock of yours deep inside me."

He felt a reluctant grin curve his lips. Seems his little Stargazer didn't like her loving sweet and tender. "Yes, ma'am." He let himself go, slamming his cock deep, over and over, reveling in the way her inner muscles clenched around him, trying to hold him inside her.

He could feel his balls draw tight, his orgasm building. He fought it off, wanting her to be there with him. Wanting to share the incredible beauty of their joining.

"Oh, gods! Rylaaaaaaannnd!"

He captured her mouth, taking his name from her lips while her pussy clenched him tight and his seed jetted deep. Wave after wave of pleasure washed through him. He collapsed beside her on the sleeping platform, cradling her in his arms to hold her close, feeling every ripple of her pussy as tiny aftershocks raced through her.

They lay that way for what seemed like eons, limbs tangled together, letting their breathing slowly return to normal. Anaya opened her eyes and gave him a sleepy smile. She slipped one hand up between them and wrapped her fingers around the sapphire pendant.

"A star for a Stargazer," she murmured softly. "I don't remember the last time anyone gave me a present."

* * *

Anaya sat on the hard deck, her legs crossed in a lotus position. Eyes closed, she focused deep inside herself. She ran through each of the mental exercises that she'd learned. Her breathing slowed and she felt a sea of calm surround her.

Rising, she stripped off the robe she'd draped around her shoulders. She still wore the star pendant around her neck, and she brushed her fingers against it. She approached the image of Thor. Ryland had left an untidy pile of straps beside it, and she picked up two of the shorter ones, using them to strap her ankles to those of the statue. She rifled the pile and picked out two more of the short ones and a longer one for her waist.

"I'll need you to fasten my hands for me." She knew Ryland waited just out of her sight. She could feel his mind, full of concern, teasing the edge of her consciousness. She found the rough touch comforting. She snugged the makeshift belt tight around her waist and lifted her arms, placing them along Thor's.

She watched Ryland bend down to retrieve the last two straps. She couldn't afford to let her confused feelings for the handsome bounty hunter surface just yet. She needed to stay focused, centered, to work with the energy lines.

He moved her left arm slightly and fastened it with one of the short straps. Crossing in front of her, he attached her right hand to the statue before walking over to the captain's chair and belting himself in. His hands flashed over the console while he worked his way through the pre-flight checklists.

Anaya pulled her attention away from Ryland and closed her eyes. She could feel the energy swirling around her. The lines glowed brightly behind her closed lids, brilliant blues and greens, with a few vibrant reds showing the way to the singularity. She let her consciousness expand, and searched the lines, calling them up one by one, examining them, discarding one after the other when she knew they weren't the one she sought. She clenched her hands, arching herself upward into the sparkling lights.

The feeling of power was incredible. Seductive. It teased her, beckoning, tempting her to absorb more and more of it. Sometimes, it was all she could do to resist. If she let them, they'd swallow her whole, absorb her consciousness into the interplanetary web. She sent a tendril of her mind out, searching for Ryland. There. She could feel him. Solid. Grounded. Reliable.

The temptation lessened and she went back to her search. This line went back to the Colony planets. That blue one led to a lovely asteroid, devoid of life. The green one held promise. Yes! That was the one. She couldn't explain how she knew, but there was no doubt. She pulled the energy to herself, using her outstretched hands to capture the sparkling line. Diverting the energy through her body, she sent it pouring into the engines. She could feel them revving up, gaining power. She pulled more of the energy and directed it to them.

The search over, she let the joy of the ley lines rush over her and through her. It made everything worthwhile. She reveled in her power. Only a Stargazer could know the amazing feeling of being one with the energy of the universe.

She sensed the planet growing closer and she knew it was time to let go. She reached out for Ryland, a tiny tendril, to make sure he stood guard over her body. Waiting for her to return. She held his presence in a tiny corner of her mind while she reluctantly let the line slip away from her. She felt the giant engines slow.

She opened her eyes, breaking her trance and the connection to the vast network of energy. For just a second she felt lost, bereft of the power. She sagged against her restraints, wincing. The straps chafed against wounds that hadn't quite healed yet.

Ryland growled out an oath and reached up to release her hands. Droplets of blood splashed onto his arm from the wounds that had reopened on her wrists. She draped her arms around his shoulders, careful not to let the open wounds touch anything. She sighed contentedly, leaning into the comfort of his hard body while he fumbled with the strap wound around her waist.

If she'd had enough energy left, she would have smiled at his clumsy attempts to release her. He might think himself a hard-assed bounty hunter, but she knew better. He cared too much, so he tried to wall himself away from feeling.

He finally managed to get the strap off her waist, and she found herself slipping over his shoulder while he bent over to free her legs.

"Thor's had enough fun for one day." He wrapped his arm around her legs and straightened up. Anaya found herself dangling over his shoulder, with a nice view of his tight butt.

She closed her eyes and listened to him grumble about Stargazers and energy lines and serial killers who didn't know enough to stay put so he could deal with them. He strode into his cabin and slid her gently onto the sleeping platform. He rummaged through the cabinet on the wall and produced a tube of ointment. Squeezing a generous amount of creamy stuff onto his palm, he massaged it into her chafed wrists and ankles.

"You should have stopped when they opened up." He scowled at her. "A few more days won't make any difference. Sooner or later we'll catch up. I don't want you pushing yourself." He lifted her wrist to examine the welts. "Promise me that next time you'll stop before I have to stand there and watch blood dripping from you."

Anaya gave him a tired smile. "I promise." Later she'd explain it to him. How she didn't feel the pain until afterward. How the energy of the lines seduced her, taking her away from herself. Later. Now, she needed to rest.

She felt Ryland's lips brush gently across her forehead as she drifted off to sleep.

* * *

Anaya opened her eyes, trying to figure out what had woken her. Slipping the blanket off, she sat up and looked around sleepily. Ryland was nowhere to be seen. Not surprising. He'd probably headed up to the bridge plotting his next move. The man was nothing if not methodical. She considered calling him, but decided to clean up first. Using her talent had left her feeling sweaty and Ryland had a real water-based shower on his ship instead of the plasma-ray-based ones favored by frugal captains. She hummed happily. She grabbed a towel from the cabinet and headed into the shower.

The hot water cascaded over her naked body in welcome sheets and she lifted her face to the spray. She stood there reveling in the wet warmth until the water started to cool. With a contented sigh, she turned the taps off and stepped out, reaching for her towel.

"Damn idiots."

She turned, lifting a brow in silent query when Ryland strode into the cabin. He gave her an apologetic smile. "The governing body on this godforsaken pile of rocks doesn't seem to think a woman-hating killer is a problem. They concede that there have been two women found dead and mutilated since Grunner arrived, but they just don't care. The women were past their prime childbearing years." He slammed his fist into the bulkhead. "They've declined to help with the capture and went so far as to caution me that my activities better not interfere with their society." He rolled his eyes in disgust.

"So now what?" Anaya draped the towel around her and picked up her hairbrush.

Ryland crossed to stand behind her, taking the brush from her hand and running it through her long hair with firm strokes. "I'll have to go and find him myself. The authorities aren't going to be any help." He smoothed the hair back from her temples. "I'll have to find some way to flush him out into the open."

"Flush him out? Didn't they even tell you where

he is?"

"No." Disgust sharpened his voice. "They don't keep track of visiting psychopaths."

"I could try to find him for you," she offered softly.

"I'm not using you for bait." Ryland stopped brushing her hair, and she could feel the tension in him.

"Not for bait. Sometimes I can find people by their energy signature. It doesn't always work, but Grunner would have a very distinctive aura. I might be able to locate him if you take me down to the surface with you."

Ryland twirled around so they were face-to-face. "No. You heard what Joe said about this place. Even without factoring Grunner in, this is not a planet you ever want to set foot on. I won't risk you."

Anaya tilted her head sideways, smiling sweetly into his angry face. "You'd rather wait until he kills half a dozen more of those poor women?" Ryland glared at her, and she knew she'd won. "You'd be right beside me all the way. I know you'd never let him hurt me."

"Damn straight." He continued to brush her hair. "But if I let you do this, you have to promise to do everything I say. Immediately."

"Well, of course." She gave him her best innocent smile. "I wouldn't dream of disobeying you."

"Yeah. Right." He tugged gently on a lock of hair. "Promise."

Anaya sighed. "Fine. I promise."

He patted her on the head. "There now, that didn't hurt at all, did it?"

She rolled her eyes and didn't bother to reply.

Chapter Five

"Remember, you promised to obey me." Ryland adjusted the pack strapped to Anaya's back. Using women for pack animals was just one more of the quaint local customs. He'd made sure it appeared full, while actually holding very little.

"How could I forget?" She slanted him a mischievous look from under her lashes. "You've reminded me eight times since we docked."

He gave the pack one last tug and slapped her on the butt. "Mind your manners." He used his neural net to tap into the ship's computer and call up a grid map of the area. He also checked to make sure the tracking chip in the star pendant was functioning properly. Having her down on the planet's surface was making him very nervous. "The latest murder was down in the lower section of town, so we'll start there." He strode down the middle of the street, leaving Anaya to follow a step behind. He would have preferred to have her beside him, but they needed to blend in.

They'd arranged a series of signals so they could communicate without drawing attention to themselves. If Anaya sensed Grunner's presence, she'd fake a twisted ankle to allow Ryland to turn back and confer with her. He'd also made sure she wore the star. He'd been telling the truth when he said it concealed a tracking device linked to his nano system. What he hadn't told her was that he'd inserted the device into the star just for her. He could have just as easily planted the device directly beneath the surface of her skin.

He'd found the star at a bazaar on one of the outlying Colony planets, and the shimmering facets had captured his imagination, bringing back memories of all those days he'd spent studying the heavens. He'd paid a goodly sum for the gem, taking it back to the ship and suspending it from the bulkhead in his study where he could sit and stare at it for hours. It pleased him that she loved it so much.

He wandered through the streets of the lower town, passing by the scene of the latest murder from several angles, and Anaya remained silent, trotting meekly along behind him. The twin suns were directly overhead, and he could see a small inn up ahead, offering midday meals for reasonable rates.

He slowed and let Anaya catch up. "We'd better get something to eat. I'll go in and order. You wait at one of the tables." Women weren't allowed in shops or eateries, so the inn provided tables in a small courtyard in front of the inn for those who were traveling with females and preferred not to just leave them waiting at the door.

Anaya nodded and then picked a table, shrugging the pack off her shoulders before she sank into the seat. Ryland hesitated at the doorway, glancing back to make sure she was all right before he entered the inn.

He ordered two bowls of stew and a tankard of the local ale. A young woman with a shy smile took his order. She passed him the ale and two mugs, promising to bring the food out to their table. He thanked her and hurried back outside. He didn't feel comfortable with Anaya out of his sight.

She smiled up at him when he placed a mug in front of her and filled it with the cool liquid. The waitress brought out the stew and the two of them dug into the delicious smelling food.

They ate in silence, watching the locals bustle about their business. The women seemed like women everywhere, some happy and smiling, others scowling as they followed the men.

"I'd like to sit here a while and see if I can get a fix on his position." She took a sip from her mug. "I might be able to point us in a general direction."

Ryland shrugged. "It's worth a try. Walking back and forth doesn't seem to be doing us any good."

He watched her lift her chin and close her eyes. The slender shoulders relaxed and he imagined she'd entered the trance state. She looked so beautiful, so serene. He looked around, automatically checking for threats. The street was almost deserted; most of the populace was inside enjoying their midday meal. He smiled at a stray cat darting out from behind a potted plant to snag a scrap of bread. If it weren't for the bizarre religious customs, this would be a nice colony.

Anaya opened her eyes. "I can sense his presence, but I'm having trouble getting a direction." She ran one hand through her hair in frustration. "Maybe if we move to a different location I'll have better luck. There could be something here blocking me."

Ryland grinned. At least they knew they were close. After having had Grunner elude him time and again, that was good news. "How about we try for a couple of blocks in that direction." He gestured to the left. "If that doesn't work we can always move again."

She nodded, giving him one of those smiles that always managed to send heat racing through him. "I'll just go use the facilities first. That ale seemed to go right through me." She got to her feet and headed in the direction of the ladies' room sign. Amazingly, those little symbols seemed to be the same throughout the universe.

* * *

"Well, well, what do we have here?"

Anaya stiffened in horror when a man's arm wrapped around her throat. Not just any man.

Grunner.

The disturbing tattoo on his arm was unmistakable. No wonder she hadn't been able to get a direction. He'd been right here all the time. She could feel the evil tainting the air around him. She opened her mouth to scream, only to choke when he viciously tightened his grip, cutting off her air. The points of the star pendant dug into her skin, the pain distracting her.

She let herself go limp. She couldn't fight him in this position, so her best bet was to trick him into thinking she'd lost consciousness. She could see no point in trying to talk to a madman.

"That's it, you little slut. You just go to sleep and let me take you to my playroom." He slapped a piece of tape over her mouth so she couldn't scream. "I've been following you and your master for most of the morning. He's going to have to find himself another female. I'm afraid you're not going to be much use to him when we've finished playing."

It was all she could do not to shiver at his touch. She wondered how long it would be before Ryland noticed her missing. She concentrated on her breathing, keeping it slow and steady. He'd have to loosen his grip around her neck at some point. Maybe she'd be able to run. All she'd need was enough time to get outside where someone would notice her. She tried to block his aura. The oily taint of evil made her stomach lurch in protest.

She opened her eyes a crack. All she could see was the wall of the bathroom, completely devoid of windows or anything she could grab and use as a weapon. Grunner stayed behind her, using his superior body weight to push her toward the doorway.

"Stupid bitch. Didn't even see me watching you, did you?" Grunner kneed her in the back of the legs unexpectedly and she fell forward. Her eyes flew open, a startled oath escaping her as she put her hands out in front of her to break her fall. She hit the packed dirt floor hard, jarring the breath from her lungs in a whoosh.

With an evil laugh, Grunner dropped to his knees beside her, wrenching her arms out from beneath her and tying them behind her back. He jerked hard on the ropes and Anaya whimpered, pain shooting through her recently healed wrists. He gave the ropes another hard tug before he rolled her over. He bent down and ran his hands over her body, squeezing her breasts painfully.

"A little on the small side, but they'll do." He leered. "Does your master like you to strip for him? Does he like to play with your little titties before he shoves his cock into you?"

Anaya shivered. Grunner's eyes held no hint of sanity.

"Time to move. Don't want that big master of yours to find us before I have time to appreciate you." He picked her up, hoisting her over his shoulder.

Anaya could feel herself starting to panic. This man had murdered twelve women. Murdered them and cut them into little pieces. She sent a tendril of awareness out, searching for Ryland's presence. It connected immediately and a soothing calm flooded through her, grounding her. He would find her. The panic shrunk to manageable proportions.

Grunner stepped out of the bathroom and strode down the street. He didn't bother to hide, carrying her over his shoulder like a rolled-up rug. No one questioned him, or even bothered to give her a second glance. Her only consolation was that faint connection to Ryland's aura.

She knew he would follow. He wouldn't let this madman harm her.

* * *

Ryland glanced in the direction of the bathrooms. Anaya hadn't been gone long, but he felt uneasy. He'd never felt good about letting her accompany him down to the surface, and having her out of his sight for any length of time was pure hell. He tapped his fingers on the table. How long did it take a woman to use the facilities? Damn, he should have made her stay onboard the ship.

She should have been back by now. Standing, he downed the last of his ale and grabbed the pack that Anaya had left leaning against the table leg, slinging it over one shoulder. Where the hell was she?

It didn't take him long to locate the bathrooms or to realize that Anaya wasn't there. The door hung open, swinging gently in the breeze. Ignoring the startled look of a passerby, he cursed loudly, not sure if he was mad at himself or at Anaya for taking the opportunity to escape. He'd been so sure she'd honor her bargain and stay with him.

He looked around, wondering which way she might have gone. The foot traffic had picked up a bit, but not enough to hide a woman alone. And how did she think she'd get off this woman-hating planet without a man accompanying her?

He couldn't believe she'd pull a stupid stunt like this. He closed his eyes and tapped into the ship's computer, accessing the tracking chip in her necklace. He hoped she'd forgotten its purpose and still wore it.

"Did thou need some help?" A young girl, barely

out of her teens, stopped to look up at him and he put the ship's computer on hold. She hastily looked down when he noticed her. "You seem distressed."

"I'm looking for a woman." Maybe the girl had seen which way Anaya had gone. Might prove useful if the chip didn't pinpoint her location. "Full grown, but a stranger to this land. She had long, dark hair and green eyes. She wore a blue dress down to her ankles and she would have been alone. Did you by chance see a lone woman leaving here?"

The girl raised her head. "No. A woman of that description was taken away by a dark-haired man, but I saw no woman alone." She shuddered, then added, "The man was from off-planet. He had the most horrible pictures colored on his arm, and he carried the woman over his shoulder like a sack of grain. I think she was sleeping. She didn't move."

Ryland felt his blood run cold. "Which way did they go?" Her description of the tattoo meant the man had to be Grunner, and he had Anaya. He cursed himself for doubting her, for thinking she'd run away from him.

The girl pointed down one of the many narrow laneways behind him. "That way. May I go now? My master will be mad if I am late returning."

"Of course. And thank you." Ryland smiled reassuringly at the girl before she hurried off. He reestablished the link to the ship and set up a link to the tracking chip. The signal was faint, fading in and out. The planet's magnetic field must be strong here; it was interfering with the directional sender. He snarled out an oath. Damn tech gadgets never worked right when you needed them.

Pivoting, he took off at a trot in the direction the girl indicated, searching every doorway and alley he passed for some sign of the pair. The tracking signal continued to cut in and out, but at least he knew he was headed in the right direction.

He had to find them before Grunner decided it was safe to stop. The girl had said she appeared to be sleeping and he didn't know if that meant she'd fainted, or that Grunner had drugged her to keep her quiet. His mind shied away from the thought of Anaya on the receiving end of the serial killer's manic attention.

He paused several times to ask people if they'd seen the couple. Invariably they had, although it disgusted him to know that no one had felt compelled to question a man's right to carry a woman through the streets of town like so much baggage.

As he got farther from the center of town the shops and markets thinned out to be replaced by warehouses and deserted shop fronts of a poorer district. The tracking signal gained strength, although it still fluctuated at random intervals. He needed it to stabilize. When he got off this blasted planet, he was going to go visit the trader he'd bought the tracking chip from and feed him the damn thing one metallic piece at a time.

Ryland felt his heart sink. They could be anywhere in this maze of buildings. He could search forever and not find her. He stopped and stood still, looking around.

Which way?

He became aware of a light touch in his mind, a feather-light caress. Anaya. He could sense her!

He turned in the direction of the touch and started to walk. Slowly. The tracking signal strengthened, confirming he was headed in the right direction. He concentrated on Anaya, trying to keep that slight feeling of connection. He passed an old cheese store, a dry goods and a deserted laundry. He turned left onto a narrow boulevard lined with warehouses and buildings in various states of decay.

The sense of her presence filled him, more substantial now. He ignored the tracking signal; he no longer needed the device to help him. He walked faster, more confident, sure that he would find her. He could sense her anger and her fear. She was close.

He turned down a narrow alley that came to a dead end in front of a rickety warehouse, the windows boarded up and graffiti scrawled across the walls.

There. She was in there. He was sure of it. He slowed down, keeping to the shadows close to the buildings. He couldn't hear any sounds, any screams, and he hoped that meant he wasn't too late.

He glided quietly forward, heading for one of the boarded-up windows. Reaching up, he pried one of the loose boards off and peered through a gaping hole in the filthy glass.

Anaya lay on a crude wooden platform in the middle of the room. He could see her hands bound behind her and her mouth was covered with some type of tape. The star pendant hung around her neck. Ryland's breath caught in his throat. She seemed okay. Scared, but not yet hurt. He looked around the room, searching for the killer. A movement in the far corner caught his eye and he could see Grunner digging around in a box.

Chapter Six

The room reeked of blood and fear. Anaya found it hard not to move, to pretend to be paralyzed by fear. Grunner had dropped her onto a hard platform in the middle of the room, and then went to rummage around in a box over in the corner. He giggled and mumbled to himself, already anticipating the pain and horror he had planned. She listened to his sick ramblings and was horrified to realize his victims hadn't been dead when he'd mutilated their bodies.

She hung on to the tenuous link to Ryland, but she couldn't tell how close he was. The connection seemed to be getting stronger. What if he arrived too late?

Grunner placed several items on the floor beside the box, grumbling while he searched for an elusive item.

She had to face the fact that Ryland might not be close enough to save her. She searched for ley lines, knowing the chance of tapping into the interplanetary net from an unfamiliar planet was slim -- especially given her heavy clothing and her bound position.

She sensed something below her and redirected her efforts. There! A rich brown line shimmered into view below her, with many lesser lines intersecting it.

The building sat on the nexus of the planet's ley lines. Tentatively, she touched the line. It felt different to the ones she used in space, but similar in some ways. Right now she was desperate enough to try to use it.

She cautiously drew a small amount of the power, careful not to let it flood her. The energy flowed brightly, cleanly, bolstering her spirit with its earthy taste. Her link to Ryland strengthened. She could sense his fear and his determination to reach her in time.

Grunner turned, an evil leer on his face and a long dagger covered with reddish-brown stains gripped in one hand. "Playtime." He advanced toward her slowly, watching the expressions on her face, giving her time to realize what he had planned.

Anaya held tight to her link with Ryland and let the power of the ley line flood into her. She sensed that Ryland was aware of the link.

Grunner stepped closer, holding the blade up so it sparkled in the light, the dark blotches of dried blood a sickening contrast to the glittering metal.

Ryland burst through the door with a loud crash, anguish and determination on his face.

Grunner wheeled to meet the threat, the dagger brandished menacingly in front of him.

"No!" Anaya directed the energy toward the blade, watching the brilliant light dance down the metal conduit and enter Grunner's arm. An eerie light flared, and Grunner let out an unearthly howl. The energy ran through his body, the line absorbing him into itself before it grounded back to the earth through her link with Ryland.

Ryland stared in disbelief as the dagger dropped to the floor, no longer having anything to hold it up. A wisp of black smoke curling lazily up from the floor was all that remained of the man who'd terrorized women across three galaxies. Ryland raised his head and met Anaya's gaze. She could read awe in his eyes. Awe and relief.

Without a prisoner, or at the very least, a body, he wouldn't be able to claim the bounty. But then again, she knew this had never been about the bounty. It was about right and wrong and justice.

Grunner was dead. Justice was served.

"I'm so sorry." Ryland moved to her side,

stepping over the scorched spot on the floor. "I never should have left you alone, even for a second." He pulled the tape off her mouth, wincing at her whimper of pain. He kissed the raw red marks left by the adhesive. "We need to get out of here in case anyone noticed that flash of light. We don't need to be pulled into any kind of government inquiry." He gave her a lopsided grin. "Knowing their history, they'd probably find you're to blame for the demise of one of their upstanding citizens."

Anaya raised her eyebrows. "Because I'm female?"

"Exactly!"

"Then perhaps you could untie my hands so I can get up."

Ryland obliged, grumbling when he noticed a few new sore spots on her wrists. "Do you need a few minutes to rest? I know how drained you get when you manipulate the lines."

She sat up on the hard surface. "This was different." She paused, remembering the way the energy had grounded through the link to Ryland. She recalled stories from her childhood, about the witches of Old Earth and the Druids who partnered with them to control the ley lines.

"I accessed the planet's lines, not the interplanetary ones. It felt softer, smoother." She looked him in the eye. "And you grounded the flow, so there was no backlash. I've never heard of a man being able to ground."

Ryland stared at her. "I could sense what you were doing, which in itself is a little weird, but I didn't do anything."

Anaya frowned. "I saw it. I sent the energy to the metal blade, and I expected it to run through Grunner, throwing him off balance. I was more surprised than you were when it absorbed him into itself. But then, instead of lashing back at me, it ran through you into the ground. That's why I'm not exhausted."

She needed to look into the Druid connection. But not now.

Ryland shrugged. "Who knows? Maybe earth-based lines react differently than interplanetary ones. Whatever the reason, it's over and we need to get out of here."

She hopped down off the platform, wincing when her wrist brushed the hard surface. She picked the pack up off the floor where Ryland had dropped it. "Got to agree with you there. Nice as it is to feel solid ground beneath my feet, this place gives me the creeps. At least ten people saw him drag me through the streets and yet no one tried to stop him." She shook her head. "The sooner we blow that docking ring, the better."

* * *

Anaya watched Ryland stir the little pot hanging suspended over the heating laser. "What is that?" He'd laid her out on the mess hall table, securing her arms and legs to the corners with his favorite toys, the immobilizer cuffs.

He turned to answer, smirking when his gaze strayed to her pussy. "It's chocolate. I read somewhere that ancient earthlings used to use it for an aphrodisiac."

"An aphro what?"

"Aphrodisiac." He lifted the spoon to his lips and tasted. "Just about done. It needs to be at just the right temperature."

She felt like a kid at the first day of school. "Right temperature for what?" She really didn't care. When he'd ordered her to strip, she'd expected him to screw her. Make that wanted him to screw her. A lesson in cooking definitely wasn't on her agenda.

Ryland tasted it again and a slow smile spread across his face. "Perfect!" He poured the hot liquid from the pot into a serving dish and then added a little ladle. "Ready for me?"

She watched him strip off his clothing, dragging out the suspense by folding it carefully and piling it on one of the chairs. "I've been ready for ages. Get on with it already."

"Tsk, tsk." Ryland shook his head. "You need to work on your attitude. You should be grateful I plan to bestow my attention on you."

"Oh, I am. I just wish you'd hurry up."

He picked up the serving dish and sauntered across to look down at her naked body, spread wide for his pleasure. "Very tasty looking." He tweaked one of her nipples, smiling approvingly when it puckered.

"Please." Anaya did her best to look submissive.

"That's better." Dipping the ladle into the mixture, he lifted it over her belly and carefully drizzled the warm chocolate across her breasts, making sure each nipple was thoroughly coated.

She gasped at the incredible sensation. Liquid darts of pleasure ran from the tip of each breast down to pool low in her belly.

Ryland bent over and began to lick the sticky mixture off, sucking each nipple into his mouth in turn and swirling his tongue around to get every drop. "Mmmmm. Tasty." He dipped his finger into the serving dish and held it to her mouth for her to taste.

She licked it clean, sucking it into her mouth suggestively while she swirled her tongue around to make sure she didn't miss any. She couldn't remember chocolate ever tasting this good.

Ryland dipped the ladle back in and dripped chocolate over her belly. He lowered his head to lick it off, and Anaya bucked and whimpered under the double pleasure of the smooth, warm chocolate and his talented tongue. Ryland lifted his head and gave her a mischievous grin. "And now for dessert."

He held her gaze and loaded the ladle up yet again, before holding it suspended over her pussy. She could feel herself cream in anticipation. Ryland used his other hand to part her labia. Slowly, watching her reaction, he trickled the warm, sticky chocolate over her eager entrance.

Anaya closed her eyes and let out a startled breath at the incredible feeling. Desire clawed at her, driving darts of erotic heat through every nerve in her body. "Oh, dear gods, I need to feel you inside me. Please." She opened her eyes to stare imploringly at him. She didn't know how much more of this she could take.

"Not yet." Ryland stroked his hand down his enormous erection, and Anaya found herself picturing it covered in chocolate. A tasty snack.

He released her ankles and lifted her legs, placing them on his shoulders. With a cheerful grin, he swiped his tongue across her sex, getting a mouthful of chocolate and cream.

"Mmmm. Tasty." He lowered his head and started to feast.

Anaya responded with a wild thrashing of her hips, bucking and twisting beneath him while she ground her aching pussy against his tongue, his teeth, his face. He stabbed his tongue deep inside her and she went wild. She wanted her hands free so she could run them across the bulging muscles of his shoulder. Force his head tighter against her sex. Rake her nails down his back.

She could feel his fingers probing the tight bud of her anus, and she remembered the feel of him riding her hard, his thick shaft pistoning in and out of her butt. He nipped her clit with his teeth and threw her into a violent orgasm. She screamed incoherently as wave after wave of pleasure washed over her.

With one last swipe of his tongue, he dropped her legs back onto the table and climbed up to straddle her. He closed a fist around his hard shaft and slowly stroked down the length. "I'm going to fuck you until you scream for mercy." He stroked the length again, and while Anaya watched, fascinated, a single drop of pre-cum glistened on the tip. She licked her lips, and he pressed the plum-shaped head to her sex. Leaning forward, he braced himself on his elbows and entered her slick channel with a single thrust.

"Yes!" Anaya wrapped her legs around his waist and he started to shaft her with long, hard strokes of his massive cock. She matched him thrust for thrust, eyes closed, arms still outspread.

She felt the heat slowly building, rising, driving her up toward the stars. She could still feel the connection to him, the joining that had strengthened on the surface of the planet. Then he let out a hoarse shout and plunged deep one last time, his seed spurting inside her while her channel convulsed, holding him in, clenching tight while she soared up and over the edge and her world shattered into a million vibrant explosions of color.

Ryland reached up to release her arms, dropping a soft kiss on the tip of her nose. "Happy?"

She nodded. "Ryland?"

"Yes?"

"Are there any Druids back in your family tree?"

Ryland laughed. "I've no idea. If there were, it would have been centuries ago. Why do you ask?"

She thought about the way the energy had flowed through him instead of lashing back at her. She thought about the tales of witches and Druids in the ancient oak groves. "No reason. I just wondered." She fingered the star pendant on her neck and snuggled into his warm arms, her head resting in the hollow of his shoulder.

Ryland stroked his fingers through her hair. "I guess I'm going to have to take a trip to Colony Five."

Anaya started, rising up on her elbows to look at him in disbelief. "You're going to turn me in?" She couldn't believe he'd even consider it. "I thought we had a deal. Not to mention the fact that I was beginning to feel like maybe you actually liked me."

Ryland cupped a hand behind her head. "We do have a deal, and I have no intention of turning you over to Colony Five or anyone else. You're mine." He pulled her head down to kiss her very thoroughly. "They put a bounty out on you, and I don't intend for us to spend the rest of our lives avoiding hunters who are trying to capture you. They need to cancel the bounty and they might as well know you won't be returning to them."

Anaya relaxed. "They won't be happy about this. What makes you think they'll go along with it? Those government officials aren't used to people telling them what to do." She paused. "And my handler is going to be extremely pissed off. He gets a lot of perks just for keeping me in line."

Ryland shrugged. "Your ex-handler should be happy I've decided to let him remain alive." He ran a finger across her lips. "As for the official government of Colony Five, let's just say I can be very persuasive. Want to see?" He reclaimed her lips, and Anaya had to agree.

He could indeed be very persuasive.

Wayward
Sci-Fi Action & Intrigue Romance
Anne Kane

Katarina and Abbie are twin Stargazers, and their mother, fearful of the pirates who run rampant in this part of the galaxy, has been hiding their abilities for years. But when Abbie is kidnapped, Kat boldly offers her services to a very sexy pirate captain in return for his help.

Tore is fascinated by the sexy young Stargazer, but how far is she willing to go to save her sister?

Chapter One

Kat perched atop the barstool and took small sips of her cocktail, assessing the other drinkers in the popular portside bar. She needed to find a man. The door made a whooshing sound as it slid open, and she turned her head.

The man strode through the doorway like a conquering Viking, and she studied him with interest. He was well over six feet tall, and his wavy blond hair hung loose to his shoulder blades, held in place by a thick strip of leather around his forehead. His eyes were like chips of ice-blue rock, sharp and hard. He walked with the loose, easy gait of someone who spent more time off planet than on. Thick ropes of muscle covered his arms, with more outlined beneath the tight material of his heavy uni-suit. He slid onto a barstool at the far end of the Last Chance, and the bartender immediately bustled down to take his order. No waiting for someone like him.

Kat motioned to the bartender after he had served the Viking look alike his drink. "Who is he?" She tilted her head toward the newcomer.

A smirk lit his dark features while he gave her a quick once-over. "That's Tore, captain of the *Sun Runner*. Usually stops in here when the ship's in for maintenance. Rumor has it he's a pirate, but I'm not stupid enough to ask him if it's true. He generally doesn't pick up any female companions here, but for a class act like you, he might make an exception. You want an introduction?"

Kat grimaced at his suggestive tone. She did, but not for the reason he had in mind. "No, thank you. I'm perfectly capable of introducing myself."

The bartender shrugged and drifted over to a

group of miners playing cards. Kat waited a few seconds, gathering her courage. This Tore fellow looked like he might be just what she needed. Now all she had to do was convince him to help her. She wasn't sure the credits she'd accumulated would be enough to buy the loyalty of a pirate. She took a deep breath and slid gracefully off her stool.

She almost made it to his side before the huge stranger turned his head. She felt a dart of pure lust lance through her as his gaze swept her from head to toe. Up close, she could see the rows of scars on his arms and face, evenly spaced so you knew they weren't inflicted in a fight or by accident. Those kind of marks bespoke deliberate torture. She shuddered. It was the kind of torture the Intergalactic Council liked to call rehabilitation.

"How much?" His deep voice reverberated through every nerve, causing moisture to gather deep inside her pussy.

She knew exactly what he meant. He thought she was one of the whores who frequented the bar looking to pick up new clients. She should be insulted, but the smoldering passion deep in those gorgeous blue eyes made her consider, just for a second, taking up the ancient profession. A man like this would generate so much power. And so much passion. Unfortunately, she didn't have time right now to slake her thirst for sex.

She let her regret show briefly in the smile she flashed him. "I'm not a whore. I'm looking to hire a ship, one that's fast and able to fight." She paused, realizing she should be careful about how much information she divulged. She knew nothing about him or his connections.

He lifted one eyebrow, a spark of interest lighting his eyes. "Really? And what would you need a ship like that for?"

Kat held out her hand. "My name is Katarina. My friends call me Kat, and I have my reasons. Are you available?"

He stood, towering over her, and Kat found herself tilting her head to keep eye contact. A cynical smile hovered on his lips as he reached out and took her hand, holding it just a fraction of a nanosecond longer than necessary. She wondered if he knew what he did to her pulse rate.

"Name's Tore. Perhaps we should get a private booth if we're going to discuss business." He glanced over at the bartender who nodded toward the back of the bar.

Kat licked her suddenly dry lips, feeling unexpectedly nervous. Perhaps this wasn't such a good idea. "Certainly."

Tore grabbed his drink and led the way, threading through the crowded room with the arrogance of a man who knows people will get out of his way. Kat trailed behind him, admiring the taut slide of well-honed muscles under the tight uni-suit. He didn't bother to look back and see if she was following. It probably never occurred to him that someone might not do exactly what he instructed.

"After you." He stepped aside to let her slide into the booth ahead of him. She put her drink down on the table before she slid onto the slick pseudo-leather seat, trying to look composed.

An old saying popped into her head. *Never let them see you sweat.*

Tore palmed the privacy settings, waiting for the digital readout to glow a reassuring green before he sprawled across the bench opposite her. He took a deep draft from his bottle before placing it on the table.

"So exactly what is it you need?"

Kat looked into those deep blue eyes. They gleamed with calculating intelligence, and she could feel the confidence radiating from him. Although her twin was much better at reading people's auras, Kat's Stargazer talents lent her a certain advantage in negotiations. She'd be able to tell if he was lying and if his intentions toward her were dangerous.

"First I need to know if you are affiliated with the Intergalactic Council." She watched his body language. His answer was crucial to her plans. He tensed for the barest fraction of a second, and her gaze flickered to those scars. She wished she had the nerve to ask him where they'd come from.

"They'd like to catch me. I don't intend to let them." He sat a little straighter. "If you're working for them, this conversation is over."

Kat relaxed and shook her head. "No. They don't even know I exist, and I'd like to keep it that way." She made a split second decision, her gut instinct telling her she could trust this man. "I'm a Stargazer, and I'm sure they'd do whatever it took to get me to work for them." She shuddered in spite of her resolve not to show fear. "I've heard stories."

"And they're mostly true." He gave her a piercing look. "They have spies everywhere, and most Stargazers end up under contract to them, either voluntarily or through other venues. How did they manage to miss you?"

"My mother's been hiding us since we first started to show signs of talent." She took a sip of her drink, remembering all the times they'd picked everything up and moved on a moment's notice. "Our father left before we were born, so it was just the three of us. No one else knew."

Tore held up a hand. "Hold it. Three?"

"Yes, I have a twin sister, Abbie. She's missing."

"And you think the Intergalactic Council kidnapped her?"

Kat set her drink down on the table. "No. She was kidnapped by a pirate, some type of reptilian alien."

"He sent a ransom demand?"

She shook her head. "No. No ransom demand."

"Then how do you know she was kidnapped? Maybe she ran away with a lover."

Kat hoped he had an open mind. People didn't always believe how close she and Abbie were. "We're twin Stargazers. When we want to, we can concentrate and 'see' through the other's eyes. I saw the abduction."

She stopped and took a deep breath, willing the panic away. She needed this man to take her story seriously. Being dismissed as a hysterical female wouldn't help her save Abbie. "She was on her way home from a shopping trip when they lured her into an alley. The alien was big, stocky, with green scales all over him. He didn't knock her out so I was able to see the ship they dragged her aboard, but I haven't been able to get a response from her in over seven cycles. Either she's drugged or they're using an energy shield to block her. Usually I'd be able to make contact with her, but all I'm getting is a vague sense of direction."

"Probably a shield." He tapped his fingers on the table. "From your description, I'm guessing she was taken by one of the Aviroan slaver ships, and they routinely use energy shields to block detection by the authorities. Keeping captives drugged is expensive, not to mention risky. Not all sentients react the same way to chemical input."

For the first time in days, Kat felt a flicker of hope. "Do you know where to find these Aviroans?"

He shook his head. "Not that easy. Their home planet is in the Basal system, but that's not where they'd be heading if they were picking up slaves. Can you describe the ship you saw?"

Kat concentrated, trying to recall every detail that might help locate her sister. "It looked like one of the Council's supply shuttles, only smaller. It had reflective strips across the bow and the wings were sloped backward, as if they planned to cut through a narrow channel."

"Something like this?" He traced invisible lines in the air above the table and all of a sudden, the image of a shuttle appeared, floating in the air.

Kat gulped, looking from the image to Tore and back again. A human couldn't manufacture images out of thin air. "What are you?" she whispered.

His eyes narrowed to cold slashes of blue ice. "I'm human. Just not quite as human as some." A faint aura of red fury tinged the air surrounding him, sending shocked recognition through her. His aura. She didn't have the ability to see auras, but there it was. Tore took a long pull on his drink, and Kat sat quietly, wishing she had the nerve to ask him to explain.

As if reading her thoughts, he relaxed and gave her a wry smile. "A long time ago, the Intergalactic Council thought it would be interesting to genetically alter some of the orphans under their protection. After all, who cared what happened to a bunch of throwaway kids? My body adapted well to their tinkering, so I became one of their special projects." He fingered the bottle idly, and she could feel him forcing his emotions under control. "A cyborg named Tarik rescued me and took me under his wing." He regarded her thoughtfully. "His mate, Krystal, is a Stargazer as well. Seems like there's a lot of you running around loose."

Kat jerked her head up in surprise. "I didn't know there were others. We thought the Council contracted any Stargazer they knew about except those the slavers managed to get hold of and sell in the free space auctions."

"So who else knew about your talents? Besides your mother?"

Kat glared, not liking his sudden change of direction. "She wouldn't have betrayed us."

He shook his head. "That's not what I'm getting at. It sounds like your mother did a fine job of hiding your talents all these years. Has it occurred to you that maybe your twin wasn't kidnapped for her Stargazer abilities?"

Kat frowned. "No. I just assumed..."

"Well, don't, it's dangerous. Assumptions have caused more grief in the universe than religion." He made a point of sweeping her body with his gaze. "Sometimes slavers are interested in other things."

Kat felt the blood draining from her face. The thought of gentle Abbie being sold as a sex toy terrified her. Her sister wasn't the type to cope under those circumstances. Kat wasn't even sure she'd survive.

"If you're identical twins, I'm thinking it's quite likely. At first glance I mistook you for a pleasure worker."

"But Abbie isn't like me." Kat felt her cheeks heat for the first time in ages. "She's the quiet one. She even refused to take a lover to increase her powers. She said she wanted to wait until she fell in love before she would consent to sex. She wanted it to be special."

Tore jerked upright and stared at her in horror. "You can't mean she's a virgin?"

Kat nodded slowly. The look on his face sent a sick knot roiling through her stomach.

Tore got to his feet. "We need to find her, and fast. I'll call the maintenance techs and get them to push *Sun Runner* to the top of the list. Do whatever you have to, and meet me at the Docking Ring in an hour."

"Wait." Kat grabbed his arm, feeling her world spinning out of control. When had he offered to help her? And when had she agreed? "We haven't discussed fees yet. What if I can't afford your services?"

Tore looked down at her with something akin to pity in his eyes. "Mature female virgins are very rare. There are special auctions for them, and you don't want your sister to be in one. We'll come to some type of arrangement for payment, but right now you need to get your little butt in gear and get ready to depart." He ran a finger down her cheek. "One hour. Don't be late."

* * *

Kat hesitated, her finger hovering over the activation button on the voice transmitter. Her mother was suffering enough with Abbie missing. Her imagination was probably working overtime as it was. She hit the transmit button. She knew it was cowardly, but her mother would be at work right now, so Kat wouldn't have to answer any questions. She crossed her fingers.

"Hi, Mom. I picked up a short contract out of the space dock, so I'll be gone for the next two cycles. I'll keep my eyes and ears open for any news on Abigail. Don't worry, from what I'm hearing the Intergalactic Council treats their Stargazers well once they've signed on, and I'm sure Abbie wouldn't do anything to annoy them. You know what a gentle soul she is. Not like me at all. I'll let you know if I hear anything. Don't worry, it'll all work out for the best. Got to run, the ship's waiting."

She signed off, feeling slightly guilty about misleading her mother. Why was it that whenever she decided to do the right thing, it started out with her feeling guilty?

Grabbing her rucksack, she wondered what one packed for a spontaneous space voyage with a genetically altered pirate that she'd met a scant few hours before. She could feel a ghost of a smile curving the corner of her mouth. Given the circumstances, packing was the least of her worries. The ship should be able to synthesize anything she forgot, and if she was working she'd be naked, so clothing wasn't terribly important. Opening the closet, she started stuffing in items haphazardly. One hour didn't give her much time to pack.

She wondered why Tore had been so willing to help. At first glance, he didn't look like a man given to charitable gestures. On impulse, she set her pack aside and went to the vid interface. Palming the access panel, she called up the search engine.

Search system activated. State the parameters. The mechanical voice sounded bored.

"Tore. Pirate. Genetically altered humanoid." She wondered if she'd get any hits with such sketchy information. She didn't even know his family name, but then again she hadn't supplied hers, either. She kept packing, making sure she got the basics stuffed into her pack.

Information located. Awaiting instruction.

"Proceed. Verbal download." Kat stood and

walked over to the vid screen, chewing nervously on her lower lip. A picture of a younger Tore, sans scars, flashed up on the screen.

Tore. Intergalactic ID number 9653247. Level ten security lockdown. Please contact district militia for further information or to report sighting.

Kat stared at the screen. Level ten? Serial killers and mutant aliens who attacked in droves only got a level eight. What the hell had she gotten herself into?

* * *

Tore finished checking over the maintenance specs and closed the vid display. The techs had worked their magic and the *Sun Runner* was ready and raring to go. He glanced down at the time display. Kat should be along any minute now, and he'd have to go meet her at the Docking Ring bay. Security wouldn't let her through without a pass and he hadn't had time to get her one.

He shook his head, striding out the door and palming the locks on his way out. The chances of them finding her sister before anyone hurt her were slim. The universe might look neat on those intergalactic star charts, but in reality things were messy, and people got hurt. Usually the nice ones got hurt the worst.

He pondered what he knew of Stargazers. He'd had a Stargazer platform installed when Tarik and Krystal had borrowed the *Sun Runner*. Tore worked alone whenever possible and had never needed it. He'd actually been using it as a handy rack to toss various items onto when he got too lazy to put them away.

He wasn't sure why he'd agreed to help the young Stargazer. Perhaps it was the slightly panicked look in those witch-green eyes of hers, or the concern she showed for her missing sister. Or perhaps it was because the mere sight of her had his cock swelling harder than a moon rock from his home planet, and he knew what the Stargazers did to increase their power. He looked forward to making sure Kat had all the power she could possibly use.

"Tore! This nice man seems to think I'm some sort of threat to intergalactic security." Kat waved at him from behind the security barrier, a determined smile plastered on her face. His enhanced sense of smell detected the fear behind it.

"I'm sure he's just doing his job." Tore gave the security man a friendly smile before he reached for Kat's wrist and drew her through the barrier. "This all you brought?" He scooped up her pack and led the way to the *Sun Runner*.

"Yeah. I travel light. You do have synthesizers on your ship, don't you?"

She seemed a little more restrained than she had in the bar, but then he'd dropped quite a bombshell on her. He'd heard that twins were closer emotionally than normal siblings, and he'd wager Stargazer twins would be even more so. He felt a twinge of loneliness. He had no idea who his parents had been, let alone if he'd ever had any siblings.

He stepped up to let the *Sun Runner*'s security scanner read his retinal pattern before it opened the hatches. "Welcome aboard." He stood aside to let Kat enter.

"Thank you." She moved through the airlock and stopped to look around. "This is nice. Compact and tidy."

Tore came in behind her and the hatch cycled closed with an audible click. "The sleeping quarters are through here." He walked into the narrow corridor and led the way. "This will be yours." He opened the door and set her pack down on the large sleeping platform. "There's a synthesizer in the mess hall, and the head is at the end of the corridor." Kat gave him a wary look again, and he stopped, exasperated. "What?"

"What do you mean, what?" She looked like a bird ready to take flight at the slightest provocation.

"Why are you looking at me like I just sprouted a second head, or a nice set of wings?"

She opened her mouth, and then snapped it shut with a tired sigh. "I tried to call up your data on the comp, and it said there was a level ten security lockdown on it." She gave him a strained smile. "That either means they want you really badly, and I might have just put myself in the hands of a psycho, or you work for them, in which case you're probably going to get a nice bonus when you hand me over. I haven't decided which alternative I prefer."

She looked so cute, standing there trying not to look terrified. "There is a third option, you know."

"Really? What would that be?" She tilted her head inquiringly.

"I'm one of their experiments that got away, and they want me back in their lab so they can figure out how to program me to follow orders."

She snorted inelegantly. "You want me to believe you're a victim?"

He shrugged. "I really don't care what you believe. If you want a chance to save your sister, you're going to have to work with me. Unless you know of some other pirate with a spaceship who'd be interested in a quick voyage to the outer fringes of the galaxy?"

He stood stock still as she walked up to him, very aware of his body's reaction to her proximity. She lifted her hand and traced the line of his lips with the tip of one finger. "There's one way for me to be sure I can trust you."

The feather-light caress of her fingers on his lips sent tendrils of flame running through his entire body. He didn't want to move for fear it would break the spell and she would stop touching him. "How's that?"

"You can fuck me. It will give me a closer link to you and I'll be able to read you. I can't read minds, but I'll be able to sense simple things. It's hard to explain."

Tore reached out and ran his fingers through the long silky locks of her hair. "Or I can hack into the Council's system and let you read the file they have on me."

Kat looked up at him, and he could see she'd already relaxed. He wondered just how much of his intentions she could read just by touching him, because right now, his intentions involved a lot of bare skin sliding against his.

Mischief danced in the depths of her witchy green eyes. "I like my idea better."

Tore lowered his head to taste her lips, his cock straining against the tight fabric that imprisoned it. "So do I."

Chapter Two

He tasted her lips, teasing them apart to slip his tongue in and explore. Kat responded with an unbridled lust, sending heat clawing through him. Her sister might be a virgin, but Kat knew exactly where to touch him, how to use a feather-light brush of her fingers to send heat racing through his body. He angled her head to give himself better access, sliding his tongue across the roof of her mouth.

Kat moaned, using her own tongue to follow, running it down the side of his, engaging in an erotic duel as he thrust deeper into the moist sweetness, tasting the honeyed depth. She pressed herself against him, her well-toned curves brushing against him and causing his heartbeat to race.

He pulled back a bit, unsettled by her unfettered passion. He was used to women who calculated how much to give, what to do to elicit the response they wanted from his body. Kat just threw herself at him, all soft curves and feminine need.

"We need to pace ourselves here, Kat. You'll have me going up in flames." He whispered the words in her ear while her cloth-covered breasts pressed against his chest, tempting him to explore their lush curves.

"Can't take the heat?" A thread of wicked amusement wound through her voice, and he chuckled. She liked to control the situation. He could see they'd have to work out who was boss. His gaze drifted to the platform, and a wicked idea slid into his mind. Stargazer platforms were designed to hold the witches strapped spread-eagled while they worked.

He wrapped one arm around her waist, and the other arm beneath her legs, scooping her up into his arms while he nibbled his way from her ear down to the tender hollow of her throat. Despite her well-toned muscles, she felt light as air to his enhanced strength and he cradled her against his chest, enjoying the warmth of her body pressed against him. He nuzzled the loose neck of her collar aside and couldn't resist running his tongue across the top of one firm breast.

Stepping onto the platform, he put her down, holding her against him so that her ripe young body slid down his, the friction driving his lust higher. He fastened his mouth on hers, distracting her while he lifted her hand and tied it to the loop above her head, repeating the process with the other arm. Crouching down in front of her, he ran his hands down her sides, holding her hips firmly in place while he secured the belt at her waist.

"What are you doing?" Kat frowned as she stared down at him out of passion-clouded eyes. "I'm not going to work yet."

"No." He nudged her legs apart to slide her feet into the straps especially formed to hold them. "I am. And when I'm done, you are going to be one very satisfied witch."

A sexy smile curled her mouth. "I didn't know you were into bondage. I wonder what else is in that locked-down file of yours."

She certainly didn't take long to catch on. He didn't blame her for checking up on him; she'd be insane to trust him. Insane or desperate.

He stood, testing the straps to make sure she couldn't move before he cupped the back of her head and took her lips in a quick hard kiss. Letting her go, he stepped back and grinned. "Now we're going to play my way." He stripped the top of his uni-suit off. Kat stuck her tongue out at him in a childish gesture of defiance, and he laughed. "You've got quite the attitude for a tiny little thing that's all tied up."

"Size isn't everything." She screwed up her nose in a haughty gesture.

He grasped the waist of the suit and skimmed it down over his hips, letting his engorged shaft spring free. He watched her eyes widen, and a slow flicker of heat started deep in his groin.

"Then again." She licked her lips. "That's quite impressive."

Tore kicked the suit off to the side and came to stand in front of her. Circling his shaft with one fist, he casually stroked down the length. "Haven't had any complaints."

She shifted in her bonds, flexing her fingers. "I'd hate to be the first."

"Oh, I'm not worried." He stepped forward and undid the leather strap holding the bodice of her suit together. "Let's see what you have hidden under that skimpy little outfit of yours." The edges of the bodice parted, and a dusky pink nipple peeked out. He unsnapped the shoulder straps and the lacy material fell to the deck. Her breasts were high and firm, just the right size to fit in his hands. He spread his palms over the mounds, covering the silky flesh. "You must work out."

She sucked in a lungful of air when he stroked his thumbs over the nipples, bringing them to taut attention. "In a zero-G chamber. Good workout without the impact stress. The discipline helps me to focus."

He squeezed gently, watching the mounds come together. "There's a chamber on the lower deck. We'll work out together."

"You like to give orders. Don't you ever ask?"

"Why? You know you want to."

"But I like to be asked."

He smirked, and lowered his head to score his teeth across one nipple, pleased by the whimper of pleasure that slipped out of her lips. He grasped the waistband of the sassy scrap of material that passed for a skirt, and twisted it, ripping it off her hips. A red lace thong rode jauntily on her hips, the lacy wisp barely covering her pussy. He could smell her excitement.

"Krystal told me Stargazers fuck to increase their power." He slanted his head to watch her reaction. For some reason, the thought of her looking at some other man with her eyes clouded with passion made him want to hit something. Hard.

"Who's Krystal?" He wasn't prepared for the anger that tinged her voice. Jealousy?

"She's Tarik's mate. You didn't answer the question."

"Sex between two consenting sentients creates a great deal of positive energy. We can harness the energy for our own use." She sounded as if she were reciting a star route.

Tore raised one brow. She still hadn't answered the question, but her wording intrigued him. "Two consenting sentients? As opposed to what?"

She shivered as he licked across the tip of her breast. "There are stories that tell of a time, way back in the beginning of our history, when the Intergalactic Council forced Stargazers to mate against their wishes. It was basically rape, and the negative energy backlashed through the Stargazers and nearly leveled the compound they were being held in, as well as most of the rest of the star base."

"Reiger One." Tore licked a wet path from one breast to the other. He'd heard the story, but he'd thought it was just another legend.

She nodded. "Hence the consenting. And of course, two space amoebas just don't generate anything except a need to detour the ship around the gooey mess."

Tore grinned reluctantly and scored his teeth across her second breast. "You're supposed to be mindless with lust by now. My ego is taking a bruising here."

She grinned back, and his heart did a little flip-flop at the sparkle in her eyes. "Not quite mindless, but you've got a hell of a way with that mouth of yours. If my pussy gets any wetter, there'll be cream dripping down my thighs. Can I quit with the witty repartee now?"

Tore pretended to growl, and slapped her lightly across the side of her ass. He'd never had a woman tease him like this during foreplay. He could get used to it. His cock was rock hard, and he had to resist the urge to rip the sexy little scrap of lace off her sex and just plunge himself deep inside her. He gritted his teeth, imagining the feel of her cream-slicked channel gripping around his cock while he thrust into her.

He sucked the tip of one breast into his mouth and started to feast. Licking. Sucking. Nibbling. He switched his attention to the other breast and continued, listening to her low moans and whimpers. He explored her captive body with his hands, the smooth silky texture of her skin, the tight muscles of her tummy, and the hollow of her hips.

Kat whimpered, thrashing against the restraints holding her in place. Tore loved the deep-throated sounds she made every time he scored his teeth across the tip of one of her nipples. He slid the palm of his hand under the lace of her thong and cupped her bare mound, pausing as she squirmed wildly, incoherent words slipping out of her mouth. She was so responsive, so sensitive to each touch, each caress.

He flicked the catch on the restraint at her waist and the straps fell away, leaving her free to move her hips, to arch and buck against him. A quick flip of his wrist snapped the lacy strap of her thong, and he tossed it aside.

He slipped a finger into her slick channel, and she screamed out his name, her voice hoarse with need. The inner walls of her pussy clamped down hard around the finger and he withdrew it slowly, and then thrust two fingers back in, lust building deep inside him when she matched his rhythm, riding his hand with every thrust, circling her hips to force his thumb over her engorged clit. He pulled his fingers out, and she let out a low keening sound. "Don't stop." Her voice, needy and desperate, vibrated through him.

He sank to his knees and wrapped his arms around her hips. Pulling her tight against his face, he thrust his tongue between the soft folds of her labia and stabbed deep, feasting on the sweet cream dripping from her pussy. He could feel an intense shudder go through her, and he gripped her firmly, shocked at how fiercely exultant he felt. Just to feel the pleasure rippling through her, to feel her body responding with such enthusiasm to his attention, was almost enough for him.

Almost. His cock felt ready to burst, rock hard. He needed to bury it deep inside her. He wanted to take her over and over, and feel the tight clasp of her channel while it milked the seed from his shaft. He wanted to feel her body convulse around him as orgasms swept over both of them. He swiped his tongue across her entrance one last time, curling it around the hard bud of her clit, and then rose to his feet.

Kat's eyes were open. She stared at him, dazed with passion, a soft moan of protest escaping her lips. He ran his hands down her sides, stepping in toward her so their bodies pressed against each other, skin to skin. He took her lips in a fierce kiss that betrayed his raging need. The head of his shaft prodded the moist entrance to her sex while he ravaged her mouth with barely controlled lust. His tongue stabbed deep, and he knew she could taste herself on his lips.

He grasped her hips and slowly began to sink his aching cock into the damp heat of her sex, inch by slow wonderful inch, feeling her channel stretching to accommodate him, welcoming him.

Kat moved against him, whimpering incoherently when he withdrew his cock and then slammed it back into her. Heat swept through him, a fiery raging need he could no longer control. He shafted her with the hard length of his cock. Harder. Deeper. Feeling her hips moving, meeting him thrust for thrust. Feeling her hot breath fanning across his chest while she gasped out his name when she came.

Her tight inner muscles clamped down hard, pulsing over and around his cock, holding him deep, sending fiery darts of carnal pleasure ripping through his body. His balls drew up tight and he gave a hoarse cry as his seed spurted into her.

He reached up and released her hands, and Kat wrapped her arms around his neck, twining her fingers in his hair as shudder after shudder wracked her body. He could feel the waves of aftershocks racing through her as her tight channel continued to pulse around his cock. She nuzzled her face into the crook of his shoulder, and he marveled at how well she fit against his body.

He buried his face in the silken mass of her hair and inhaled, feeling oddly protective of the diminutive Stargazer. Kat threw herself into lovemaking with a joyous abandon that left him breathless. The universe could be a cruel place, and he didn't want her to find that out firsthand.

* * *

"Our first priority is to find out exactly where your sister is." Tore linked his fingers behind his head and leaned back in his seat. "Tell me exactly what you saw in your vision of the kidnapping."

"It wasn't a vision." People often had a hard time understanding her connection to Abbie. "I saw what she saw."

"Which was what? Give me as much description as you can."

Kat narrowed her eyes and called up her memories of that awful day. She could still feel the terror running through Abbie when she'd realized what was happening. "There were three of them. They were big, about as tall as you, and stocky. One of them lured her into an alley by making noises like an injured animal. Abbie always had a soft spot for anything needing help, so she didn't even stop to think that it might be a trap. When she went behind a metal storage bin, she didn't find the injured animal she had expected. One of the aliens grabbed her and held her while the other two wrapped some sort of restraints around her arms and legs."

Kat paced restlessly as she spoke, clenching and unclenching her hands. "They had a hover car, and they shoved her in it, keeping her between them so no one could see she needed help. With the restraints immobilizing her, she couldn't call out for help." She bit down on her bottom lip and looked up, blinking rapidly to stop herself from breaking out in tears. She didn't want him to think she was weak.

Thankfully, Tore wasn't looking in her direction. His fingers tapped out an agitated rhythm on the console as he stared out the window, his brow furrowed in thought. He glanced up when she stopped talking. "The reptiles. Can you describe them? Color? Eyes? Anything that might help us to narrow their destination?"

Kat took a deep breath to steady herself. "I thought you said you knew what they were. Aviroans?"

"That's like saying I'm humanoid. There are different types of Aviroans, and each race has its preferred planets and destinations. We need to narrow it down so we don't waste time looking in the wrong places."

She frowned. "They had shiny green scales, and they were tall, and really wide. The one who grabbed her appeared to be the leader. His eyes were black with yellow diamond-shaped pupils. They wore some sort of light chainmail type of suit." She shuddered. "They all hissed when they talked, like snakes in those old vid shows."

"Their clothes? What color were they?"

Kat paused, trying to picture the three. "Gray. Dull gray with some kind of black edging. Why?"

Tore sat up straight and ran his hands over the console. Images flashed up in the air, cycling so fast that everything was a blur of color. "There!" An image of a reptile materialized, so lifelike that Kat took an involuntary step backward. "Does this look like it?"

Kat's stomach tied itself into a queasy knot. "Yeah. That's him." It was powerful and ugly, but those flat black eyes, with their total lack of emotion, were what scared her. "What the hell is it?"

"Like I said in the bar, it's definitely an Aviroan. They're sentient reptiles. These are the Omari Aviroans, a particularly nasty bunch. Officially, they have no ties to the Council. Unofficially, they are the Intergalactic Council's pet slavers. People that annoy the Council just disappear. The Council uses them when they don't want to get their hands dirty. No one's sure where their home planet is -- but it's somewhere outside Council space."

He snagged her wrist and pulled her down to his lap. "They make a lot of money off the slave trade. They'll land on a planet, kidnap some of the locals and disappear before anyone realizes what's happened. The upside to this is that they probably don't know your sister is a Stargazer. The Council would never condone grabbing a Stargazer like that; they would have sent the militia. She must have been targeted for her looks."

He paused, and Kat's heart sank. Pity shone in his eyes. "But what?"

Tore ran a finger down her cheek, tracing the bone structure. "They'll likely be headed for one of the auction houses outside Council territory. And if they find out she's a virgin, it will be that much harder for us to get near her."

Kat cringed. She really didn't want to ask this. "How would they find out? Reptiles and humans aren't compatible, and I can't see it being the type of information that Abbie would volunteer."

"Reptiles and humans aren't genetically compatible." He wrapped his arm around her and held her close. "But that doesn't mean they won't rape her. Just that she won't conceive if they do."

She lifted her head to stare at him in horror. This just kept getting better and better. She sucked in a deep breath and tried not to give in to panic again. "So, at least, if they find out, it might buy her some time. If they rape a virgin, her value on the auction block drops."

He nodded, and she could see a glimmer of respect in his eyes. "We'd better get cracking. Do you have any feel for where she is?"

Kat closed her eyes. As a twin, she could often pinpoint Abbie's whereabouts. And as a Stargazer, she should be able to locate her by her energy signal. The fact that she hadn't felt any hint of Abbie's presence in over a full cycle had to mean they were blocking her. Kat refused to consider any other explanation.

They would find her. Before anyone hurt her.

Chapter Three

Kat looked up as Tore strode into the chamber. Although she was starting to get used to them, the multitude of scars visible on his arms and face caused her to wince. She hadn't asked him exactly how he got them. She wasn't sure she wanted to know.

"We're at the edge of the space controlled by the Intergalactic Council. Are you ready?" He held out his hand.

She could feel him, a light touch in the back of her mind. She could feel his anxiety, his worry about her sister. He thought the genetic experiments had made him something other than human. He was wrong. She nodded, rising gracefully from her lotus position. She'd been meditating, getting herself centered before she attempted to locate her sister. "Yes. I can feel Abbie's presence, but only as a general direction. Normally I'd be able to share her consciousness, feel what she was feeling, and see what she saw." She refused to let that distract her.

Tore led the way to the bridge in silence, and Kat appreciated his thoughtfulness. She concentrated on her breathing. Slow, deep breaths to help keep her calm and centered.

She stepped up onto the platform, feeling a slight smile curve the corner of her mouth at the memory of the passionate union they'd shared here. The energy she'd gained from that torrid session surpassed anything she'd ever managed while coupling with casual partners in the past.

She removed her clothing, one piece at a time, folding it carefully and laying it aside. She slid her feet into the straps on the bottom of the platform, pulling them tight. The padded belt at her waist was next, and she made sure to fasten it firmly around her. She needed to be able to count on it to hold her up if exhaustion overtook her, so that the energy would continue to flow unimpeded in the correct direction. Satisfied that the belt would hold, she reached up and threaded her arms through the loops over her head, pulling them snug. They were precisely spaced, keeping her arms outstretched to capture and control the energy of the lines.

She glanced over to where Tore watched, his chair swiveled to face her. Warmth and worry vied for position in his eyes, and she could feel his concern. She nodded to him, secure in the knowledge that no harm would come to her while he watched. She closed her eyes, and let her consciousness expand.

The ley lines shimmered into view behind her closed lids, flooding her with their warmth, tempting her with their vibrant energy. The colors always astounded her. Here at the outer reaches of the system, they were brighter, greens, reds, and vivid golds vying for her attention. She reached out to each in turn, searching for the one that felt right, the one that would lead her to her sister. She couldn't explain how, but each line filled her with energy, with knowledge of its origin, its planet and the systems it traveled through to get here.

She let the brilliant green flow through her. It told of an ice planet with strange alien beings, sentient, but not evolved. It enticed her. *Come. See my world. Meet my peoples.* She discarded it quickly, before the invitation became a trap she couldn't avoid. There was danger in the seductive call of the ley lines. They could absorb her essence; tempt her to merge completely with their joyous energy.

She sent a tendril of thought out, seeking the

comforting aura of Tore's solid presence, reassuring herself that he was there. Stargazers needed an anchor, someone to hold them firmly in this world so that they didn't give in to temptation and let the ley lines devour them. She'd always used Abbie to anchor her in this reality, and the loss of her sister's calming presence left an empty spot in her heart. She stroked an imaginary finger down Tore's scarred cheek before she turned her attention back to the glittering maze of the lines.

She touched each lightly. Searching. Discarding. Looking for the one that would lead her to Abbie. Time slowed to a crawl as she worked her way through the tangled web. She'd never felt so many strong lines, pulling at her, tempting her. The lines connecting the planets within the Intergalactic Council were weaker, their energy siphoned off by the many Stargazers who worked them.

There! She felt Abbie's faint presence in the shimmering gold of the line. It would lead her straight to her sister. She opened herself up, gathering the sparkling energy into her, capturing it with her outstretched arms and directing it to the engines idling below deck. She could feel the moment the engines powered up, roaring to life. The *Sun Runner* started to move, following the line across the vast emptiness of space. To Abbie.

Kat reveled in the power of the line as it flowed through her. Once she let her shields down, let the glorious power flow into and through her, the temptation to merge completely with the line, to let it absorb her very soul, became almost impossible to resist. If Abbie were lost to her, she wasn't sure she'd even try to resist the temptation. Her twin was like the other half of her soul, the good half, the one who didn't take chances or flaunt her differences with scanty outfits and multicolored streaks in her hair.

Other Stargazers used their mates to anchor them to this world. She'd never felt the need for one. There were more than enough unattached males available if she felt the urge for sex. She reached for Tore, felt his concern. He felt her sorrow. And he wouldn't let her go.

She relaxed, and concentrated on the ley line. The energy out here had a different flavor. It tasted cleaner, brighter, spinning off in unknown directions. Time ceased to exist. The engines ate up the energy as fast as she channeled it, and the *Sun Runner* continued to travel smoothly through the void of space. Eventually, their destination came closer and she could sense many different sentients crowded together on a planet. The kaleidoscope of emotions swamped her senses. Reluctantly, she let some of the energy bleed off, slowing the ship. Even with Tore to anchor her, she felt a wrenching loss and she was grateful for his calming touch.

She sent out tendrils of energy, searching for Abbie amongst the many life forms on the surface. Although she could sense her sister's presence, she still couldn't contact her directly. She could feel her own power waning, drained by the long journey. She let herself slip out of the trance, her tired body sagging against her restraints. In a moment, Tore was at her side.

"Engage autopilot. Stationary high orbit." He bit the words out between his teeth as he reached up to release her hands. The belt took longer to undo, her body weight holding it taut. When he finally managed to free her, he scooped her up, cradling her against his chest while he strode off the bridge. His cabin was closest, and tired as she was, she marveled at how quickly he managed to cover the distance, carrying her extra weight. She might not be as tall as him, but she wasn't frail by a long shot. Many long practice sessions in zero-G had layered sleek muscle over her bones.

She was tired beyond anything she could remember, but she opened her eyes. Tore stared down at her, worry and something else flashing in those gorgeous blue eyes of his.

"Don't you ever," he ground out between clenched teeth, "ever do that again. I thought you weren't coming back. The damn lines had some kind of hold over you."

She smiled weakly. He cared, and she could feel his fear. Fear that she'd lose the battle and let the lines absorb her into their wonderful energy. He didn't understand, but he'd felt her slipping away.

"I'm okay. Just depleted." Her gaze dropped to his groin. There was only one way to replenish her energy quickly, but she didn't think she had enough energy for sex just yet.

* * *

Tore let himself relax, just a bit. When she'd sagged against her bonds, he'd wanted to rip her from the damn platform. Nothing was worth losing her for, not even the twin sister she was determined to rescue. He didn't understand it, but he'd been able to feel her energy dwindling, and that scared the hell out of him. When had he become so attached to the green-eyed witch?

There was no future for the two of them. Stargazers were highly valued and could have their pick of any male in the galaxy. Thanks to the Intergalactic Council and their amoral research department, he wasn't entirely human anymore. She deserved a real man, one who would cherish her and give her everything she wanted.

The sleeping platform sagged under their combined weight, and he dipped his head to place a chaste kiss on her lips before he drew the blanket back and laid her down. His protective instincts flared into full gear at the sight of her limbs falling limp, her gaze sliding over him in one last wistful caress before she succumbed to the sleep she so desperately needed.

He pulled the cover up to her chin and rose to his feet, pacing across to the doorway. Even at rest, her body called to his in a way he'd never experienced before.

He'd hacked into the comp system at the Intergalactic Council's research facility after his escape. He'd been almost feral then, on the verge of maturity and unable to control his impulses. He couldn't recall interacting with other children much, and had virtually spent his childhood in isolation while the scientists studied his reaction to their computer manipulations. Much of what he learned meant nothing to him -- formulas and notations so complex that he sometimes wondered if they'd made them up to confuse anyone who managed to infiltrate the mainframe.

He knew a cargo ship had found him huddled beside the dead crew of an ore freighter. They'd estimated his age as two or perhaps three galactic standards. From samples of his DNA, they'd assumed his rootstock came from the Vikings of Old Earth. After the Troubles, tribes of Norse had taken to the stars, looking to recreate their origins. Most of them had disappeared into the vastness of space. As an orphan, he was officially taken in by the Intergalactic Council and assigned to a research station specializing in genetic manipulation. The staff called him Tore, a joking reference to a warrior from ancient Norse mythology.

Most of the records from that point forward had been encrypted. He knew they'd experimented on his basic cell structure, splicing in strands of animal and alien DNA. He remembered times when he'd been so sick that he'd been unable to rise from his sleeping pallet. Other times, his emotions raged out of control, and the scientists watched with detached clinical interest while he raged in the plas-steel holding cell and tried to claw his way out to them with his bare hands.

He'd eventually learned to control the beast raging within him, to keep it in check and pretend to go along with the scientist's games. He hated the head of the facility, a human female named Smith, more than the rest.

She often came to observe him, never saying a word, her eyes flat and emotionless while her underlings poked and prodded him. She dictated notes to her record pad, her voice clinical and detached, describing the torture of the day and how his frail child's body reacted. He'd vowed that one day they'd meet without the protective plas-steel between them, and he'd make her pay for each and every indignity inflicted at her cruel command. His only regret when Tarik rescued him was that she'd been off planet and hadn't died in the fiery explosion that ensured no other child would have to endure the same living hell.

He stepped onto the bridge, sliding into the pilot's chair. It sensed his presence, folding itself around his bulk. Kat had brought them to one of the outer planets in the Triangulum system. The autopilot had parked the *Sun Runner* in high orbit, out of sensor range of the port below. He moved his hands with practiced skill across the control panel, and a schematic of the port facilities shimmered into view above the console. He studied it carefully.

The Docking Ring extended in an arc to the left, and all of the amenities were listed. Besides the usual places for food, lodging, and recreation, there were three separate auction halls. The holding area for slaves awaiting the block was huge, hinting at a lively trade. They'd have to hope they found Abbie quickly, before someone purchased her and whisked off planet. Then again, maybe it would be easier to see her in less crowded conditions.

No! We get her now.

Tore's head jerked up. What the hell?

Kat had said having sex would give her a connection to him, allowing her to read his intentions, but she hadn't mentioned anything about being able to communicate telepathically. He concentrated, trying to feel her presence. *Kat?*

It's not me! I'm not telepathic. You're invading my mind. And this is giving me a headache.

He felt a reluctant smile play around his mouth. His little Stargazer sounded tired and grouchy. Tore stood and let the chart fade. He didn't recall Tarik mentioning telepathy when he talked about Krystal and the other Stargazers, but then again, this felt intimate, maybe not something they'd want to share. Tore had never been able to communicate telepathically, so it must be Kat's talent. If she'd been hiding all these years, she wouldn't have had much chance to explore her abilities.

He checked to make sure the *Sun Runner*'s orbit was stable before he exited the bridge and headed back to his stateroom. Kat wasn't the only one who needed some rest before they mounted a rescue.

He felt a mischievous grin curve the corner of his

mouth. He wasn't averse to sharing his bed.

* * *

Kat darted her tongue out to wet her lips as she watched Tore's firm butt disappear through the hatch. The black ship-suit he'd donned looked like it was painted on his muscular frame and did nothing to hide his many masculine attributes. If anything, it accentuated the breadth of those massive shoulders and the bulky muscles that roped his upper torso. She felt a tiny shiver of want slide through her. That quickie when she'd awakened to find him sharing her bed had been like an appetizer, priming her for the main course.

Then, instead of the prolonged romp she'd expected, he'd announced they needed to explore each other's fighting skills. Somehow, until he'd produced the ship-suits and shimmied into his with absolutely no sexual overtones, she'd assumed he'd been kidding. There were a whole lot of things she'd like to explore with this mountain of a man, and fighting wasn't one of them. He turned and looked at her through the open hatchway, one brow lifted in challenge.

Taking a deep breath, she stepped through the circular opening and into the zero gravity tube. The floor fell away beneath her feet and she closed her eyes, taking a few seconds to center herself and allow her body to adjust to the feeling of weightlessness.

The tube was smaller than the one she normally worked out in. Not surprising considering this one needed to fit on a spaceship. She could sense Tore hovering above her near the top of the tube. When she opened her eyes, he pushed off and drifted toward her. He managed to look mouthwateringly tempting, even in zero-G. She kicked a foot out, angling her body in his direction.

"How about some light sparring first to warm up?" And to give her a feel for his style, although she didn't mention that. She'd learned early on that what she lacked in sheer bulk and muscle, she needed to make up in strategy. Fight smart, not hard.

He shrugged in agreement, and brought his hands up in a classic defense mode. "Sounds good to me." He pushed off the side of the tube with one arm, drifting to her right. "Have you tried to contact your sister since you woke up?"

She let a smile slip onto her face. Distraction. Always a good tactic. Usually she was the one initiating it. "Yes, but no luck. She must be behind some kind of force shield. Even if she's out cold, I should be able to read her with us this close." She pushed off with her foot, sliding away.

He kicked off, gliding toward her. "You may have better luck once we're on the surface."

She kicked her feet to slip farther away. "When are we going down?"

"As soon as we get clearance. I'm well known in this sector, so it's only a formality." He gave her a wry smile. "Paperwork. Ever the downfall of civilized men."

She darted forward, tapping the side of his face with one hand before she drifted back out of range. "You know the slavers?" She'd been under the impression he'd disapproved of the slave trade.

"No. This is a way station for anyone not wanting to attract the attention of the Council. The Council knows they're outnumbered in this sector, and most of these beings will attack first and ask questions later." The lazy grin on his face warned her he wasn't about to let her get away with that tap on his cheek. "I use it as a place to rest and refuel when I'm too far to make it to my home base."

Where was his home? Kat had a feeling he wouldn't answer that question. She kept her guard up.

Tore feinted right, and when she flinched, he reached out and tapped the side of her butt with his left foot. "One for me."

"That makes us even, then." She toed the wall and angled her way below him. Sparring in zero-G negated the advantage of his larger frame. A mischievous impulse caused her to twist in mid-flight and shoot her right leg out to trace the hard edge of his shaft that was outlined beneath the tight material of his suit. A swift intake of breath let her know he'd felt it. She grinned from her position below him. "Two for me."

Molten heat lit his eyes, reminding her of the big cats on her home planet. He bared his teeth in a wicked smile that promised retribution. In a blur of movement so fast she had trouble following it, he slid closer and trailed his fingers over the tip of one breast.

Kat gasped as delicious darts of pleasure curled through her. The big pirate grinned at her and she stuck her tongue out at him. He laughed, a deep-throated sound that started all the way down in his belly and bubbled up to spill out of those full, sensual lips. "I can think of a lot better uses for that tongue of yours."

Her eyes widened as he ran a hand suggestively over the massive bulge at his groin. "I thought we were sparring."

"We are." He flicked his foot against the side of the chamber to come tumbling toward her. Before she had time to avoid him, he stuck one hand out to deliver a stinging slap on her ass cheek. "I think that gives me three."

They continued to exchange strikes, but the focus had changed from inflicting damage to erotic stimulation. Kat trailed a foot across his wide chest. Her next pass, she managed to slide her fingers between his massive thighs to feel his balls drawn up tight.

Need and want built within her as he darted in time and again, his hands and feet trailing paths of liquid heat across her belly, her breasts and between her thighs. They both worked their way from the bottom of the tube up to the top, then back down again, teasing and tempting each other in turn. Kat's breathing grew ragged, and her response time slowed as Tore's superior muscle mass began to tell.

She saw Tore push off to start another run at her. She tucked her head in, intending to roll down the tube and avoid him, but at the last second, he twisted and wrapped his arm around her, bringing her in hard against his muscular body. She lifted her head just in time to see his lips swoop down.

Chapter Four

Tore attacked her mouth with the same blend of skill and brute strength that he used to fight. Lips and teeth scraped across hers in a thorough exploration that left her breathless and wanting more. He tasted clean and male, and the heavy bulge pressing against her belly assured her that he was every bit as aroused as she was. She tilted her head to allow him better access, enjoying the feel of his hard body against hers. She wrapped her arms around his neck and pulled him closer.

His hands wandered down her body, large and warm, tracing the curve of her hip, the flat plane of her stomach. Arousal roared through her, sending sparks of lust running down her spine. She wrapped one leg around his, holding him in tight. The thought of fucking Tore in zero-G excited her.

Tore slipped a hand in between them and released the seal on his ship-suit. The front edges parted with a muffled *whoosh*, and his muscular chest came into view. Her eyes followed the smooth ropes of hard muscles that gave way to a flat stomach, and a dark V of hair disappearing lower to where the suit covered his groin. He shrugged the material off his shoulders, holding her firmly against him with one arm while he skinned the suit down over his hips and legs. His shaft sprang free, hard and thick, rising from the dark nest of curls between his thighs. Her breath caught in her throat as she remembered exactly how it felt buried deep within her.

The suit floated beside them, reminding Kat of a fledgling butterfly with its discarded cocoon, and she couldn't help giggling at the thought of the muscular Tore in the role of a delicate butterfly.

The giggles died in her throat when he busied himself at the front of her suit, easily releasing the seal and parting the front to let her breasts spill out into his hands. He growled softly, the sound wildly arousing in its total lack of civility. He dipped his head to swipe his tongue across one nipple, teasing it into a rigid peak before he moved to its twin, licking and nipping. Teasing. Tempting. Tormenting her with featherlike strokes of his tongue.

She wound her arms around his neck, arching her back to offer herself up to his caresses. His breath feathered warm across her naked chest, adding to the fire that slowly built along every nerve, sliding with fiery intent to center deep within her belly.

He gripped her hips and shifted her upward, his mouth trailing a path of liquid heat down her sensitive skin, pausing to explore her belly, nipping the tender flesh with sharp teeth. "Goddess, you're so beautiful. I could spend a lifetime exploring you." He lifted his head to stare deep into her eyes.

She whimpered, unable to form a coherent thought. Want and need thundered through her, robbing her of the ability to think clearly. The hard length of his shaft pressed against her thigh, teasing her with its hard presence.

"Tell me what you want." He let one hand stray to the silken flesh of her bare mound. She stared at him mutely. "Come on," he coaxed, cupping her sex with one large palm. "Tell me."

"I want you." She managed to whisper the words out past the growing need building inside her.

He shook his head, his eyes glittering darkly. "Not good enough. What do you want from me?"

Kat whimpered and tried to rub her aching sex against his palm. "I want you to fuck me, damn it!"

He laughed then, a rich deep laugh of male satisfaction. He slid one finger down and plunged it into the waiting heat of her pussy, sending flames of pure lust rolling through her every cell. She writhed and grabbed at his hips, trying to force the finger deeper. *Damn zero-G!*

Tore grinned and stroked the finger in and out, scoring his thumb across the aching bundle of nerves at her entrance. Kat groaned, and managed to hook one foot behind his knee, using the leverage to rotate her hips on his finger, grinding herself against the palm of his hand.

Tore pushed his body lower and withdrew his finger, ignoring her cry of distress at the loss. Wrapping one arm around her hips, he stuck out his tongue and gave her a nice wet lick across the slick entrance of her sex.

Kat yowled, squirming against his face in mindless want. He thrust his tongue deep, lapping at the cream that dripped from the eager lips of her pussy. He circled the hard nub of her clit with his talented tongue, suckling and teasing until she writhed beneath him, her ankles locked behind his neck. She could feel herself riding the waves of lust, each one building upon the last until they detonated over her in a glorious explosion of pure feeling.

Tore fastened his mouth over her slick entrance, licking every last ounce of dew from her as she trembled through a multitude of aftershocks.

She opened her eyes to stare down at the top of his dark head. "That was…" She paused, not sure what to say. She'd had her share of sexual encounters, some better than others, but she'd never felt this kind of connection, that burst of pure feeling. "Wonderful." She sighed. Somehow, that didn't begin to convey the heights to which he'd sent her. Without, she conceded, any thought to his own pleasure.

"Thank you. I do aim to please." He reached up to hook an arm around her neck, drawing her down until they were floating eye to eye. "But I'm not done yet."

Kat's gaze followed his hand as he lowered it to circle his thick shaft. A single drop of pre-cum glistened on the tip, and she had a sudden urge to taste it. Tore ran his hand down the long length in a slow, erotic motion that sent heat coiling deep in the pit of her belly.

He pulled her in close for a kiss that turned into a long, slow exploration of her teeth, her tongue, her lips. She heard a low moan, and realized it came from her own throat. His practiced lips made her wonder why she'd settled for all those mediocre sexual partners who only cared about their own pleasures.

He ran a hand between her thighs and stroked her clit, making little shushing noises against her lips when she moaned deep in her throat. Lust started building within her again, sending flames of need dancing along her nerves. She felt the broad head of his cock pushing against her slick folds and she spread her thighs in welcome.

"Passionate little witch, aren't you?" A very male look of pure satisfaction crossed his face.

"I did say Abbie was the good sister, didn't I?" She rotated her hips, sliding her clit along the hard flesh of his shaft.

"That you did." He grasped her hips in a firm grip, preventing her from impaling herself on his cock. "I've always admired a woman who knows what she wants and goes after it." He thrust forward, driving himself deep inside her aching pussy.

Kat gasped at the sensation of his thick shaft stretching and filling her. Pleasure lanced through her every nerve. Her sex gripped the invading flesh as carnal hunger drove her inhibitions into hiding. She threw her head back, rotating her hips to make sure she captured every inch of that delicious cock.

Tore kept a firm grasp on her hips as he worked his shaft in and out, his heavy muscles gleaming with a thin coating of sweat. His eyes glowed a molten blue, and Kat could smell his warm male scent tempered with a hint of musk. She spread her thighs, opening herself wider to accommodate all of him.

"Goddess, you're tight." He dipped his head to nip one turgid nipple.

"And you're huge." She gasped as he rotated his hips and sparks of desire flared across her sensitive skin.

A dark grin flashed across his face and he started to drive into her with long lustful strokes. She writhed and whimpered, lifting her hips to meet him thrust for thrust. She could feel another orgasm starting to gather, liquid heat rolling from her breasts, to her thighs, her belly, before roaring through her sex.

She opened her mouth and screamed out his name as hundreds of sparkling lights exploded behind her eyelids. Tore plunged into her one last time, burying himself balls-deep, and she could feel his hot seed spurting inside her as wave after wave of intense pleasure roared through her.

They floated in the zero-G tube for a long while, wrapped around each other while tiny aftershocks rippled through their bodies. Surrounded by the warmth of Tore's arms, Kat relaxed, letting her head rest in the hollow of his shoulder.

She could feel the energy gathering around her,

seeping into her and strengthening her for the ordeal that lay ahead. Abbie needed her, would be counting on her to find her and save her from whatever horrible fate those damned reptiles had in mind. But first, Kat needed to rest and let her body assimilate the energy produced by her mind-boggling coupling with Tore.

She ran her palm down the hard flesh of his arm, feeling the scars that marked him. Were they a byproduct of his days in the research facility? Or something else? Whatever secrets lurked behind those brilliant blue eyes of his, Kat knew deep down in her gut that he'd do everything in his power to help her rescue her sister.

She breathed in the scent of his warm male body, and a contented sigh escaped her as she slipped away into a dreamy future where a brawny blue-eyed pirate took care of her every carnal need.

* * *

"You want me to wear that?" Kat stared at the straps of soft leather hanging from Tore's hand. How had she ever thought him one of the good guys? "Are you insane?"

Tore just stood there, his expression implacable. "If you want to go down to the surface with me, this is the way it's going to be." He shook his hand and the ridiculous... thing... did a little jig.

"And if I refuse?"

He shrugged those massive shoulders of his. "You stay onboard ship. How badly do you want to save your sister?"

Kat took a step forward, eyeing up the offending article. "That's not going to cover anything at all."

Tore looked at her with a blank expression and then burst out laughing. "It goes over your suit! You thought I planned to parade you around a space station in nothing but a couple of straps of leather?"

Kat felt the color rising in her cheeks. That's exactly what she'd thought. "That's what you said," she pointed out.

He tossed the offending item on the console and reached for her. "I thought you understood and were just balking at having to play at being my slave. I'm not sure my sanity would survive watching you parade nearly naked in front of a whole planet."

She slipped out of his grasp, and crooked a smile up at him. "So explain to me how this works." She picked up the harness and tried unsuccessfully to untangle the dangling straps.

Tore took the harness from her and deftly twisted the straps until they hung straight. "Hold your arms out straight from your sides."

Kat did as he instructed, watching as he dropped the contraption over her head and adjusted the various buckles. "I feel like a Bali-dragon getting harnessed for a parade." She tried to ignore the sparks that flew when the back of his hand brushed against her breast. Sheesh. You'd think she was the virgin. He only had to look at her, and moisture gathered in her pussy. "You'd better not be getting any ideas."

"Oh, I've got lots of ideas." He waggled his brows at her in an exaggerated leer. "Want to hear some of them?"

"No." She gave him her best *don't mess with me* look. "I'm sure they're very wicked."

"Oh, very," he assured her.

He checked the tension on the shoulder straps, and his expression sobered. "The people on this planet can be dangerous. Some of them are wanted by the Intergalactic Council. Probably most of them. You have to promise me that you'll do everything I tell you to.

Immediately. No exceptions."

Kat nodded, worrying her bottom lip with her teeth. She'd do whatever she had to, to help her sister. She still hadn't managed to connect with Abbie, had barely been able to sense her presence since the abduction. She'd always taken their connection for granted, and its absence left an aching hole in her heart.

* * *

Tore clipped a soft leather lead to the belt around Kat's waist, wrapping the excess around his hand. "This really is the safest way to get you in there. Most creatures will think twice about challenging me, even for a tasty morsel like you. So long as they believe I own you, you're relatively safe."

Kat raised her brow, a wry smile on her luscious lips. "Uh huh. I believe you, but why do I get the feeling you're enjoying this?"

Tore grinned wickedly, reaching out a hand to stroke the outline of her breasts beneath her tight suit. "I wouldn't be male if I didn't enjoy the sight of you bound on the end of a lead."

"Only because I allowed it."

He noticed she didn't flinch from his hand. "You might learn to enjoy it."

She snorted. "I doubt that."

He stared pointedly at the sharp outline of her peaked nipples, enjoying the color that flushed her high cheekbones as she followed his gaze. She lowered her eyes, and he chuckled. She had a lot to learn about the relationship between men and women, he thought, and he'd enjoy teaching her.

He sobered as he considered the task before them. He still hadn't decided whether to try to free her sister and make a run for safety, or simply buy her when she appeared on the block. Sometimes the simplest plan was the best. A lot depended on what they found on the surface.

"All set?" He reached out to adjust the top of her suit, allowing the creamy tops of her breasts to peek out. She nodded, and he could read the worry in her eyes. "Just stick with me, and remember to act like a slave."

"I'll try, but I don't know how a slave acts," she pointed out. "We don't have any on my planet."

"Simply, really. Just keep your mouth shut, and follow my orders." He tilted her chin up and took her mouth in a hard kiss. He'd promised to save her sister. He hoped he could keep that promise.

Chapter Five

They made it through the port docking facility without incident. The guard greeted Tore by name and flicked a disinterested look at Kat. "Good to have you return to us. Your regular berth is available should you wish to stay portside."

"I thank you for your service." Tore bowed formally, and tugged on the lead, herding Kat through the portal and into the main facility area.

Huge crowds of both humans and aliens filled the main corridor, and he watched Kat stare in amazement at the many different species milling about. A giant creature that would resemble an Old Earth teddy bear if not for those blood-red eyes turned to look at Kat before he addressed Tore in a guttural tongue.

Tore answered in the same dialect, tugging on the leather lead that circled Kat's waist. "He thinks you need discipline." An amused smirk curved the corner of his lips. "You hold your head up too high, and haven't learned to drop your eyes when looking at your superiors." He couldn't suppress the thread of amusement that ran through his voice. If looks could kill, the glare she shot him would have stopped him in his tracks.

"Yes, master." She kept her voice low, but he could see her clenching her hands.

He found himself wishing they were here on a social visit. He'd enjoy showing her around the station and pointing out the more bizarre residents. He couldn't remember ever feeling this relaxed around another being, except perhaps Tarik. He found it hard to trust people he knew, let alone strangers. He mentally shook his head and headed down a side corridor that led to the slave auctions. There'd be time to daydream later, when Kat's sister was safely stowed on the *Sun Runner*.

He shortened the lead so that Kat walked beside him. "Can you contact her?" He kept his voice low.

"No. We're close enough I can sense her presence, but not a direction." She gave a half shrug. "We'll have to go with your Plan B."

Fine by him. He led the way to a large doorway. As they got closer, a huge guard stepped out to intercept them. "Greetings." He flicked an assessing glance at Kat before directing his question to Tore. "Buying or selling?"

"Looking for something to pair up with this one." Tore gestured at Kat. "Heard there was some new stock up for sale. Got anything suitable?"

The guard turned to study Kat more closely, and Tore had to give her credit for her composure. She didn't flinch under the guard's appraisal.

"Most of what came in were darker-skinned. Unless you're interested in contrast, I don't think there's anything that would interest you, but you can go in and have a look. Maybe something will strike your fancy." He moved back to let them pass through. "If you're interested in bidding on any of them, you'll need to register."

"Thanks. I'll keep that in mind." Tore held Kat on a short leash as he passed through the doorway.

The room was a huge circle, with a square platform in the center to serve as the auction block. Small cubicles lined the walls, each one fronted with a force field that blocked the entrance while allowing the prospective buyers to see the slave inside. A digital readout above the cubicle gave the details of the person offered for sale.

"Guess we start here and work our way around." Tore glanced down at Kat. A frown creased her forehead as she looked at the beings in the cubicles, both human and alien. "Don't even go there. You can't save all of them." He gestured at a dark-skinned man flexing his muscles for a silk-clad woman of diminutive stature. "Some of them don't even want to be saved. Being owned means guaranteed food and lodging. There are a lot worse things in the universe." Like being an orphan under the Council's care. He left the words unsaid.

He paced the perimeter of the auction hall, checking out each of the cubicles, but Abbie didn't appear in any of them. He could see the tension building in the anxious line of Kat's shoulders. "This is just a beginning. Don't start worrying yet. There are still a couple more auction halls, as well as some smaller establishments. If she's here, we'll find her."

"She's here." Kat looked up and he could read the certainty in her eyes. "I know she is."

"Well, then." He pushed his way through a crowd of short furry creatures who were chattering excitedly amongst themselves as a tall, redheaded slave posed in a very suggestive position for them. "Let's keep looking."

* * *

By the time they'd toured the fourth auction hall, Kat could feel herself becoming inured to the sight of endless cages full of slaves being exhibited and prodded like animals. As far as she could see, it bothered her a lot more than most of the slaves.

"Time to change tactics." Tore waved off the slaver who'd been heading over to them. A sales pitch was the last thing they needed right now. "We'll go back to one of the bars and see if anyone has any info on an Aviroan ship landing here within the last couple of cycles."

"Whatever master wishes." Kat kept her head down to hide her tired smile.

"Good girl!" Tore patted her on the head. "You fit right in."

"Thank you, sir." Kat gave him her sweetest smile, and stomped on his foot. It would have had a lot more effect if she'd been wearing her boots instead of these pansy slippers. "Oh, I'm sorry, master. Did that hurt?"

The gleam in his eyes told her he knew exactly what she was up to. He leant down and his warm breath wafted gently across her ear. "No, but if you keep it up, I might just turn you over my knee and paddle that sexy little ass of yours. No one here would stop me."

Kat let her eyes widen innocently. "Oh, please, master. Don't punish me. I'll behave." Despite her worry over Abbie, she couldn't remember ever enjoying herself this much. Just his proximity made her feel content.

Tore plastered a mock severe look on his face. "See that you do." He reached down and cuffed her lightly on the butt. "My favorite watering hole, the Nebula, is just around the next bend. We'll try there."

"Hey, Tore!"

A large man with the blondest hair Kat had ever seen waded his way through the crowds toward them. Tore looked over and a big grin lit up his rugged features. "Tarik!" Kat took a step backward as the two men threw their arms around each other in an exuberant bear hug.

"Where the hell have you been hiding your mange-eaten hide?" Tarik slapped Tore on the back.

His gaze dropped to Kat, and a surprised look crossed his rugged face. "When the hell did you start keeping slaves? Krystal's going to chew your ear off when she hears about this."

Tore glanced at Kat, fingering the lead. "Not what you think, buddy. Let's go grab a drink and I'll explain."

"Okay." Tarik dropped an arm around Tore's shoulder and the two men rounded the corner, with Kat doing her best to keep up. They entered the Nebula and pushed through the crowd at the front of the bar, heading for the booths in the back. "It's been ages since you dropped in to visit." Tarik slid into the booth. "Krystal planned to mount a search party if you didn't surface soon. You know how that woman worries."

Tore motioned Kat into the booth, and then slid in beside her. "I was planning on coming back for a visit but while I was waiting on some repairs to the *Sun Runner*, Kat here roped me into helping find her sister."

"Looks like you're the one doing the roping." Tarik stared pointedly at the harness and leash. "What gives?"

Tore glanced at Kat, and she could read the question in his eyes. He wanted to know if she was okay with him telling Tarik the whole story. She nodded. Anyone who managed to gain Tore's confidence must be okay.

"It all started when I went into the Last Chance bar on Luna One. I'd just taken the *Sun Runner* in for an overhaul and thought I'd have a few drinks before I turned in. That's when I met Kat."

A gentle smile curved his lips as he ran his hand down her arm in a soothing gesture while he explained the situation to his old friend. Kat sat quietly beside him, content to let him do the talking. She remembered Tore telling her that Tarik's mate was a Stargazer as well, and she wondered where the other woman was. Once this nightmare was over and Abbie was safe, she'd love to be able to talk to another Stargazer.

"Wow." Tarik ran his hands through his thick mop of blond hair. "You sure manage to get yourself in some tight spots. Are you sure that the Aviroan took her?"

Tore nodded. "Kat could see them through Abbie's eyes. They were Aviroan all right."

"Well, I've been here for a couple of cycles now, and I've only heard of one of their ships making port here. Not sure exactly what they have, but I do know they're holding a private auction tomorrow. Invite only, and no viewings beforehand." He looked over at Kat with sympathy in his eyes. "If they're the ones who took your sister, that doesn't give you much time."

Kat felt her stomach lurch. She shifted closer to Tore, gaining reassurance from his warm body. "Now what?"

"We get ourselves invited to the auction." Tore gestured the serving-bot over and ordered a round of drinks. "Shouldn't be hard. I'll just flash some credits around and let it be known that I'm in the market for another slave."

The serving-bot returned, hovering over the table until they'd each taken their drink, and Tore threw a handful of credits on the tray to cover the bill.

"I'd stick around and help you, but you don't want to make them nervous." Tarik took a deep gulp of the purplish liquid in his mug. "My views on the slave trade are too well known around here to get me invited to that kind of party."

Kat sipped cautiously at the fizzy drink Tore had

ordered. He didn't look too worried, and she hoped he knew what he was doing. She was way out of her league here. She tried not to think of Abbie, alone and surrounded by those damned reptiles. A picture of the slaves on display in the auction halls earlier flashed through her mind, and she shuddered. Abbie just wasn't tough enough to survive the kind of brutality that seemed commonplace here.

"We'd better head back to the slave markets and start making enquiries. Will you and Krystal be around for a while in case I need some backup?" Tore asked.

Tarik nodded. "We're not scheduled to leave for a couple of moon cycles. We docked on the second tier. You know my call sign, I haven't changed it since the last time you visited." He stood and downed the rest of his drink in a single swallow. "I haven't been in a good fight in ages, so don't hesitate to call if you need help. We'll lie low until we hear from you."

"Appreciate it." Tore rose to his feet with a sinewy grace. "Say hi to Krystal for me."

"Will do. And I'll tell her you're bringing another Stargazer to visit. That'll make her happy." Tarik turned and started to wind his way toward the exit.

Tore looked down at Kat. "Ready to go? We may as well start fishing for that invite."

* * *

Kat sat quietly on a cushion at Tore's feet and looked around the auction hall. His hand rested lightly on the top of her head, and she found a small measure of comfort in the gesture. Just before they'd taken their seats, she'd felt the subtle brush of her sister's presence in her mind for the first time since the kidnapping. Abbie was alive. Kat hadn't realized how terrified she'd been for her sister's safety until that moment.

Getting an invitation to the auction proved to be

as easy as Tore had presumed, but they hadn't managed to get a look at the slaves awaiting their turn on the auction block. Given the tight security and relative lack of time before the auction, they'd realized that a rescue would be problematic, so they decided to go for the simplest strategy. Tore had a sizeable amount of credits stored up, and when Abbie was put on the block, he'd simply outbid the rest of the buyers.

Kat knew the credits she had saved probably wouldn't be enough to pay him back, but she wasn't worried. She'd do whatever he asked so long as her sister was safe. Secretly, the thought of how he might require her to work off her debt sent wet shivers straight to her sex.

Tore's hand tightened on her shoulder as the stage lit up and the auctioneer stepped out of the shadows. An expectant hush fell over the crowd. An attendant led the first slave onto the stage, a young female with a pale blue tinge to her skin. Her exotic looks caused a flurry of initial bids that trailed off as the stakes grew higher. She turned and posed seductively throughout the bidding, and Kat realized she'd been bred for this, conditioned to it from birth. The auctioneer finally banged his gavel to signify the winning bid of twenty-four thousand credits, and the girl grinned and curtseyed, obviously happy to have been valued so highly.

One after another, the slaves stepped up to the platform, some more cooperative than others as the buyers made their choices known. Abbie had yet to make her appearance, and Kat started to fidget. The crowd thinned out as the winning bidders departed with their purchases, and the losers went to drown their disappointments in the adjoining bars.

Tore bent down to whisper. "Can you still sense

her?"

Kat nodded. "She's close, and she's scared."

"She's a smart girl." He looked up as another slave stepped up to the platform. "Does she know you're here?"

Kat shook her head. "I don't think so. There's still something shielding her, although we're close enough that I have a better connection."

The auctioneer banged his gavel loudly to get the audience's attention, and they both looked up. A dark-skinned attendant led Abbie up onto the auction block. Her brown hair flowed down her back, caught up in a delicate web of lace that held it back from her face. A cloak of shimmering green silk hung loosely from her shoulders, hinting at the supple form beneath it. Kat could have cheerfully choked the auctioneer as he leered at her beloved sister.

"And now for the crowning jewel of our offerings." The auctioneer smiled down at his audience. "Something rare, dare I say almost impossible to find. You could search the entire galaxy and not come across another such as this." He gave a slight nod to the attendant, who stepped up behind Abbie and removed the cloak.

Abbie's eyes had a glazed look, and she stared resolutely over the heads of the crowd. Beneath the cloak, she wore a harem harness of soft leather and silk. The cleverly placed straps covered just enough of her figure to inflame the crowd. A silver collar circled her slender neck, and by the way her head hurt every time she looked directly at it, Kat surmised that it contained the dampening field.

Tore laid a warning hand on Kat's shoulder, and she shrugged it off, not caring how it would appear. Watching Abbie being treated like an animal, she barely managed to contain her anger. She knew better though. Now was not the time to lose control. She concentrated on her breathing, attempting to bring her emotions under control and center herself. Abbie needed her, and she wouldn't let her twin down.

She listened to the bidding. The prospective buyers were beginning to thin out as the numbers climbed into the double digits. Quiet descended in a momentary lull, and the auctioneer nodded to the attendant, who began to lead Abbie around the perimeter of the stage, showing off the young Stargazer from every angle.

"Did I mention this young slave's most appealing feature?" A sly, oily smile crossed the auctioneer's face, and Kat clenched her fists, digging the nails into her palms. "This lovely creature is a certified virgin."

"Shit!" Tore swore softly as an excited murmuring swept through the crowd.

A stocky man in the second row stood and waved excitedly. "Twenty thousand." Kat's heart sank.

"Twenty-one thousand credits."

She looked up at Tore, but he gave her a slight shake of his head.

"Twenty-one thousand five hundred." The tension in the room was palpable.

"Twenty-one thousand seven hundred fifty credits."

The numbers rose at a staggering pace until the offerings topped thirty thousand credits. "Thirty-one thousand credits."

The auctioneer paused to look around the now silent room. "Going once." The attendant stepped behind Abbie and reached around to run his hands over her body in a lewd display.

Kat started to rise, and Tore put his hand down to forcibly restrain her. "Take it easy," he murmured. "You don't want to blow this now."

Kat bit her lip, and settled back down on the cushion. This was the hardest damn thing she'd ever done. Closing her eyes, she concentrated on sending encouraging energy toward her sister. The shield had a tangible presence, a huge wall of energy preventing her thoughts from penetrating. She let her consciousness slip along the wall, looking for a weak spot, a hole, anything that would allow her to get in and comfort Abbie, let her know that help was here.

"Going twice." The auctioneer's oily voice penetrated her focus.

Not a whisper sounded in the room. The audience stared in fascination at the attendant fondling the helpless woman.

"Forty thousand credits." Tore stood, his voice ringing out loudly in the silent hall.

Chapter Six

Kat looked up, startled, and Tore spared her a quick glance. Murmurs of disbelief swept through the auction hall as people craned their necks to see who had offered so many credits.

"Forty thousand credits. I have forty thousand from the discerning gentleman in the third row." The auctioneer's eyes lit with greed. "Do I hear forty-one?"

Abbie turned her head to stare, and Tore could tell the exact moment that she recognized her twin. Relief and hope flittered across her face.

"Forty thousand going once." Abbie reached up to tug absently at the collar on her neck. "Forty thousand going twice." The man didn't bother to try to get the crowd riled up again.

"Fifty thousand."

The hair on the back of Tore's neck rose at the gravelly sound of that hated voice. He turned his head and searched the crowd until he found him. *Drago!* The keeper of the orphan's compound run by the Intergalactic Council, the place where he'd learned that hell wasn't an abstract place made up by wandering religious nuts; it was a room in the research facility. He'd had nightmares about this man for a long time after his escape.

The asshole inclined his head, and a cold smile curved his thin lips. It was the same evil smile that Tore had learned to hate as a child. The one that said Drago was in a mood to hurt someone, to make them scream. Tore took a deep breath and forced his face to remain blank. He was no longer a terrified child unable to defend himself. Drago would not be using Kat's sister for his sick pleasures.

"Who the hell is that?" Kat hissed in alarm.

"The man who carved each of these scars on my body. Relax. I'll deal with him."

He signaled the auctioneer. "Fifty-five thousand." The crowd let out a collective gasp.

"Sixty thousand."

Tore laced his fingers through the silky length of Kat's hair. He swore he could feel her inside his head, calming him, supporting him. Giving him the strength to confront his past. "Sixty-five thousand credits."

"Seventy thousand. You should know better than to challenge me, Tore." Drago's despised voice cut across the crowded room. "I see your scars healed after all. I didn't think you'd survive that particular punishment."

Tore rose to his full height, chin held high as he turned to face the demon of his childhood. "I'm no longer the helpless child you amused yourself by torturing, Drago. I suggest you gather your pathetic gang of child abusers and leave quietly. While I'm still in the mood to let you live."

He stared into the eyes that had haunted him for his entire life. Dead, black pools of evil, they bore into him, looking for a weakness, for something to exploit. He met that gaze and held it, refusing to look away. He could feel Kat's warm hand on his thigh, feel her in his mind, feeding him her strength as the silent battle of wills raged.

Drago was the first to look away. He dropped his gaze to the floor, and Tore continued to stare at him for a few minutes. Then he turned to the auctioneer. "Seventy-five thousand credits. Final bid. This auction is over."

The man must have seen something in Tore's ice-blue eyes that scared him. His eyes widened and his gavel hit the podium for the last time. "Sold to the gentleman for seventy-five thousand credits. That's all for this round. Buyers, please pay the cashier at the back of the hall before you claim your merchandise." With a last furtive look at Tore, he hastened off the stage.

Tore grasped Kat by the wrist and helped her to her feet. He turned his head to watch Drago hurry out of the auction hall, his eyes filled with hatred and humiliation. He shook off the urge to follow, to take vengeance for the endless years of pain and torment he'd suffered at Drago's hands. Now was not the time.

Right now, he had Abbie and Kat to look after. A reluctant smile tugged at his mouth. If Abbie was anything like her twin, he'd have his hands full. He threaded his way up to the stage and picked up the discarded cloak, wrapping it around Abbie's shoulders, covering her body. She stared at him warily, her wide eyes so much like her twin's.

Then Kat stepped forward and threw her arms around her sister. "Oh, Abbie! I was so afraid for you."

Tore stepped back and watched the two. The attendant took a step toward them, but the glare Tore gave him had him remembering pressing business elsewhere.

"This is Tore." Kat let go of her sister and pulled him forward. "He helped me find you and rescue you." She paused sheepishly. "Actually, we were going to rescue you but it seemed easier to just buy you."

Tore cleared his throat, feeling unusually reticent. It mattered to him, whether or not Abbie approved of him. "It's nice to meet you, Abbie. Kat has told me a lot about you. I don't want to break up this reunion, but I need to pay the cashier and get you two out of here. The sooner we're safely back on the ship, the better I'm going to feel."

"Me too. I've had enough of crowds and strangers to last me a lifetime." Abbie gave him a shy smile. "Nice to meet you, Tore. And thank you." She pulled at the silver collar at her neck. "Any chance you can make them take this off? I can barely think with it on." Her eyes widened, focusing on something over his shoulder.

"I bet you think that little witch has the hots for you just because you're such a big stud, don't you?"

Tore whirled around to find a smirking Drago right behind him, flanked by two of his cyborg guards.

"I'll let you in on a little secret. When we screwed around with your DNA, we tried a little concoction to see if we could make a male irresistible to the Stargazer whores. The Council hoped to keep them in line by linking them to males under our control. Looks like that particular experiment was a success." An oily smirk crossed his disgusting face. "I'll be sure to inform the Council. I'll bet the little bitch begs you to do her, doesn't she?"

Tore snarled softly and turned his back on the man in a deliberate insult. Someday, he'd deal with the asshole, but right now he had more important things to worry about. Drago wasn't worth the time it would take to teach him a lesson.

Then again…

He pivoted sharply and brought up his right hand, landing a solid punch directly on that supercilious sneer before the startled guards could step in to block him. The satisfying crunch of breaking bone, combined with the high-pitched squeal of agony from his childhood tormentor, brought a satisfied smile to his lips.

* * *

"Dear goddess of light! How do you plan to

handle two of them?" Tarik stood beside Tore while Krystal went to introduce herself to Abbie and Kat. The three Stargazers wandered off in the direction of the galley, leaving the men to their own devices.

Tarik and Tore had agreed to travel in tandem until they were out of this galaxy and safe from any chance of attack, especially since Drago was somewhere in the area. Kat suspected that it was just an excuse for the two old friends to spend some time together. Men! They couldn't just come out and say they missed each other. She felt a warm, melting sensation in the vicinity of her heart as she watched the two.

She turned her attention back to her sister. "So what do you want to do now? Tore and I would be glad to have you aboard ship with us."

Abbie raised her eyebrow and regarded her twin, an amused smile on her face. "Tore and you? Did I miss something?"

Kat felt her cheeks flush. "Well, I'll have to work off your purchase price and that'll take a good long time." She glanced over at the pirate's smooth features. He hadn't said one word about her repaying him.

"Uh huh." Her sister rolled her eyes. "I'm not that naïve, and besides I can see inside your head. You think he's yummy."

Kat giggled. It felt so good to have her sister back. "He is yummy! And he knows exactly what to do with that big body of his." She changed the subject before Abbie could ask what their plans were. She and Tore needed to have a serious talk. Soon. "So what are your plans?"

Abbie glanced over at Krystal. "I think I'd like to spend some time at Star Haven. I've always wanted to know more about the other Stargazers, and it'll give me some time to decide what path I want to choose." A shudder ran through her slight body. "After having those reptiles and the slavers handling me like I was an animal, I'm not sure I want anybody touching me for a while."

Kat tilted her head. "What is Star Haven?"

"A planet colonized by Stargazers." Krystal joined in the conversation. "They spend their time studying their talents and piecing together our history. Not much is known about the origins of the Stargazers, or why some women exhibit signs of the talent while others don't." She smiled gently at Abbie. "It's also a very good place for a Stargazer to go when she needs a peaceful place to recuperate and decide what she wants to do next. Tarik and I visit there from time to time. The planetary administrator is a good friend of his."

Abbie nodded. "It sounds perfect. I may not stay there, but I really need time to think, without Mom hovering over me."

"Well then." Kat hugged her sister. "I guess Tore and I can drop you off at Star Haven. But first, you'd better contact Mom and tell her you're okay."

* * *

Kat lay sprawled naked on Tore's sleeping platform, watching him toy with the food replicator. He'd just come out of the cleaning unit, and the towel draped around his hips gave her all sorts of ideas. Most of them involving sweat-slicked bodies sliding against each other. She licked her lips as the towel slipped a fraction of an inch lower. "What are you doing? I'm getting lonely over here."

"This is an old recipe Tarik shared with me. He said it is used as an aphrodisiac on Ancient Earth."

"Really?" Kat propped herself up on one elbow

and tried to see what he was doing. "What's it called?"

The replicator beeped cheerfully and a tray appeared on the platform. Two long-stemmed glasses full of a light amber bubbly liquid flanked a bowl of bright red round berries with short green stems above a cap of leaves. Kat wrinkled her nose. "What is it?"

"Champagne and strawberries." Tore deftly scooped up the tray and brought it over to the table by the sleeping platform. Plucking up one of the strawberries, he held it in the air above her mouth. "Open up." Kat opened her mouth obediently. Tore picked up one of the glasses. Holding the berry by its green stem, he dipped it in the liquid before he held it just above her waiting lips.

An explosion of flavor hit Kat's taste buds as she crushed the sweet fruit between her teeth. The slightly tart flavor of the champagne made a teasing contrast to the sweet flesh of the strawberry. "Mmmmmm." She licked her lips. "Yummy."

A darkly wicked grin lit up Tore's rugged face. "Feeling like attacking me yet?"

Kat giggled. "Not yet. Maybe you'd better feed me some more." He picked up the next berry and dipped it into the pale amber liquid, but instead of feeding it to her he popped the tasty morsel into his own mouth. "No fair!" Kat sat up and reached for the tray. "You're supposed to be feeding me."

Tore laughed and grabbed her wrist. "I didn't say that. I just said it was supposed to be an aphrodisiac. Maybe it'll make me want to attack you."

"You always want to attack me," she pointed out. "You don't need any help."

Tore pounced onto the sleeping platform, the towel slipping off his hips to expose his cock at full attention. "Then I guess the foreplay is over." He straddled her hips and leaned forward to pin her hands above her head.

Their gazes locked and Kat went still as she stared into the molten depths of his eyes. Who ever told her blue was a cold color? Heat coiled around her spine as he slowly lowered his head. She found herself staring at his lips. Full. Soft. Sensual. She loved the way he used them. Kissing her with a searing passion. Roving across her bare flesh to taste and tease. And then there was the feel of them clamped on her sex…

His mouth made contact, open and demanding. His tongue thrust in to swirl around hers, sliding along the side in a caress so sensually hot she was amazed she didn't come on the spot. Ye gods, the man knew how to kiss.

He lifted his head. "So I guess you're going to become a permanent fixture on the old *Sun Runner*." He covered her breasts with the palms of his hands, kneading the tender flesh before he took each nipple between a thumb and forefinger, tweaking just enough to make her gasp.

Kat whimpered and arched up off the sleeping platform as pleasure combined with pain. "You mean because I owe you for rescuing Abbie?" She was having trouble concentrating with darts of liquid heat sliding along her every nerve. "I have some savings, and the rest won't take that long to work off."

Tore grinned and sucked the tip of one breast into his mouth, licking the hurt away with his tongue. He moved to the other and repeated the procedure. "Got nothing to do with Abbie. I freed her because I couldn't bear the thought of you being unhappy, and having your sister sold as a slave definitely didn't make you happy."

Kat threaded her fingers through the soft locks of

his hair. Following a logical conversation took almost more brainpower than she could muster with his mouth busy at her breast. "Then why am I going to be a permanent resident here?"

He raised his head and those gorgeous blue eyes twinkled with mischief. "Because I'm irresistible to Stargazers and since you're a Stargazer, you'll just keep begging me for more."

Kat frowned. "Doesn't that bother you? What that evil man said? The Council deliberately manipulated your DNA to make you more useful to them. And more appealing to me."

Tore grinned, that irresistible little boy grin that made her heart melt. "Honey, they may think they're all powerful and can influence the outcome of all sorts of things in the universe, but the fact is that you and I were made for each other. No research, no Intergalactic Council, nothing can change that."

Kat raised her brows. "You are the bossiest, most arrogant male I've ever met." She let a shy smile curve her lips. "Now quit talking and start being irresistible."

"With pleasure." He turned his attention back to her breasts, licking and teasing with tiny bites and long wet swipes of his tongue. Kat closed her eyes and let the sensual feel of his tongue and hands wash over her. The sheer carnal pleasure caused her pussy to cream in anticipation.

Tore worked his way lower, his warm, callused palms sliding over every exposed part of her. She bucked and writhed beneath him, flickers of lust dancing across the surface of her skin. He nibbled a circle around her belly button before he paused to explore the shallow indent with his tongue. Kat gasped as a jolt of sheer pleasure lanced through her. "Damn, you are irresistible."

"Why, thank you." He slid his hand down and parted the moist lips of her pussy. His questing fingers found the hard nub of her clit, pinching the tight little bundle of nerves between thumb and forefinger.

Kat screamed out an incoherent word as need and lust blasted through her. To hell with the damn foreplay. She wanted that big, thick cock of his buried deep inside her, and she wanted it now.

Tore slid a finger into her wet passage, lifting his head to give her a look that was pure lust. "You're so hot you're practically melting." He raised himself up on muscular forearms and positioned his cock at the entrance to her sex. The swollen head pushed eagerly through the wet folds of her labia, and he grinned darkly at her eager whimper.

Slowly, he started to thrust his thick shaft into her, inch by inch, driving her mad with want and need. She arched her back, trying to take more, trying to force him deeper inside her, but he refused to be hurried. "Fuck me, damn it!" Frustration edged her voice.

"I am." He had the nerve to sound amused. If she weren't so desperate to feel the hard length of him buried up to the balls in her sex, she would have slapped him.

"Faster. Harder." Damn, he shouldn't be needing direction. The teasing feel of that swollen head working its way deeper was driving her insane with need.

"You need to learn patience."

But she could hear the strain in his voice. He wanted this every bit as much as she did. She opened her eyes to look into the beloved deep blue of his. "I can't wait to feel my pussy clench tight around that huge cock when you drive it balls-deep into my hot tight channel." She darted her tongue out to wet her lips.

"Witch!" He reared back and drove his cock into her eagerly waiting sex with one hard thrust, forcing her channel to stretch to accommodate his massive girth.

Kat howled in lustful abandon and wrapped her legs around his waist, meeting him thrust for hard, deep thrust as he pounded into her. The musky smell of aroused male and the feel of flesh sliding hard against her combined to inflame her senses. She could feel her orgasm starting deep within her belly, liquid fire rolling through her body as each stroke of his cock drove her higher and higher.

He pulled back, his lips descending to hers in a kiss that seared her to her soul. He thrust back in through her wet folds, driving his cock deep, and her climax spun through her, wave after crashing wave of indescribable pleasure. She screamed his name out against his mouth as his hot seed bathed the tight walls of her pussy. She arched her back, making sure she had every wonderful inch of him. Her sex clenched around his shaft, rippling in sensuous waves.

"Sweet goddess of light!" She wrapped her arms around him, holding him tight. They lay tangled in each other's arms while their breathing slowly returned to normal. Kat rested her head on his naked chest, his heartbeat echoing soothingly in her ear.

When her breathing finally returned to normal, she slanted a look up at him. Her lover. Her partner. "Does it bother you, what that horrible man said?"

He nuzzled the top of her head. "What did he say?"

"That they bioengineered you so I'd want you? So that any Stargazer would want you?"

Tore laughed. "Drago is a consummate liar. He can say whatever he wants, it doesn't make it true. You want me because I have a yummy body, and I know exactly how to use it."

Kat gasped, spluttering indignantly. "You were eavesdropping!"

"No," he corrected her smugly. "I have enhanced hearing, which means I heard you bragging about me to your sister and Krystal. I'm sure the word yummy was used. More than once."

Kat felt a reluctant grin tugging at the corner of her mouth. "I might have been talking about your cooking."

Tore raised one sculpted eyebrow. "I don't cook. I program the replicator."

Kat giggled. "Things seem to sizzle when you come near me."

"Yes, they do." He tilted her chin up with one finger and gave her a very thorough kiss. "And it had nothing to do with Drago or the research facility or the experiments they tortured me with."

He propped himself up on one elbow to look directly into her eyes, his expression sober. "You are the most amazing female I have ever met. When I'm with you I feel so many things that I never thought I'd ever feel. Hope. Happiness. Contentment. But most of all, I feel love. For you. I know you deserve better. Hell, after everything they did to me I'm not entirely human, but I promise, if you stay with me, I will do everything in my power to make you happy, and to protect you and provide for you."

Kat could see the uncertainty in his eyes as he held his breath waiting for her reply. She'd gone looking for her sister, and in the process found the keeper of her heart, the other half of her soul. She reached up to trace the outline of his lips with one finger. "Of course I'll stay." Her voice quavered with emotions she couldn't quite control. "I love you too."

Sinful
Sci-Fi Action & Intrigue Romance
Anne Kane

When Roark captures the sexy Stargazer, he has no idea how quickly she'll capture his heart.

Breanne is furious when she's captured by an interstellar bounty hunter. Her mission is to rescue a fellow Stargazer who fell prey to pirates, and she can't do that from the brig of Roark's spaceship.

When Breanne convinces Roark they should join forces, though, they find out just how powerful they can be together. The pirates don't stand a chance against their combined wrath.

Chapter One

Breanne twisted and turned, attempting to loosen the man's grip. "What the hell do you think you're doing?" She let out her breath in an exasperated hiss. "I'm not some little station bitch you can pick up and use for your pleasure." Her legs flailed helplessly in the air as she dangled from his broad shoulder, his arm wrapped around her midsection like an iron band.

The man just laughed and shifted his grip a little higher, his biceps pressing hard on her ass. "Feisty little thing, aren't you?" He pointed an access card at the barricade, pausing for a brief moment while the computer scanned the card. The barrier dissolved to allow them into the outer ring of the space station that housed the docking rings for travelers' spaceships. "I can see how you managed to get this far. You bluff better than a moon-cat trying to scavenge food for her kits. Your bond-master warned me about your acting skills."

"My bond-master?" Breanne stopped squirming and tilted her head to look over her shoulder at him. If he wasn't busy kidnapping her, he'd be just the kind of man she drooled over. At least six and a half feet tall, he had the broad shoulders and wide chest of a man who didn't spend his days riding herd on a desk. Long and luxurious, his dark hair brushed his shoulders in thick waves. She let her gaze slide down to his groin, where the skintight uni-suit stretched over the thick bulge of his cock. Possibilities danced through her mind and she felt heat staining her cheeks.

She gave her head a mental shake, and met his amused gaze. "You've got the wrong person. I'm a free woman. I don't have a bond-master."

"Right. You just happen to be a dead ringer for

an escaped bond-servant who was last seen heading for this station aboard a stolen flitter craft." He chuckled, the sound deep and rich. "We'll see what Mr. Keiro has to say about that when I call to collect the bounty on you."

Oh, great. Breanne rolled her eyes in exasperation. This Keiro person would confirm the mistake, but not before she lost precious time. And time was not on her side.

She'd hoped to meet up with the Stargazer she'd been tracking before Talia was whisked off-station again by her dubious crew. Rumor had it that Stargazer Talia was not with the crew of the *Alpher* of her own free will. As a member of the ruling Triad of Star Haven, it was Breanne's sworn duty to protect all Stargazers, and she took her duty very seriously.

"Perhaps you can contact this Keiro by vid-call and have him identify me?" That should end this little farce in a hurry.

"Nice try. You know he abhors the use of vid-tech." The behemoth ran his hand across her thighs in an overly familiar caress. "He set up the bounty by remote server-bot. You'll be home soon enough. You might want to consider how you plan to work off the reward he offered for your return. Bond-masters generally aren't the generous type."

Breanne groaned. She could see her chance of intercepting the *Alpher* and talking to Talia slipping away. She twisted her wrists, hoping to loosen the plas-tek he'd wrapped around them. No luck. The damn man knew how to tie a bond. Frustration flared in her. "You're not listening, you jerk. You have the wrong woman!" She shrieked, more in surprise than pain as the idiot had the audacity to bring his hand down on her ass in a stinging slap.

"You need to learn some manners, Breanne. Calling me names is not going to put you on my good side."

"I don't want to be on your good side." She glared at him. "I don't want to be anywhere near you."

The man took a sharp right turn and headed down one of the access corridors. "That's too bad, because I'm the only person you're going to see for the next ten solar cycles. You might want to reconsider your attitude. Life could be a lot more pleasant if you cooperate."

Breanne opened her mouth to make a quick retort, then hesitated. It might not be wise to antagonize the bounty hunter any further. It looked like she was going to have to put up with his company for a while. She swallowed hard and attempted to inject a note of sincerity into her voice. "How do you know my name? You didn't stop to introduce yourself before abducting me, so I'm at a disadvantage. I have no idea what your name is."

"Where were my manners?" He stopped in front of an access door and tilted his chin to let the security field scan his retinal patterns. A subdued whooshing sound signaled its acceptance of him and the airlock cycled open to allow them access. "Your name was on the bounty posting. Mine is Roark Danning, freelance bounty hunter. Welcome aboard the *Blazing Star*. If you behave, we could have a very pleasant voyage."

The suggestive note in his voice, along with the way his fingers caressed the back of her thighs, left little to her imagination. The fact that her name and the missing bond-servant's name were identical puzzled her, but the metallic clang signaling the outer hatch shutting behind them distracted her from commenting on it.

Once they left the station, she'd be at his mercy.

"Don't panic. I'm not going to hurt you." Roark strode down a narrow passageway and entered a room to the left. Breanne glanced around the sparse furnishings. The brig she surmised, by the lack of amenities and single entranceway. She took a deep breath.

He loosened his grip to allow her to slide down to her feet, while holding her close enough that she could feel every luscious inch of his hard male body, including that intriguing bulge at his groin. Standing, she had to look up to see the smoldering expression in his eyes. He had to be at least six and a half feet tall, she estimated. At six foot even, she rarely had to look up to a man, and the experience was unsettling. A member of the ruling Triad of Star Haven, she was used to being the one in control of any given situation.

Amusement danced in Roark's smoke-gray eyes, and she knew he could sense her uncertainty. She felt her temper rising, but this wasn't the time to indulge in a tantrum. She needed to get on with her mission, and to do that she needed to outsmart this sinfully sexy bounty hunter.

Reaching behind her, he released her wrists, wrapping the length of plas-tek into a neat coil and tucking it into a pocket. The feel of his turgid shaft digging into her soft belly gave her a sinfully delicious idea. As a Stargazer she could harness the power generated by sexual encounters, and if she seduced this bounty hunter, she could use his own arrogant power against him. She felt the corner of her mouth curve up as she let her lashes sweep down to hide the calculating gleam in her eyes. "My, you're a big man. Maybe we can work something out." She let a note of breathless anticipation creep into her voice while her left hand moved over his chest in a practiced caress.

His eyes darkened as he pulled her in, and his shaft swelled even larger. Breanne relaxed, molding her body against his, and tilted her head. She parted her lips slightly and let the tip of her tongue slide along the edges, leaving them wet and glistening.

"Now that's more like it." His arms tightened around her, drawing her even closer as he lowered his head to take her lips in a searing kiss that sent lust coiling deep in the pit of her belly. His tongue slid along the seam of her lips, demanding entrance. Breanne acquiesced, opening her mouth to allow him to plunder at will.

He took immediate advantage, his tongue sweeping in to explore every nook and cranny, sliding along her teeth and probing deep. Not submissive by nature, Breanne used her tongue to challenge him, letting him know how much she wanted him. She felt the heat slide along every nerve when he refused to back down. Most men deferred to her status as part of the ruling Triad, letting her take the lead in sexual encounters.

Roark broke off first, nibbling his way down her neck. His sharp teeth sent darts of liquid heat sliding down her spine, and a soft whimper escaped her.

"Like that, do you?" He chuckled softly and scooped her up in his muscular arms. "I told you I wouldn't hurt you."

She blinked, and then realized he was referring to his earlier comment. Making a conscious effort to relax, she raised her arms to wind them around his neck. "I won't hurt you either." She favored him with a full smile. "Unless you want me to."

"You are a feisty little morsel, aren't you? I can see why Keiro is in such a hurry to get you back." He bent to toss her onto the sleeping platform.

Breanne rolled over and stretched out on the firm surface. Looking up, she saw the bounty hunter's amused expression as he stripped off his clothing with a minimum of wasted movement and tossed it carelessly on the floor. She studied his nude body with interest as he stalked toward her. She'd seen her share of naked men, and he was impressive. Heavy muscles covered a large frame, and a jagged scar ran from beneath his left nipple to the edge of his hip. Her gaze went lower, to where his thick shaft jutted out from a nest of dark curls. She licked her lips in anticipation of the energy their union would produce.

"Strip."

The single word, uttered in a husky growl, sent a shiver of lust spinning down her spine. She got to her feet in the middle of the sleeping platform, letting the natural buoyancy of the platform cause her body to sway seductively. Making eye contact, she let a smile play across her lips while she raised her hands to the tiny seals that held the uni-suit closed down the front. Humming an ancient fertility song, she toyed with each seal before releasing them one by one. The taut material sprang apart as each seal gave way, opening a path from neck to thigh.

She watched his eyes darken as her full breasts spilled free of their restraints, and her smile widened. Seduction was one of the first things a Stargazer learned. The bounty hunter didn't stand a chance. She continued to release the seals, letting her hips sway in time to her humming, and soon she stood before him completely naked. She lifted her arms above her head, the move lifting her breasts.

Roark let his breath out in a loud whoosh, his gaze devouring her full figure. "We may be taking the long route back to Keiro's." He reached out and grasped her wrist to gently tug her toward him.

Breanne stepped into the circle of his arms and sank to her knees, putting her lips only inches from his. His warm breath feathered gently across her face as they stared at each other. His eyes, dark with want and need, started a familiar tightening deep in her belly. She let her eyelids flutter down as she licked her lips, patiently waiting for him to make the first move.

His lips were firm and hard, covering hers to take possession of her mouth. His tongue invaded, probing deep, and Breanne parted her lips to allow him full access. He tasted fresh and male and dominant, the combination triggering her most basic needs. She could feel moisture gathering in her sex. Bringing her arms up, she wound them around his neck, her fingers twining in his dark, crisp hair. She ran her tongue across his sensuous bottom lip, teasing him.

His response was immediate, deepening the kiss and wrapping his muscular arms tight around her. Breanne leaned into him, reveling in the feel of a hard male body pressed against her. Roark feathered kisses from the corner of her mouth to her ear, pausing to nibble on the sensitive lobe with his sharp teeth. Breanne sucked in a deep breath, her pulse racing. He worked his way lower, trailing his lips across her cheek and down to the hollow of her throat.

Breaking off his moist exploration, he picked her up and laid her down in the middle of the bed, climbing up to straddle her. "You are so beautiful. If you didn't have a price on your head, I'd be tempted to keep you for myself." He cupped her breasts in his big hands, kneading the firm mounds.

Breanne arched her back, moaning softly. The feel of his warm skin against hers sent ripples of pleasure coursing along her entire body. She lifted her hand, stroking the scar that bisected his chest. The thought of someone deliberately trying to harm him raised an unexpected flicker of alarm in her. She let her fingers drift to his hard nipples, gliding across them in a gentle caress.

He shuddered deeply, then lowered his head to suck one nipple into his mouth. Warm, liquid heat enveloped her and her body reacted instantly, her nipples rising to sharp peaks under his attention. He licked and sucked, feasting on each breast in turn. Never had her body reacted so quickly to a male. Need and want lanced down her spine with agonizing intensity.

He scored his teeth across one nipple before working his way lower, nipping and licking his way down to her belly. He detoured around her navel, his tongue trailing a fiery path to the sensitive hollow of her hips.

Breanne wasn't sure exactly when she lost control, when her calculated seduction became an unabashed surrender to his hands and his mouth. She writhed beneath him, low moans escaping her lips as his sinfully sexy mouth pushed her lust even higher. His hand brushed across her bare mound, and she whimpered, arching up against it.

Roark chuckled, the sound low and very male. He slid one finger between the lips of her pussy, stroking the tender flesh before he plunged it deep inside her slick sex. "Tell me you like it, little one." He whispered the words against her belly.

"I like it." She couldn't lie. Not to him. Not to herself. She moved her hips in time to the rhythm of his finger as he plunged it in and out. And all the time, he watched her, his dark eyes narrowed and focused.

"I knew you would. I could see it in your eyes the minute I found you. You were born for this, born for sex." He shifted lower, swiping his tongue from her clit to her anus in one long, wet stroke that sent her libido soaring to the stars before he settled himself between her thighs and fastened his mouth over her sex. His tongue was nothing short of pure magic, coaxing her higher and higher, sending curls of liquid heat racing along her skin.

Just when she felt her climax building, Roark removed his mouth and got up on his knees. She gasped in protest at the sudden absence of warm pressure, opening her lids to look up into his dark eyes.

He grinned and flipped her over with a casual strength that made her realize the bounty hunter might not be entirely human. Then, all rational thoughts fled as he grasped her hips from behind, pulling her up onto her hands and knees. She gasped as she felt his cock push eagerly against the entrance to her sex.

Roark entered her with one hard thrust, plunging his cock balls-deep in her slick channel. Breanne whimpered as darts of erotic heat fanned throughout her entire body.

He began to shaft her with long, deep strokes of that magnificent cock. Slow at first, he let the pace build as she matched him stroke for stroke, moaning and pushing back against him. In. Out. Harder. Faster.

She felt the climax building again, starting at the tips of her toes and sweeping throughout her. Wave after wave of exquisite pleasure washed over her, and she writhed in ecstasy. Dimly, she heard him growl out in triumph just as his hot seed jetted inside her.

The two of them collapsed onto the platform in a tangled heap of limbs, their ragged breathing sounding loud in the confines of the small room. Breanne could feel the energy seeping into her, and she let a sleepy smile curve her lips. Soon, his energy would aid her in escaping, while he would still be exhausted from their exertions. An unfamiliar tinge of regret swept through her as fatigue overcame her and she drifted off to sleep.

Chapter Two

Roark frowned at the call log. He'd sent a message to Mr. Keiro to let him know that he'd found and detained Breanne. He'd expected to receive an immediate confirmation with the coordinates to a meeting spot by now, but the message terminal remained stubbornly blank. Unless the man was a computer geek and could mask his online presence from Roark's cyborg senses, he hadn't even bothered to pick up the incoming message. Strange. The reward posting had made it sound like the bond-master was sitting on the edge of his console chair waiting for someone to bring back his wayward slave.

He checked the relays to make sure there wasn't a problem with his system, and then sighed. Hopefully, Mr. Keiro hadn't found himself a new distraction. Roark had been counting on that bounty, and he wasn't sure he'd be callous enough to put Breanne up for auction if her bond-master refused to pay for her return.

Shrugging in annoyance at the pitfalls of his trade, he passed his hand over the control panel and called up the brig surveillance display to see how his cargo was faring. A three-dimensional display of the brig shimmered into view, and his gaze fixated on the Stargazer's fabulous legs flashing enticingly as she paced the length of the small room. She didn't look thrilled to find herself alone in the brig.

He felt a wry smile curve the corner of his mouth. No doubt she'd thought she could seduce him and use the resultant energy to enable her to escape while he slept it off. Unfortunately for her, he knew how Stargazers operated. He'd spent enough time on an ore cruiser with a resident one when he'd first taken to space. He'd been more than willing to take his turn supplying the nubile female with the energy she needed, but he'd also learned how to use his cybernetic implants to block her before she drained him completely.

He watched the woman slam her hands against the locked door. "What the hell are you?" She glared around the room, as if expecting him to materialize at any moment. From her bearing, he'd be willing to bet hard credits that she wasn't used to being thwarted. The thought of going down there and forcing the blue-eyed witch to submit to him made his cock jerk in anticipation. He wondered how her bond-master managed to control her, and then shrugged. It really wasn't his problem. He just needed to deliver her and collect the bounty.

Turning his attention to the control panel, he keyed in jump coordinates. Sitting dead still in the heavily traveled shipping lanes was an invitation to disaster. He'd take the *Blazing Star* out into space, and wait for Mr. Keiro to reply.

He reached up to pull the safety netting over his seat, and opened the brig's com-link. "We're on countdown to launch. I'd advise you to buckle in."

The woman's head came up and she scanned the walls of her prison. "Damn cyborgs! That's what you are, aren't you?" She paced across the small room, stopping in front of the launch chair. "Only a cyborg would be able to walk away after last night."

Roark chuckled. It hadn't taken her long to figure that out. He had to give her credit. Most women, when confronted with the reality of a cyborg, would be terrified, or at least scared. He'd had more than one working girl run when they realized what he was. Breanne was just plain mad. "If it makes you feel better, my legs were just a wee bit shaky. You're an even better lover than the last Stargazer I bedded."

The anger on her face turned to thoughtful calculation. "So you've had occasion to consort with some of my sisters. Then you must know about Star Haven and the Triad." Her gaze drifted around the room as if trying to locate him. "The Triad of which I am a member."

"I've heard tales. A mythical planet that only the Stargazers can find." He watched the annoyance flash across her face. "As for the Triad, to the best of my knowledge, no one has ever seen them so your claim to be one of the three is pointless. I told you we're about to make the jump to hyper-space, so unless you want to find yourself thrown around that cell, I'd advise you to strap yourself in."

He cut the audio link to the brig before she could respond. It never paid to let a witch get in the last word.

* * *

"It's not mythical, it's hidden and for good reason. Men like you would love to get your hands on a whole planet full of Stargazers." Breanne glared around the room, wondering where the surveillance bots were hiding. It galled her to follow orders but her common sense overrode her stubborn nature and she plunked herself into the chair and pulled the safely netting over her. She could feel the deck beneath her feet starting to vibrate as the engines revved up for the jump.

Time for Plan B. Pity she didn't have one.

She settled herself into the seat and made sure the harness was snug. The whining of the hyperdrive engines hit an excruciatingly high note just before the ship flung itself into the vast void of space. Breanne found herself plastered against the netting for a brief second before the artificial gravity field kicked in and her body fell back into the seat. Lord, how she hated the first few seconds of a hyperdrive flight!

She closed her eyes and considered her options. Obviously, seducing the bounty hunter wasn't going to work, although their lovemaking had boosted her energy levels, and she had to admit she'd enjoyed herself immensely. He might be a cyborg but he certainly knew his way around a woman's body. Those big hands of his were just the right size to... She shook her head and tried to concentrate on the problem at hand. The longer she stayed here, the smaller her chances of finding and helping Talia.

The sound of the engines faded into the background as the ship settled into hyperspace, and the gravity field leveled off. She released the safety net and stood, stretching her arms above her head. Her only hope was that they'd reach their destination quickly and the bond-master would verify what she'd already told Roark. He had the wrong woman.

"So what does one do for food around here?" It had been ages since her last meal on the station, and her stomach was making its needs known. She wandered the perimeter of the small cell, running her hands along the smooth metal walls. If there was a food synthesizer anywhere, she had yet to locate it. "Are you listening to me?"

"But of course." The bounty hunter's deep voice sounded from behind her. Breanne whirled around to see Roark lounging insolently in the open doorway. A sexy smile curved the smooth lines of his lips. "There's only one food synthesizer on my ship, and it's in the galley. This isn't a pleasure cruiser. Do you want to come get some dinner, or would you like to spend a little more time cursing me?"

Determined not to let him see how much he rattled her, she stalked across the small space with her head held high. "I'm sure I'll have plenty of time to curse you later. Which way to the galley?" She refused to acknowledge the deep male chuckle that rumbled up from his chest.

"Not so fast." He extended an arm to grasp her wrist as she tried to sweep past him. "You really don't think I'm going to let a Stargazer wander around my ship unrestrained." He drew her up against his hard body. "Especially one who's recently absorbed a good deal of energy from me. I'm not an idiot."

"Really?" Breanne held her chin high, refusing to acknowledge the heat flooding her skin at his proximity. "Then you might want to consider that I'm not the woman you were sent to recover, and you are holding a member of the Triad against her will."

"A member of the mythical Triad? How naughty of me." A hint of disbelieving mockery tinged his voice as he ran a hand down her back to rest on her buttocks, the contact sending a wave of lust rolling through her belly. "If you promise not to do anything to disrupt the ship, I'll leave the restraints off."

She arched a brow and gave him a look she hoped showed her distain. "I'm not a complete fool. If I damage the ship, I'll be stuck out here in the middle of space with you. Not a fate I'd deliberately court."

A sinfully dark smile crossed his lips, and his strong arms wrapped around her, drawing her up against him until she could feel his thick shaft pressed into her belly. "And would that really be such a hardship?" He dipped his head and his lips brushed across hers, scattering all thoughts of food.

As the familiar heat started to coil deep inside

her, she closed her eyes, parting her lips to allow him to plunder at will. She'd never reacted this strongly to a male before, never felt this overwhelming urge to surrender, to let him do whatever he wanted with her. His tongue probed deep and she tilted her head to accommodate it, bringing her arms up to wrap around his neck. Arching her back, she pressed her breasts against him and felt his cock jerk in response.

"You have got to be the hottest female this side of the Nebula." He muttered the words against her lips while his hands roamed her body, pushing impatiently against her clothing. "I can barely resist the urge to rip that uni-suit off you and bury myself deep inside you, even though I know your kind just use men to gather energy."

He went still against her, and Breanne opened her eyes. His smoke-gray eyes narrowed, studying her. "Are you bonded to your master? Is that why you ran, to escape his hold?"

The tension in his body as he waited for her answer puzzled her. Why would he care? "I don't have a master. I told you, you have the wrong woman. I'm not bonded to anyone, and I intend to keep it that way. The last thing I want is some dumb-assed male trying to dictate to me."

The tension in his body increased, and he picked her up and turned to press her back against the wall. "Maybe you need someone to take a little of that attitude from you." He drew her arms up over her head, caging them with one big hand while he nudged her legs apart with his knee.

She opened her mouth to object, and he brought his head down to sear a soul-destroying kiss across her lips before he proceeded to strip the clothing off both of them.

"Maybe I'll just keep you naked and available for the rest of the journey." His eyes smoldered with lust. "It would save a lot of time."

"Mmmmm." That sounded like an excellent idea to her. He leaned into her, and the slide of his flesh against her bared breasts sent want coiling through her like warm honey. "Aren't you afraid I'll drain your energy?"

"Not sure I care at the moment." He picked her up and held her against him, her feet dangling in the air as he positioned her sex a hairsbreadth above his engorged shaft.

Breanne wrapped her legs around his waist, locking her ankles behind him as Roark slid his hands down to her butt to steady her. He stared into her eyes as he lowered her onto his cock with agonizing slowness.

She moaned softly as his hot flesh stretched her inch by inch. The cold metal wall at her back contrasted sharply with the hot slide of his muscular chest against the sensitive flesh of her breasts. Darts of erotic heat danced along her every nerve, and she writhed against him, wanting to feel more. More of his hard male body. More of his thick pulsing cock. More of his big hands on her soft flesh. More.

He rocked on the balls of his feet, using his hands on her butt to hold her in place while he rammed his shaft into her again and again. He picked up the pace, sending her lust spiraling higher as he plunged in and out of her slick sex.

It felt so good. Pleasure so intense it bordered on pain slid along every nerve, and she squirmed against him. The feel of his hard body, his big hands holding her, his warm male presence, drove her lust to a fever pitch.

Reality narrowed and Breanne lost track of everything but the feel of his cock in her slick channel. Heat flared in every cell of her body and she felt her orgasm building, rolling over her with the strength of a moon-called tidal wave. She threw her head back and screamed, giving voice to the overwhelming feelings.

Roark's deep growl mingled with her scream and she felt his hot seed jetting into her. She arched her back, tightening the muscles of her sex around his enormous shaft as she greedily milked every last bit of his seed.

Finally spent, she released her ankles and let her legs sink to the floor, glad that he kept a firm grip on her, holding her upright. She had a feeling that if he let her go she'd sink to the floor, her legs unable to hold her.

"That was incredible." She looked up into those smoky gray eyes, still clouded with passion. "No one's ever managed to make me come twice in such a short time."

"Glad to be of service." The gruff sound of his voice told her he was every bit as surprised as she was. "I can see why your bond-master is in such a hurry to get you back." He paused and an odd look crossed his face.

"Not having second thoughts about dragging me to see this guy, are you?" She let herself hope. "I'm not lying. I'm the wrong woman and this trip is a waste of time for both of us. If the money's a problem, I can match whatever he's offering."

Roark shook his head but continued to stroke her hair in a calming rhythm. "I'm the best bounty hunter in this quadrant. I'm not going to risk my reputation by letting you go, so you can forget that. Besides, he's offering a small fortune -- ten thousand credits for your safe return. I'm just wondering why he hasn't responded to my hail. I told him I'd apprehended you, and given how frantic he appeared when he put the bounty out, I would have expected him to be chomping at the bit to get you back."

"He isn't responding to your hail?" Breanne felt a sinking feeling in the pit of her stomach. "Did it ever occur to you that this might just be a ruse to get me out of the way?"

"Out of whose way?"

Breanne hesitated, not sure how much she should tell this man. He seemed like an honorable sort, for a bounty hunter. She decided to risk putting her mission on the line. "I've been tracking a pirate ship that's got a Stargazer on board. Rumor has it she's not there by choice, and it's my job to make sure she isn't being held against her will, or to free her if she is."

His eyebrows shot skyward. "And why would that be any of your business? If they're holding her illegally, the pirates aren't going to turn her loose without a fight." His gaze slid down her slim figure. "No offence, but you aren't going to be able to defeat a ship full of pirates, even if that Triad thing is true."

She rolled her eyes, frustration tempting her to stomp her foot in a childish display. The man just wasn't paying attention. "The Triad thing, as you call it, is true. I'm one of the three, and it's our sworn duty to protect all Stargazers."

She didn't bother to add that her current mission might have been ill-conceived. When she'd set out alone, she'd hoped to intercept Talia on the space station, where she'd be able to call on help from the authorities if she needed it. Thanks to the bounty hunter, she'd missed her chance. Even if he let her go now, she wasn't naïve enough to think she could track the pirate ship and force them to set Talia free.

"Won't do her much good if they take you too." A hint of sympathy crept into his voice. "How about this? You promise to behave yourself while I wait to hear back from Mr. Keiro, and I'll see what I can find out about your pirates. If they're anywhere in this sector, I should be able to track their co-ordinates."

Breanne looked up at him. "You'd do that? Find the pirates for me?"

He shrugged, and the muscles on his massive chest rippled under her hands. "Sure. It'll give me something to do while we wait. And..." a grim smile curved the corner of his lip, "if what you say is true, and the bounty is a ruse to get you off their tail, I'll be wanting to talk to them. I don't take kindly to being played for a fool."

Chapter Three

Roark watched Breanne wander around the bridge. The sight of her trim figure sent the blood rushing to his groin despite his resolve to maintain his distance. Stargazers were bad news. You could become addicted to their sensual nature, and if he had any sense at all, he'd lock the little witch in the brig until he arranged to turn her over to Mr. Keiro. He felt a rueful smile curve his lips. Caution had never been his strong suit.

Dragging his attention away from the enticing sway of her hips, he placed his hands palm-down on the contact grids on either side of his chair. Sensors on the grids immediately accessed the cybernetic links placed just beneath his skin, allowing him to log on to the ship's mainframe, and from there branch out to the 'net.

It had been called the World Wide Web, back in the days when mankind was restricted to one planet. There were entire banks of files in the historical libraries devoted to the precursor of the universal 'net. Over the last few centuries, the primitive electronics had been refined and expanded until a vast network of wireless signals crisscrossed the universe.

Years ago, the ore carrier he'd been working on had been hit by a stray meteor, and the med-techs had used cybernetic technology to save his life. They'd placed his body in stasis while it adjusted to the cybernetic implants; and he'd spent countless hours roaming the 'net.

Closing his eyes, he opened his consciousness to the multitudes of invisible lines. Years of practice allowed him to tune out the hum of mechanical traffic and concentrate on messages generated by sentient life forms. The most voluble contact came from the station they'd left behind, and he spent a few minutes sifting the routine traffic to make sure none of the messages bore the unique stamp of Mr. Keiro.

The little witch had sounded very convincing when she'd denied being a runaway. Combine that with the sudden lack of communication from the alleged bond-master, and he was starting to doubt the legitimacy of the bounty. It had seemed like an excessive amount at the time, but he'd put that down to a man's desire to recapture that which he considered to be his.

Satisfied that the elusive Mr. Keiro wasn't connected to the 'net using any of the station portals, he turned his attention farther afield. The lines of the data stream flowed into him via the receptors in his hands, flashing along the cybernetic pathways to his brain. He could see the encrypted data from the Federation ships patrolling the mining posts. He paid more attention to the civilian messages from the passenger vessels, but they contained nothing of interest and he let his focus widen, searching for a change in the pattern, something out of place or a quiet spot where there should be noisy data traffic.

A faint tingle and a slight shimmer in the fabric of the 'net had him tensing. A feather-light touch slipped along the edge of his consciousness, and he opened his eyes in amazement.

Breanne. She stood naked and spread-eagled in the center of the bridge, holding onto two scarves that she'd fastened to the light pods hanging from the roof. Her magnificent mane of hair streamed down her back, while her witch blue eyes stared straight ahead, unfocused. Her glorious breasts were proudly erect, the dusky nipples tilted upward as though reaching for the very stars in the sky. His cock hardened at the sight, even as he felt her presence in his mind.

The witch's eyes moved then, her gaze fastening on him, and a faint smile curved the sweet line of her lips. She stared at him intently, and he felt her slip along the pathways of his cybernetic implants until her consciousness bonded firmly with his. He could feel her every thought, every emotion. She was unsure of herself, unsure of the wisdom of this joining, but determined to do whatever she could to help locate the pirate ship and the missing Stargazer. Feminine, but with a steely determination, her character was laid bare to him in that moment. No deceit or subterfuge existed in her, and he realized she had told him the truth. Star Haven. The Triad. They existed, hidden from the rest of the world.

She led him outward to the stars, to a world of energy and color he'd never before imagined. He could feel the lines connecting the planets, pulsing with an energy that made the electronic grid of the 'net pale in comparison. A dazzling rainbow of colors washed over him and he fought to maintain his focus. His cybernetic implants quickly compensated for the overload, and he felt Breanne's admiration at his adaptability.

He acknowledged her openness and felt her acceptance of him. Turning his attention outward, he started to search for evidence of the pirate ship. He could sense planets and their inhabitants. People. Starships. Planets. Data packets zipped around the 'net. A ship packed with settlers and their gear chugged slowly along in the wake of an ore carrier heading for the outer systems. Smaller droid ships shuttled passengers between habitable planets. Single commuter ships zipped importantly between the various planets and stations, their engines thrumming with power.

Roark reset his implants to filter out these normal activities and concentrated on the anomalies. He felt a slight shift as Breanne fit her consciousness to the new parameters. If there were a pirate ship hiding out there somewhere, it would be trying to blend in with the normal interstellar traffic. Together, they would find it.

They explored each section of the quadrant, his cybernetics automatically sectioning space into a series of grids. A ship full of religious zealots lumbered amid the asteroid belt, hoping to avoid detection. A poacher used a shipment of bovine creatures to mask his cargo of exotic pets. Most of the grids held only normal traffic.

They searched each one carefully, not wanting to miss any clue as to Talia's position. They worked well together, bolstering each other's talents and strengths. Where one could see the energy signatures and calculate the size and inhabitants of the ship, the other could scan the 'net traffic to find out the purpose of the voyage.

Time passed in a blur, and Roark found himself starting to grow weary. He hesitated, not sure how to communicate this to Breanne. A ripple of amusement passed between them, and he realized she could see his thoughts just as he could read hers. He immediately concentrated on an image of her draped across his knee while he spanked her for laughing at him. The picture morphed into one of her sitting on his lap, her legs locked behind his back while she teased his lips with her tongue.

Laughing, he opened his eyes and broke contact with the 'net. Breanne lowered her arms and looked up at him. Laughter danced in the brilliant blue depths of her eyes as she stood on the bridge of his ship, gloriously naked. Blood rushed to his groin, making his uni-suit uncomfortably tight.

"That was interesting." She shook her head and the light caught the shimmering gold highlights in her cascade of hair. "I'd heard it was possible to merge minds with a cyborg, but I've never tried it. The last recorded instance of it was during the founding of Star Haven." A thoughtful look crossed her face. "There's no hiding possible in that type of union, is there? I could see your thoughts and actually feel what you felt."

He nodded. "Same here. I know that Star Haven truly does exist, and that you are indeed one of the Triad. That changes things."

She grinned. "I can hope that the accommodation will improve?"

He returned the grin. "Well, there's only one stateroom on board, but I'm willing to share."

"Nice of you, but right now I think I need some food or I won't have enough energy to fend you off."

Roark placed one hand on his chest and adopted what he hoped was a hurt look. "I'm crushed. I've never forced my attentions on a female. They all come begging me to favor them with my attention."

"Really?" Breanne raised an eyebrow. "So I can assume you have a harem of these eager beauties waiting for you somewhere?"

"No." He covered the distance between them in two long strides and scooped her up in his arms. "I was waiting for a blue-eyed witch to show up and take my breath away." He watched as her cheeks flushed a deep red. He'd never seen a Stargazer blush before, and he found it charming. He headed down the passageway in the direction of his stateroom.

"Stop looking at me like that!"

"Like what?"

"Like I'm the tastiest dessert on the replicator menu."

"But you are." He dipped his head to nibble on the lobe of her ear. "As soon as you've rested up some, I intend to taste every little inch of that delectable skin."

"We still have to find the pirates." She frowned at him. "If you hadn't snatched me back on the station, I would have been able to intercept Talia there and whisk her back to Star Haven with me."

"We'll find them." He found her devotion to her fellow Stargazer appealing. "But we both need to eat and get some rest before we try again. Even if we manage to locate the pirate ship, we're not going to do your captive Stargazer any good if we're too tired to stand up."

He paused in front of a hatch door. "Access." A panel above the door flashed from red to green at the sound of his voice, and the door slid silently open. A soft feminine voice sounded from within the walls. "Access granted."

He stepped into the room and gently laid her down on his sleeping platform. He couldn't resist letting her silky hair slide between his fingers before brushing a chaste kiss across her forehead. "I'm going to go grab some food from the synthesizer in the galley. Any special requests?"

Breanne shook her head. "Just as long as it's warm and fills my belly."

He laughed. "One warm bellyful coming up. Make yourself comfortable while I'm gone."

"Some clothing would probably be a good idea." She looked around.

"I like you just fine without clothes, but if you

insist you can see if any of my things fit you." He found the thought of her in one of his shirts even more erotic than her current state, and his cock jerked in response. He headed for the doorway. If he didn't go get that food soon, it would have to wait while he sated himself in her warmth.

A mocking chuckle followed him down the hallways, letting him know she could read his thoughts.

* * *

"Ready to give it another try?" Roark tucked a stray lock of hair back behind her ear.

Breanne nodded. "I don't want to waste any time. If the pirates know I'm still on their trail, they may disappear." And Talia would never have a chance at freedom. The thought of letting her fellow Stargazer down left a sour taste in her mouth.

Roark turned those sexy eyes of his on her, and she felt a rush of liquid warmth between her legs. The man was incredible. In the two solar periods since she'd been on the ship they'd made love four times, and she'd enjoyed it every single time.

They walked down the passage to the bridge. "I've rigged up a platform for you to use. Not perfect, but at least it'll hold you when you get tired. I wouldn't want you to fall and bruise any of that delicate skin of yours."

"Thank you." A great lover and thoughtful. Breanne peeked up at him from beneath her lashes. If she were looking for a mate, he'd be on the short list. Unfortunately, she had the feeling that the cyborg didn't want any complications in his life.

"There it is!" They stepped onto the bridge and Roark gestured toward his creation with a theatrical flourish.

Impressed, Breanne circled the makeshift platform. He'd used lightweight carbon rods to fashion a frame that would hold her upright without interfering with her movements. The crossbeams held loops of synth-rope, so she could slip her hands in them without worrying about them chafing her wrists. "I'm impressed." She reached up to gauge the height of the loops. "When did you have time to do this?"

"While you were napping." He gave her a wry grin. "As I'm sure you know, cyborgs don't require as much sleep as humanoids, so I had a quick power nap, and then came up here. Is it going to be okay?"

"Definitely. Way better than last time." She unsealed her uni-suit and shrugged out of the snug material. "If it's okay, I'd like to meditate for a few moments to center myself before we start."

"No problem." He took the suit and hung it over the arm of the navigator's chair. "I'll connect to the 'net, and you can join me when you're ready."

Breanne watched him head over to the captain's chair and slide into it. Tearing her gaze away from his broad shoulders, she lowered herself into a sitting position with her legs crossed and her hands resting on her thighs. Closing her eyes, she took deep, cleansing breaths and emptied her mind of everything but the task at hand. Talia. They needed to find her.

She concentrated on everything she knew about the other Stargazer. Her light mocha skin. Her dark eyes. Her gentle sense of humor. When she had a clear picture firmly in her mind, she stood and approached the Stargazer platform. Fastening the padded belt he'd provided around her waist, she tested it to make sure it would hold her weight. Next, she slipped her hands into the loops of synth-rope and pulled the loops snug against her wrists.

Tilting her head back, she closed her eyes and reached for Roark's steadying presence. The energy of the ley-lines could be a trap, tempting her to draw more and more of it into herself until it consumed her. Most Stargazers chose a mate early in life, using his steadying presence to help them resist the hypnotic power of the lines. Breanne had never met a man who tempted her to trade her freedom for the security of a mate until Roark threw her over his shoulder and dragged her aboard his ship. Now she understood what her co-workers had meant when they talked about a bonding, but her freedom would be a high price to pay.

Roark's solid presence slid into her consciousness, and she felt herself relaxing into the bond as though they'd done this a thousand times. She could feel his resolve to find the pirates, edged with his guilt at having thwarted her attempt to intercept Talia at the space station. She sent a gentle wave of reassurance. It would be all right. They would locate the pirates.

They turned their joint focus outward and began the search. They'd already ruled out all of the better-known shipping lanes and common rest stops. This time, they searched the lesser-used paths, the shadowed sides of planets, the routes strewn with planetary debris and abandoned satellites. They took their time, not wanting to miss any spot large enough to hide the pirate ship. Roark sifted amongst the multitudes of data packets zipping around the 'net while Breanne concentrated on the energy lines and the information they contained.

They worked their way outward from the station, passing planets and asteroids and the occasional manmade structure. They learned to read each other's thought patterns and react to the subtle changes in their link. Breanne spotted a freighter hiding behind a scattering of asteroids and her hope rose until Roark read the data streaming from its bridge. An archeological expedition searching for artifacts among the debris of a former moon. Time passed, and just as Breanne felt her hope beginning to fade, Roark perked up and showed her a data stream coming from behind a giant ice planet.

Digitally encoded to loop the message whenever the transponder came into contact with a reader, the message was simple.

This is Talia, a Class 4 Stargazer. I'm being held aboard the pirate ship Alpher *against my will. Please forward this message to the Triad.*

Chapter Four

Breanne felt a surge of elation. That exact message had arrived at Star Haven last moon cycle, convincing her to investigate. She sent a cyber hug to Roark, and then began to search the ley-lines, looking for the one that would lead them to the transponder and ultimately the pirate ship. The lines were clearer out here away from the static and interference of denser populated space. It didn't take her long to identify a deep blue line that would lead them straight to the pirate ship. She drew the energy into herself, capturing it between her outstretched arms, and directed it toward the engines.

The ship began to move in the direction she wanted, and she reveled in the power coursing through her, even as she diverted it to the engines. The ship picked up speed, moving silently toward their prey. She could sense Roark's surprise. He wanted to wait, to be sure of the target before they moved in. His doubt resonated across the bond. She spared a moment to reassure him, picturing her objectives so he could understand what she was doing. She had no intention of blundering into the pirate ship and alerting them to her presence, she just wanted to get close enough to do some reconnaissance and come up with a plan.

The line began to feel shorter as they closed in on the pirates. She let some of the power of the lines slip away from her, slowing the ship. It was so much easier to do that, to let go, while she was linked to Roark. He grounded her in a way she'd never have believed possible if it wasn't happening. The addictive lure of the ley-lines was barely noticeable, and she brought the ship to a smooth stop in the shadow of a cluster of meteor fragments. Opening her eyes, she saw Roark leap out of his chair and hurry toward her.

She sagged against her bonds as the energy of the lines drained from her, leaving her weak. Roark was right there, holding her up, releasing her from her bonds and carrying her gently from the bridge.

"You should have told me you were played out." The gruff tone of his voice failed to hide his concern.

"I'll be fine. We found the pirate ship holding Talia. That's what's important."

"It's not worth risking your life for. Is it true you could get sucked into the lines, be unable to let them go?"

Breanne nodded tiredly. "Yes. But not while I'm linked with you. You anchor me to this reality. That is so cool. I've never worked with an anchor before."

He dipped his head to nuzzle her hair. "I'd never forgive myself if I lost you. We can find another way to track down your Stargazer."

"No." She roused herself to glare at him. "Give me time to regroup my powers, and I'll be ready to go."

He turned to enter the stateroom, and laid her down gently on the sleeping platform. "Okay, but you have to promise not to risk yourself like that. You scared me."

Breanne stared up at him, marveling at how quickly he'd become important to her. She had an overwhelming urge to do as he asked, just to ease that worried look from his face.

"Promise me!" A stern frown marred the line of his brow.

She felt a soft smile curve her lips. He thought he could demand her obedience. "I promise. Now get those clothes off and get down here." She watched his brows rocket skyward, and resisted the urge to laugh.

He shook his head. "You need to rest and regain your strength."

Breanne reached up to run her hand along the tight curve of his thigh. "You forget, Stargazers absorb the energy generated by sex. Right now, what I need the most is to replenish myself." She tilted her head back and looked up at him. "So how about it? Want to give me some of your strength?"

Emotions chased their way across his rugged features. Doubt. Worry. Hesitation. Then he growled low in his throat and proceeded to strip his clothes off. Breanne propped herself up on one elbow, admiring his muscular body as it came into view. Wide shoulders tapered to a lean waist, with ropes of heavy muscle covering his entire body. Scars ran every which way, some older than others. They told of a hard life, one spent fighting for his very survival.

Then her gaze took in his massive cock curving upward. This was no civilized man she could bend to her will. He looked powerful and dangerous, and yet very concerned for her. She wanted him more than she'd ever wanted a male in her life.

He closed the distance between them in a single stride and pounced onto the sleeping platform, capturing her beneath him. She looked up into his face, into those gray eyes smoldering with naked lust. He lowered his head to sear a possessive kiss across her lips. He kissed her like a man who'd waited too long, his breath hot on her cheeks, his teeth scraping in his eagerness. Their tongues dueled in an erotic dance that left them both gasping for breath. The feel of his hot skin against her sent flames of lust curling along her nerves, and she wrapped her arms around his neck to hold him close.

She could feel his barely restrained desire, and

realized that the link they'd forged on the bridge hadn't completely dissolved when she'd released the energy lines. She ran a finger down his cheek, tracing the rough scar that marred his features. She could get addicted to this, to the taste of him, to the sense of belonging, of being connected so intimately to a man of such power. Not a man, she corrected herself. He was so much more.

"You are so beautiful." He sat up, straddling her belly with his long legs while his fingers traced a path from her face to her breasts, cupping the plump mounds in his hands. He tweaked a nipple between his thumb and forefinger, and Breanne shivered with need. Her breath caught in her throat as he moved lower, toying with her belly button, exploring the soft curve of her hips. "Tell me what you want me to do."

"I want to feel you inside me." She licked her lips as she imagined the feel of that massive shaft invading her inch by slow inch. "I want you to kiss me and hold me and fuck me until I can't move."

His eyes darkened and she could see the effect her words had on him as his cock swelled to even larger proportions. Lowering himself over her, he propped an arm on either side of her head and took her lips in a slow, thorough kiss that left her gasping for air. Hot and demanding, his lips sent searing darts of want deep inside her. He shifted positions, and she felt the head of his cock pushing against the entrance to her sex. "Are you sure?"

"Yes!" She thrust her hips upward, trying to impale herself on that magnificent shaft. "Damn it, fuck me."

He drew back and entered her with one powerful thrust, his cock stretching her slick channel with a force that left her whimpering in mindless lust. She wrapped her arms around his neck, her fingers tangling in his dark hair. Flames of desire whipped across the surface of her skin, sending her spiraling out of control. She bucked and writhed beneath him as he drew himself out of her only to plunge back in. He drove her almost to the edge of madness, then deliberately slowed the pace, making her cry out in frustration.

He knew just how to keep her on the edge, playing her body like a fine-tuned instrument. Plunging deep and fast, now slow and hard. Fire began to build deep within, washing over her. She moaned and bucked, incapable of reasonable thought while her body demanded more and more. Her orgasm exploded over her, and she was unable to keep quiet, hollering his name to the stars as wave after wave of pleasure rolled over her.

A few more hard thrusts and a warm wetness drenched the walls of her channel. Roark roared his pleasure, burying his head in her hair. The two of them collapsed in a tangled heap of limbs, their breath coming in ragged gulps.

The energy gathered around Breanne, seeping into her very bones as she lay in the arms of her lover. He wrapped his arms around her and pulled her up against him. Cradling her there, he brushed a gentle kiss across her forehead.

"Sleep well, Breanne. Tomorrow, we go hunting for pirates."

* * *

"Are you sure this is a good idea?" Breanne wriggled her wrists in the plas-tek bonds Roark had fastened around them.

"It'll work." Roark gave her a lopsided grin. "You're just upset because you're in bonds. As long as the pirates think I'm selling you, they're going to let us onboard. Now hold still while I get these on your ankles." He squatted down to fasten a chain around each of her ankles, with a connecting line of stretchable plas-tek to hold them together. "You look rather enticing this way. Maybe we'll try a little bondage once we get this cleared up."

Breanne rolled her eyes. "Dream on."

He tilted his head, laughing up into her eyes. "You'd like it. I guarantee it."

"I don't think so." She shook her head and changed the subject. "How are we going to get them to give up Talia?"

"We're not." He tested to make sure the chains were secured, and then stood. "This will get us onboard. Once we're there, we find your Stargazer and fight our way back out."

She stared at him in amazement. "That's your plan? The odds are going to be just a tad against you."

This time, the smile was grim. "I'm a cyborg. That evens the odds up nicely. Once the fighting starts, you grab your friend and make a run for our ship. Don't stop, certainly not for me. Close the hatch and stay safe. Once I'm done, I'll come and find you."

Breanne shivered, remembering how he'd looked the first time she saw him: large and dark and menacing. "Okay then." She took a deep breath to calm her racing heart. "Let's get this show on the road."

"Try to look a little less satisfied with yourself." He tilted her chin up to feather a kiss across her lips. "I've captured you, screwed your brains out, and I'm about to sell you to the highest bidder."

Breanne laughed, and then schooled her face into a more somber pose. "How's this? Or should I be sniffling a bit?"

Roark grinned and swatted her on the butt.

"You've just had the best sex of your life. I don't think sniffling is in order. Maybe dazed adoration."

She lifted one brow. "My. My. Don't have much of an ego problem, do you? How's this?" She widened her eyes and let her jaw go slack.

"Keep it up and I might have to put off the rescue for a bit while I teach an ungrateful Stargazer a lesson in manners." He ran his hand through her hair, mussing up the long locks. "There. That looks a bit better. They're going to expect you to look a bit disheveled."

He turned to key the com panel. "Showtime. I want you behind me, slightly to the side so they can see you when I contact them." A vid screen appeared above the console, showing all the ships within communications range. He placed his palm down on the panel, and she watched as all the ships except their target turned a dull red, indicating they were locked out of the com-loop before he started to broadcast. Breanne moved to a position just behind his left shoulder and focused on a spot on the deck, hoping she looked suitably cowed.

Roark glanced at her approvingly and then turned back to the vid-screen. "This is Roark, commander of the spaceship *Blazing Star*. I apprehended a fugitive Stargazer and her bond-master has not responded to my request for payment, so by right of interstellar bounty laws, I'm offering her for sale. Reply to this frequency if you wish to inspect the goods or make an offer to purchase." He reached back and hauled her forward, making sure the pirates got a good look at her before he cut off the feed.

"Now what?" Breanne looked up at him.

"Now we wait." He gave her a grim smile. "I don't think we'll have to wait too long."

As if in reply, a deep ping sounded from the com panel, and he nodded. "They won't want to pass up the opportunity to acquire a second Stargazer, and they'll be under the impression I broadcast that message to every ship within com-range." He turned to the com panel and opened the feed.

The vid screen popped back up and Breanne didn't have to fake the alarmed look on her face. A Tracian, one of the most hideous of the sentient races, glared at them. "This is Dar, of the spaceship *Alpher*. How do we know the female is a Stargazer?"

"Take a look." Roark sounded unconcerned. "If you're seriously interested, I'll bring her to you to examine, and perhaps test."

The Tracian shook his ugly head. "No. We'll come to you."

"I don't think so." Roark frowned. "I'm not stupid enough to let a Tracian crew board my ship. If you want to see her, send me your coordinates." He paused. "And I'll want proof that you're able to pay the asking price. I'll accept no less than five thousand gold credits."

"Not possible. We let no one on our vessel."

"Suit yourself." Roark shrugged his massive shoulders. "I'm sure someone else will be interested." He cut the com-link with a wave of his hand, and the Tracian disappeared.

"Now what?" Breanne couldn't believe they'd already lost.

"They'll call back." He glanced over at her and his expression softened. "It's a game. They demand. I refuse. They want you and eventually they'll agree to let me bring you over."

Breanne had her doubts. The Tracian hadn't looked very interested, and he certainly hadn't looked like a creature who liked to play games. "And if they don't?"

"Then we go with Plan B."

"What's Plan B?"

He gave her a crooked smile that made her heart do a little flip-flop in her chest. "I've no idea. I've never had to use a Plan B."

Breanne gave an unladylike snort and opened her mouth to reply, but the pinging of the com-link cut her off.

"And that would be our friend the Tracian." Roark turned back to the control panel, letting the com ping several more times before he opened the link.

"We accept. You may bring her aboard for our inspection." The creature's beady eyes narrowed as he looked at Breanne. "You will dock on the starboard side and await my security team."

Roark shook his head. "The money. I want to see five thousand gold credits before I take her anywhere."

The Tracian glared and then stood aside to reveal a gold credit-string on the console behind him. "We have the credits."

"Lovely. I'll see you shortly." He cut the transmission and turned to pull Breanne toward him. Dipping his head, he kissed her hard on the lips. "See, no Plan B required."

Chapter Five

Roark maneuvered the shuttle into the docking ring. A metallic clang sounded as the ring sealed against the hull and the command console flashed an all clear. He removed his hands from the neural interface and looked over at her. "It's showtime. Are you clear on what to do?"

Breanne nodded, swallowing a nervous lump in her stomach. "As soon as Talia shows up to verify my status, get her into the shuttle, then wait for you." She couldn't hide the fear in her eyes. "What if they capture you, or worse?"

He shook his head. "Not going to happen. When the fighting starts, I can use my cyborg tech to flood my system with adrenaline. It would take a full Federation battalion to stop me. A couple dozen pirates don't stand a chance." The corner of his mouth twisted up in a crooked grin. "Besides, they won't risk having a bounty hunter running around their ship. I'm betting they'll be right there when we unseal the hatch, with Talia close by to verify you are what I claim. We'll snatch the girl, and be back aboard my ship before the engines have time to cool."

Breanne wished she felt as confident as he sounded. A thousand butterflies appeared to be practicing a new flight pattern inside her belly, and she could barely talk, her throat was so dry. She tried to straighten in her seat, but her bound hands limited her movement. Roark had fastened the plas-tek so she could snap it when she wanted, and she had to be careful not to do that too early. The bonds on her ankles would break off with a twist of her leg.

Roark unstrapped his safety harness and stood. "We need to wait until they invite us aboard. My guess is they'll make us wait, hoping our nerves will fray."

"Good plan." Breanne wasn't sure she had any nerves left.

"Hey, you'll do fine." Roark walked over and released her harness, then leaned over to rub his hand down her back in a soothing motion. The onboard com-unit squealed, and she jumped. So much for remaining calm. Roark strode to the com-panel and hit the audio switch. "Roark here."

"The security is ready. You may exit your vessel."

"Acknowledged." He shut the unit off and turned to Breanne. "Ready?"

She nodded. As ready as she'd ever be. Getting to her feet, she crossed to stand beside him, giving him a weak smile.

"Just follow my lead." He palmed the door panel and it slid back smoothly. Directly in front of them stood the Tracian, flanked by two humanoid guards, their blasters pointed directly at Roark.

"Nice touch." Roark dismissed the two with a careless wave of his hand as he stepped onto the pirate ship. A slight movement of his head signaled Breanne to move in close behind him. "We both know they aren't going to shoot, because I'd have you in a headlock, gasping for air, before they managed to pull the triggers. So tell them to back off before I decide not to play nice."

The Tracian studied him for a moment, then turned to his guard and grunted a command. "You have a lot of balls, Roark. I like that. Now, let's get down to business." He looked at Breanne, his gaze sweeping from her head to toe in an impersonal manner. "I have a Stargazer of my own, and I've ordered her up here to verify this one. If she checks out, you can have your credits and leave in peace." He frowned. "Of course, if she turns out to be a fraud, and you're trying to con me, I'll be very unhappy."

Roark stood his ground; his arms crossed on his chest and he feigned surprise. "You already have a Stargazer?"

The ugly creature nodded, his beady eyes shining with greed. "Yes. But with two, we can outmaneuver anyone. We would be invincible. I hope that little female checks out."

"No problem there." Roark relaxed his stance, his arms dropping to his sides. Breanne realized he was getting into position to move. "She's a Stargazer all right, a Class Three. I'm sure you'll be impressed with her abilities."

A noise from down the corridor drew Breanne's attention, and she let her senses flare outward. She felt Talia's presence just before the other woman came into view. She could tell the minute Talia realized there was another Stargazer onboard. Surprise, quickly followed by dismay, tinged her aura. She came down the corridor, her identity unmistakable with that long, black hair and the trademark blue eyes. Her steps faltered as she took in the scene in front of her.

Breanne sent out a wave of reassurance, which only seemed to confuse the other woman. Dar turned toward Talia, and her face turned to an unreadable mask. She moved toward Breanne, ignoring the men.

"You will tell us if she is one of your kind." The Tracian and both of the guards watched the two women intently.

Breanne kept her eyes downcast, watching both the approaching woman and Roark at the same time. She hadn't dared dream that she'd find Talia without having to leave the ship or Roark's protective presence.

Talia continued to walk toward her. Roark stood still, balanced lightly on the balls of his feet. The guards ignored him, their attention fixed on the Stargazers. Talia stepped past the pirates and reached out to place her hand on Breanne's shoulder.

The corridor exploded in a flurry of movement. Time seemed to slow. Roark took out the guard on the right with a brutal chop to the side of his neck. The man slid to the ground with a strangled gurgle, his blaster dropping with a metallic clang. Roark kicked the weapon back toward Breanne and turned to the second guard. The Tracian stepped back to give the guard more room.

"Kill the bastard." Anger vibrated in the Tracian's voice. "If the female's not a Stargazer we can always sell her as a sex slave. She'd fetch a pretty load of credits at auction."

Roark didn't bother to answer, his attention on the guard. The man outweighed him, but Roark's superior skills and cybernetic enhanced speed quickly began to show. He knocked the blaster out of the man's hands with a roundhouse kick, and then turned to dance in under his guard, pummeling his unprotected belly with his fists.

Breanne snapped her bonds, kicking the discarded plas-tek aside before she reached up to grasp Talia's hand and draw her into the shuttle, away from the guards. Roark had told her to close the doors, but she couldn't bring herself to abandon him to the Tracian and his henchmen.

"What are you doing?" Talia looked over her shoulder at the guards. "Those guys are psycho and they'd love an excuse to hurt us. If the Tracian gives them the go-ahead, you'll wish they'd killed us."

"They don't have time to worry about us.

They're too busy trying to save their own asses." Breanne couldn't keep the pride out of her voice as she dragged the smaller woman into the shelter of the ship.

The fight felt like it went on forever. Crouched in the airlock of the shuttle, the two women watched anxiously. The Tracian moved in while Roark's back was to him, and Roark knocked him to the ground with a solid backhand blow. Grunts and the sound of flesh hitting flesh filled the air. Roark moved like the machine he claimed to be, his movements calculated to cause the most damage.

Why had she ever doubted him? Roark fought with deadly intent, his rugged face impassive, his movements so quick they blurred in front of her. The guard grunted, but held his ground, managing to hammer the side of Roark's head with a flailing fist before Roark retreated out of reach. The two men circled each other warily, ignoring the curses hurled at them by the downed Tracian. Roark feinted with his left, but the guard blocked him. Then the guard tried a low sweeping kick to throw Roark off balance. Roark stepped over his leg, and before the man recovered his balance, Roark hit him with a right-left combination to his face.

The guard screamed in agony, falling to his knees, and Roark jumped in from the side and finished him off with a hard elbow to the back of his head. The man dropped face-first to the floor, and Roark nudged him with the tip of his boot.

"Damned useless humans. Why do I have to do everything myself?" The Tracian advanced on Roark, the guard's blaster pointing at the cyborg's heart. "I really didn't intend to let you go, you know. The female is worth many credits, Stargazer or not. You were an idiot to board my ship."

No! Breanne looked around wildly and grabbed the blaster that the first guard had dropped earlier. Taking a deep breath to steady her nerves, she aimed it at the Tracian and gently squeezed the trigger as her instructor had taught her to do all those years ago.

A bolt of pure energy sprayed from the muzzle of the weapon and caught the Tracian square in the back of his head, burning a neat hole through it. Roark jumped out of the way as the lifeless body slid to the floor, and then turned to glare at her. "I thought I told you to lock that door and let me deal with the pirates." He advanced toward her, and she couldn't help the smile that spread across her face. He was alive, and that was all that mattered. He'd learn soon enough that she didn't take orders -- not even from a cyborg who had stolen her heart.

* * *

"I'm not going to go live on a planet inhabited by a bunch of headstrong women." Roark ran his hand down Breanne's back, loving the feel of her soft skin beneath his palm. "We can live on my ship and visit when it's absolutely necessary."

They'd taken Talia back to her home planet, where her parents greeted her with tears of joy. Now, they just needed to sort out their own future.

"But we would be so much more comfortable living planet side." Breanne arched her back, pressing her breasts against his chest. "The ship is okay, but it doesn't have the creature comforts of a planet."

"It has privacy." He dipped his head to suck one nipple into his mouth. "And I think we're going to need a lot of privacy."

Breanne giggled. "You might have a point there, but I have a job to do. I'm one of the Triad. I can't just announce I'll be unavailable because I met a sinfully sexy bounty hunter and I'm up here getting my brains fucked out."

"It's the truth." He let his hand drift lower, exploring the satiny skin of her belly. "And you like it when I fuck your brains out."

"Mmmmm." Her eyelids drifted down to cover those startling blue eyes. "And you do it so well."

"Thank you." He covered her sex with one palm, and slid a finger between the moist folds to find her clit.

"Oh, yeah." She arched her hips to push against his hand. "Keep doing that and maybe we can compromise."

Roark chuckled and plunged a finger deep into her pussy. He knew he'd do whatever she wanted. In the short time since he'd dragged her aboard his ship, the blue-eyed witch had stolen his heart. He inserted a second finger, pumping them in and out.

A low whimper escaped Breanne's lips, and she rocked her hips in time to each thrust of his fingers. Roark picked up the pace, marveling at her deeply sensual nature. She moaned, her body thrashing beneath his hand. Her breath came in short gasps, and he withdrew his fingers, ignoring her sharp cry of protest.

He swiftly moved to cover her sinfully gorgeous body with his own, his painfully engorged shaft bumping eagerly at the entrance to her sex. Breanne arched up against him, but Roark held back. He wanted this to be special. Deliberately, inch by agonizingly slow inch, he penetrated her moist depths. Her inner muscles pulsed around him, and he let out a low growl, giving up any pretence at control.

Breanne gripped his shoulders tightly, and he buried his face in her magnificent mane of hair as he plunged in and out of her tight pussy. She met him thrust for thrust, her soft cries of need sending fiery darts of want searing up his spine.

"Roark. Please. Oh, goddess, please!"

He felt her orgasm starting, the walls of her channel rippling around his cock and throwing him into his own orgasm. Wave after wave of sheer pleasure pulsed through him. With a triumphant cry, he emptied his seed into her as her body shuddered against his.

He felt whole. Complete. Bonded to this amazing witch who'd stolen his heart and brought it back to him wrapped in the glorious gift of her love.

Anne Kane

Anne Kane lives in the beautiful Okanagan Valley with a bouncy little rescue dog whose breed defies description and an Aussie Shepherd who's too smart for her own good. Anne likes to write spicy stories with sassy heroines and protective, sexy male heroes who love those women. Her stories all have one thing in common -- a happily ever after ending.

Her hobbies, when she's not playing with the characters in her head, include kayaking, hiking, swimming, playing guitar and spoiling the grandkids.

More books by <u>Anne Kane</u>

Changeling Press E-Books

More Sci-Fi, Fantasy, Paranormal, and BDSM adventures available in E-Book format for immediate download at ChangelingPress.com -- Werewolves, Vampires, Dragons, Shapeshifters and more -- Erotic Tales from the edge of your imagination.

What are E-Books?

E-Books, or Electronic Books, are books designed to be read in digital format -- on your desktop or laptop computer, notebook, tablet, Smart Phone, or any electronic ebook reader.

Where can I get Changeling Press e-Books?

Changeling Press ebooks are available at ChangelingPress.com, Amazon, Barnes and Nobel, Kobo, and iTunes.

Changeling Press, LLC

ChangelingPress.com